THE
MEMORY MAN

THE MEMORY MAN

John Griffiths

Playboy Press

For Alexander and Rachel

PART I

CHAPTER I

Ivkov awoke to a sense of vague anxiety. It was as if the effects of a bad dream the night before had carried over into his waking life, though the dream itself had been forgotten. For weeks each morning had started this way, with drowsy, unfocused apprehension sharpening, as his head cleared and memory returned, into fear.

He sat up. The clock beside him said four-thirty; but already, through chinks in the blinds, he could see strips of northern daylight, pale, fishy gray—not daylight at all but a kind of bleak phosphorescence. From the other bed, where he could make out above the bedclothes the head of Varischenko, there issued the sound of gentle and regular breathing. Comrade interpreter, he thought with envy; comrade policeman, sleeping the sleep of the just.

It was too early to get up. He had done so once since their arrival, but Varischenko had looked sour and muttered under his breath, so he did not care to try it again. Nothing had been precisely stated, but Varischenko had managed, nevertheless, to make his attitude clear. Since he had been put to the trouble of accompanying Ivkov on a trip which was both tedious and unnecessary, it was up to Ivkov not to add to his burden by keeping irregular hours. So Ivkov would begin this day, as he had begun each day since they arrived, alone and afraid.

He looked at his watch. May 27th. They had been here ten days already and not a single opportunity had been offered. There were only three days left.

* * *

"This tendency of certain particles to affect the behavior of other particles, in ways which, as I have shown, can only be called eccentric, is something we have so far been unable to explain. Lacking an explanation, we have been forced, as so often in the past, to retreat into metaphor. We have, therefore, called this tendency—and with, I repeat, a full consciousness of all that the term does not explain—we have called this tendency *charm*."

The lecturer paused, looking up at his audience and smiling with expectant, self-conscious shyness, like a child who knows he has been cute. There were answering smiles from the audience and a quick rustle of laughter, half-amused, half-polite. Satisfied, he turned back to his paper.

Charm? Berenstein yawned. Hardly. He knew little of subatomic particles and cared less. This paper was no different from any other he had heard—long, tediously detailed self-congratulation in a field far removed from his own. Nothing in it for him, or, for that matter, for the Pentagon. Coming to the conference was proving, as he had feared, a total waste of time and money. The money, of course, was not his problem—it was the Pentagon's, or the taxpayer's; but he resented the time.

In ten days now he had learned nothing. The East Europeans, as usual, had been completely tight-lipped. The West Europeans, on the other hand, had been alarmingly talkative. Perhaps this was why, then, at sessions of the World Conference for the Advancement of Scientific Knowledge, the scientific knowledge of the Soviet Union always seemed to advance more conspicuously than anyone else's. Instead of supporting the conferences, the Pentagon should boycott them.

Glancing around, he could see that his apathy was shared by others. The Russian, Ivkov, for example, whom Lowell and the MIT contingent took so much pleasure in teasing, was gazing ahead with the fixed stare of one who merely pretends to listen, while, beside him, the big bodyguard—Voroschilov or some such name—had taken his shoes off and was obviously asleep.

The contrast between them was striking; Ivkov, prim, spruce, and upright, his sense of painful duty written all over his face; the other, slumped in his seat, head back, mouth open, his appearance, all creased and rumpled, reminiscent of an unmade bed. He had met them before, at one of the parties, and been amused at Ivkov's attitude to the bodyguard. They moved as though practically chained together, yet Ivkov had acted as if the other didn't exist. If the bodyguard had noticed, however, he hadn't seemed to mind. He had just been there, a solid, imperturbable, faintly ridiculous presence.

He was still contemplating this bizarre relationship, completely deaf now to the revelations proceeding from the platform, when he realized that Ivkov, across the auditorium, was staring back at him. As their eyes met, Ivkov tilted his head backwards and rolled his eyes toward the ceiling. Then, cocking his head toward the nearest exit, he mimed the action of raising a glass to his lips.

Berenstein smiled and nodded. Ivkov nudged the bodyguard and whispered in his ear. They slid out of their seats and tiptoed to the exit.

Berenstein's doubts about the propriety of leaving evaporated. Mingle with the enemy. It was what he was there for. With a sense of relief he got up and followed.

"This is what you call 'playing hookey,' isn't it?"

It was when Huckleberry Finn was at school, thought Berenstein. He smiled and nodded.

"Unfortunately," Ivkov pursued, "I've completely lost track of all their particles. I used to try and keep up with them, but I have no time for the reading anymore. That man," he gestured toward the auditorium, "could have been speaking Greek."

Berenstein smiled again. There was something about Ivkov, his manner, perhaps, or the bright artificial chatter he had kept up since they met outside the auditorium, that struck him as nervous. He wondered if it was the presence of the bodyguard; but Varischenko—Ivkov had been punctilious about performing the introductions—had ignored them completely since they had sat down at the bar. He was more interested, it seemed, in the pitcher of dark, German beer they had ordered on arrival. He had just poured himself a third glass of it although Ivkov and Berenstein were still on their first. The pitcher now stood in front of him, half-empty, while Varischenko leaned back on his bar stool, gazing abstractedly at the rows of bottles lining the shelves of the bar. Apparently the conversation bored him as much as anything he had heard in the auditorium.

Berenstein did not blame him. For Ivkov had pointedly excluded him from the conversation and was leaning forward, both elbows on the counter, his body effectively a wall between Varischenko and the American.

Further down, to the right of Varischenko, a couple was talking loudly, laughing and flirting. The woman was blond, a big, well-scrubbed, healthy Scandinavian dressed in Levis, T-shirt, and sandals.

Berenstein leaned back to get a better look at her. Varischenko, it seemed, had also noticed, for he too turned and was staring at her in open admiration. In response to this, perhaps, or to some remark from her companion, she straightened up and thrust her shoulders back. As she laughed her breasts shook and pressed against the fabric of the shirt. Berenstein grinned and nudged Ivkov, cocking his head in her direction. Ivkov turned. As he did, his elbow sweeping in an arc across the counter caught the pitcher. It slid, met the metal rim at the counter's edge, tilted, paused infinitesimally at the point of balance, then toppled, pouring the better part of a quart of Lowenbräu over Varischenko.

Instantly Ivkov was on his feet.

"So clumsy," he stammered, ineffectually mopping Varischenko's jacket with a napkin from the bar. "So unbelievably clumsy. Please forgive me."

Varischenko brushed him aside. The beer had splashed his shirtfront and drenched his trousers to the knees. They now clung to his legs, clammy and cold. He was in a dilemma. His instructions were to remain with Ivkov always. But his instructions had not allowed for contingencies such as this. He had no desire to spend the afternoon in wet trousers, sticky and smelling of beer. He was already a figure of fun to the scientists at the conference and he had no wish to encourage their ribald speculations as to the origin of the dark stain which spread around his crotch. He thought, for an instant, of asking Ivkov to accompany him while he changed. But that also would make him ridiculous. Moreover, Ivkov was a member of the Academy of Sciences and a close friend of the Minister of Defense. He might not take kindly to such a request.

He decided to take the chance. It would take only a few minutes—five at most—for him to change. Ivkov would be safe enough. The hotel was well watched.

"Don't distress yourself." He made an attempt at graciousness, smiling a little sourly at Ivkov, then flicking his eyes, nervously, toward the girl. "It was an accident. Understandable in the circumstances. I shall change my clothes and rejoin you in a minute."

He got up and strode out to the lobby.

Ivkov glanced around the room. The bartender was at the far end of the counter. With the departure of Varischenko the other customers had resumed their conversations. He turned back to Berenstein.

"Please listen carefully. Do not interrupt or ask questions." His manner remained conversational but his voice was urgent.

"I need help."

The man in the hotel lobby was heartily sick of his assignment. It was a job, he reflected, like looking after small children—not demanding enough to occupy his attention, too demanding to permit him to do anything else. He could not let his mind wander and yet there was nothing to occupy it. Moreover, he was irritated by the thought that it was all unnecessary. If a man was important enough to need so much guarding, then he was too important to be out on the loose. Not for the first time he found himself baffled by the decisions of his superiors.

It was therefore with something approaching pleasure that he saw Varischenko emerge from the corridor and stride rapidly across the lobby to the bank of elevators at its far end. There was something confused and slightly furtive about his manner, which the man attributed to the large dark stain on the front of his trousers. That fool, he thought, has either spilled his drink or pissed in his pants. He got up and made his way toward the bar. He would go and take a look around there. It would give him something to do.

Ivkov was watching the mirror. When he saw the man framed in the doorway behind him, he neither moved nor broke off the conversation. Instead he switched subjects in midsentence.

"With regard to the upper atmosphere"—he was careful not to change the tone of his voice—"I agree there is a need for greater control, but I believe your concern over SST flights is premature. There is no substantial evidence to suggest that fluctuations in the ozone level are in any way related." He was relieved to see that Berenstein had not reacted to the change of subject.

The man walked over and stood at the counter beside Ivkov. When the bartender came over to serve him, he asked for a pack of cigarettes. Tearing the pack open, he took one out and placed it between his lips.

The lighter was outdated now. A relic of the sixties. He carried it only because it reminded him of better times, before most of the work of agents and analysts had been taken over by electronic gadgets and computers. But the pictures it took stood up well, nevertheless, retaining clear definition under considerable enlargement. He turned and bent toward Ivkov, cupping his hand around the wick to protect the flame against the draft from an air-conditioning unit directly above. In doing so he got a clear view of Berenstein in profile over Ivkov's shoulder. The scratch of the flint disguised the click of the shutter.

"But until the evidence is all in," he heard Berenstein object, "surely the best course would be to ban all flights."

"Easy for you to take that position," Ivkov was chuckling, "since the United States has no SST."

Scientific small talk. The man was conscious of having taken the photograph mostly to relieve his boredom. He decided, however, that the incident was worth reporting, if for no other reason than to embarrass

Varischenko who, he felt sure, would not report it himself. He strolled back into the lobby and picked up the telephone.

More than three hours later, a taxi pulled up at 313 Itäinen Kaivopuisto, one block away from the United States Embassy. Emerging from it, David Berenstein paid the driver and began to walk briskly away in the opposite direction. He would, he decided, walk around the block and approach the Embassy from the rear.

This maneuver, the latest in a series that had occupied most of the afternoon and left him with a considerable sense of satisfaction at his own ingenuity, was undertaken, as were the others, to placate a faint but lingering sense of guilt. Ivkov had asked him to do nothing until he returned to the States. But what Ivkov had not known—and Berenstein had not had a chance to tell him—was that Berenstein did not plan to return to the United States directly but was going instead to spend three weeks in Norway and Sweden. He believed in combining business and pleasure. A round trip ticket, courtesy of the Department of Defense, was an opportunity not to be missed.

So he had ignored Ivkov's instructions and, to set his own mind at ease, had spent the afternoon playing spies. It had been amusing and, had he been able to sustain the conviction that he really was being followed, it might even have been exciting.

He had gone first, by taxi, to Mannerheimintie where he spent half an hour window shopping and buying souvenirs. He had then retraced his steps and gone girl watching in Senate Square. Another taxi had taken him back to the hotel where he had stopped for a drink at the bar before emerging, after a journey through the bowels of the building, from a service entrance at the rear. This had led into an alley which to all appearances was deserted. It was only then that he had taken the taxi from which he had just been dropped.

He hoped it had been worthwhile. He had taken Ivkov seriously because the Russian had been so earnest. But he was not at all sure, even so, that he was not being made a fool of. Russians, he had heard, were great practical jokers. On the other hand, what Ivkov had told him, if true, would be extraordinarily interesting to the Department of Defense. And the Department was, he remembered, the hand that fed him. He could not afford to ignore it. But he was not about to pass up his vacation. He would turn it over to the Embassy and let them worry about it.

It takes a team of six men with three cars to follow someone in a large and crowded city without being seen. The man from the hotel had received his instructions with the gloomy conviction that more public money was about to be wasted. Now, three hours later, having watched Berenstein's erratic travels with a weary patience which became, as the afternoon progressed, a startled interest, he was not so sure.

CHAPTER II

It was Roskill's habit, when starting work each morning, to shuffle through his IN tray and sort the papers into piles. In the first he put what he termed "bumf"—interoffice memoranda, complaints from Accounting, and the like. These he invariably junked. If they contained anything important, then sooner or later he would surely hear about it. In the second pile went all the background reading—reports on the economic condition of Rumania or surveys of Chinese propaganda in Africa. These he transferred to a tray marked PENDING. He would look at them later, when he had nothing better to do. The last pile contained telegrams from the stations, extracts from monitored cable traffic, agents' reports in their orange folders tied with red ribbon. These he read.

On May 28th the first item in the third pile carried the highest security classification—TOP SECRET. U.S. EYES ONLY—and the top priority—FLASH. It was a cable from Helsinki.

"Roskill from Petersen," he read. "At 4 P.M., May 27, a U.S. citizen, David Berenstein, came to the Embassy and requested a meeting with the Ambassador. He was interviewed by the Second Secretary (Political), who took notes of the conversation and passed them on to me."

The telegram was several pages long and Roskill read it through carefully twice. Then he rang for his secretary.

"Miss Solveig." She was in her mid-forties and a spinster. He believed her first name was Sally, but he would never have dreamed of using it.

"I want you to make four copies of this telegram. Number them, and circulate to the following people. One, the DCI. Two, the Deputy Director: Operations. Three, the Deputy Director: Research, and four, Antony Holland. Also please open a special file—call it the Helsinki file—place my copy on file and make a note on the file of who has the other copies.

"Next, I'd like you to get hold of Olofson at Princeton and set up a meeting for late this afternoon. Don't let him put you off. Tell him it's very urgent.

"Then please go down to Records and get me everything they have on the following two individuals. Their names are Alexei Ivkov—he'll be under Scientific—and Varischenko, first name unknown. For him try the KGB." He spelled out the two names. "If you don't find them under those spellings, ask the desk for alternatives."

She took no notes, he noticed. She never did. But she never forgot anything either. Before her, he'd had several secretaries of the young debutante variety who were titillated by all the secrecy and who usually fell in love with him. They never lasted long. He preferred Solveig. She was prim, and no pleasure to look at, but she didn't expect to be taken to lunch, and she was formidably efficient. If the Soviets really wanted to screw the Agency, he sometimes thought, they could do much worse than snatch Solveig.

On Ivkov and Varischenko, Records produced its usual mixture of fact and speculation. There were a brief biography and two references for Ivkov, and a possible reference for Varischenko, but under a different spelling. He read the Ivkov material first.

IVKOV, ALEXEI GRIGOROVICH.

Born: Tbilisi, Georgia, 1930. Leningrad Polytechnic Institute 1949–55, apparently studying radio-electronics. Won two prizes for applied sciences. Tbilisi Aeronautics Research Institute 1956–63. Professor of radio-electronics, Moscow University 1963–70. Elected to Soviet Academy of Sciences 1972. Presently reported working at the top-security Lenin Research Establishment outside Moscow (formerly Lysenko Institute). Report unconfirmed.

Married 1958. 1 son, 1960. 2 daughters, 1961 & 1964.

No known publications.

NOTE. There is no record of Ivkov's having served in the armed forces or joined the Party. It would be unusual, however, for a sci-

entist of his apparent eminence not to have joined the Party at
some point.

Roskill sighed. He didn't need Records to tell him that. He looked at
the bio again. Not much to go on, but the gaps could be significant.
He'd risen very swiftly, had comrade Ivkov. Only seventeen years and
two academic appointments separated his graduation and his election to
the Academy of Sciences. And the election was not an honor they
handed around to everyone. But no publications. That was interesting.
Presumably they were classified. No military service either. Which must
mean he'd contributed something other than boot leather.

He turned back to the folder. There was a photograph, much enlarged but still quite well-defined. Clipped to it was a note which read,
"Taken at the Lenin Birthday Parade in Red Square in 1972 and subsequently identified as Ivkov by defecting GDR physicist Hans Neumann.
Unconfirmed."

The other reference was taken from the interrogation report on a lab
technician from the Lenin Research Establishment who had crossed the
Wall while on vacation in East Berlin in 1972. The relevant part read
as follows.

Interviewer: We are interested in the names of other scientists who
work at the Establishment.

Subject: There were a lot of them. The Establishment employs
more than five hundred people. I can't remember them all.

Interviewer: Just tell us the ones you remember.

Subject: Well, apart from the ones I just mentioned there were also
Professors Ivkov, Bilek . . .

Interviewer: Tell us about Ivkov. What is his first name?

Subject: Academician Ivkov? I believe his given name was Alexei.

Interviewer: What work does he do?

Subject: Classified work. That's all I know. I didn't know him well.
We played chess once or twice in the recreation center. He never
talked about his work. Nobody did.

Interviewer: You mentioned earlier that there was research into lasers going on at the Establishment. Could he have worked on that?

Subject: I don't know. It's possible. I think he worked in that wing
of the building.

Interviewer: I'm going to show you a photograph. I want you to tell me if the man in the picture is Ivkov.

Subject: It's hard to be sure. I think it's him, but I can't say for certain.

Interviewer: You don't know jackshit, do you?

Translator: Do you want that translated?

Interviewer: Yes. Tell him I don't know why we bother with him. Tell him I think we should throw him back and let the comrades take care of him.

Subject: I'm being as helpful as I can. I can't tell you what I don't know.

The reference to Varischenko was equally inconclusive. It was an extract from a monitored radio broadcast which read:

Cairo 12.21.66
An official spokesman for the UAR Foreign Ministry today announced that two Soviet diplomats, Andrei Biletnikov and Pavel Vorischenko, had been declared *personae non gratae* and been requested to leave the country within 24 hours for activities (quote) inconsistent with the maintenance of cordial relations between the UAR and the Soviet Union (unquote).

The official spokesman declined to comment on the specific reasons for the expulsion of the two Russians, but usually well-informed sources close to the Foreign Ministry reported that both Biletnikov and Vorischenko, whose official positions with the Soviet Embassy were respectively, Third Secretary (Economic Affairs), and Assistant Cultural Attaché, were known to have had repeated contacts with the proscribed Communist organization, PCE. Vorischenko, it was also reported, had made payments totaling more than $60,000 to the organization.
Voice of the Arabs 12.22.66

A note attached from the Station in Cairo stated that contacts within the UAR Foreign Ministry believed both Russians to be members of the KGB. There was, however, no hard evidence to confirm these suspicions.

Roskill closed the folder. It was always this way, the evidence confused and circumstantial, enough to arouse interest, not enough to merit any real confidence. The thing smelled, of course, worse than a dead mackerel in midsummer. But they couldn't ignore it, in spite of the obvious risks. The problem was how to act without catching a tit in the wringer.

Check all the facts. That was the first step. Think about the rest later. He'd send Holland to the Pentagon to check out Berenstein. He'd go to Princeton and talk with Olofson.

The prospect was unappealing. Olofson would refuse to commit himself, and he'd do so at inordinate length. And there was a belt of low pressure—he'd heard that on the car radio—centered around Newark. It would be hot and sticky.

He was contemplating sending Holland to Newark and going himself to the Pentagon when Miss Solveig entered to confirm the appointment and his reservations.

CHAPTER III

∎

Harry Rosen, the chief consulting psychologist to the Central Intelligence Agency, often referred to himself, in his more frustrated moments, as a prophet without honor. His work for the Agency consisted chiefly in constructing psychological profiles of people he had never met and about whom he knew, for certain, very little. Being a conscientious man, he usually accompanied his reports with the warning that since they were extremely speculative, the Agency should place no very firm reliance on them. It was, perhaps, for this reason that the Agency hardly ever did. He sometimes wondered why he didn't abandon the Agency to someone else and concentrate on his private practice. But he never pursued the idea very far. At thirty thousand dollars a year, his position was not, he realized, an honor entirely without profit.

He wondered why the head of the Soviet and East European Section needed to see him so urgently.

Roskill got up as Rosen entered and came round the desk to greet him. He was always careful to observe the minor courtesies. This was partly habit, acquired at Exeter and Harvard, and partly policy. People, he believed, produced better if they liked you.

"Kind of you to come in at such short notice, Harry. I hope I didn't drag you away from a patient. The thing is, I have a problem here and I need your advice. I didn't want to do it on the phone."

He paused to marshall his thoughts.

"I've got to find someone," he continued, "who can memorize at a single hearing what may amount to several pages of scientific information—say three or four thousand words and symbols—that he will almost certainly not understand. Can you give me any idea whatever where I might start looking for someone like that?"

Rosen made a face.

"That's awfully tough," he said. "That kind of memory is extremely rare. It's hard enough to find someone who can remember that much accurately when he understands what he's hearing. When he doesn't—" He shrugged. "I doubt there are more than two or three hundred people in the U.S. who could do it.

"What makes it worse," he went on, "is that when it does occur, that kind of ability crops up in the oddest places. It doesn't seem to confine itself to any particular occupation or social group. For example, there was a basketball player who used to play for the Knicks—Jerry Lucas, I think it was—who could recite page upon page of the New York phone book. But there's no obvious connection between that and making baskets. You might try magicians; a lot of them do memory stunts. Of course, you can never be sure they're not faking it."

Roskill frowned. Two or three hundred. He had known they were looking for someone extraordinary, but that made the odds close to one in a million. Bad enough in itself. But with the timing it was hopeless. They had twelve days—eighteen at the outside—in which to get their man in place. This was far less time than it normally took to get a Soviet visa. So unless they ran a special request through the State Department—suicide if Ivkov were fronting for the KGB—they would have to find their one in a million among the U.S. citizens who had visas for the period June 10th to 17th. There were not millions of these. There were not even thousands. Roskill had the list in front of him. There were two hundred and fifty-three.

That left him between a rock and a hard place. They could send a scientist, as Ivkov had instructed, apply for a visa through State, and pray that they wouldn't get caught with their heads up their asses. Or they could forget it.

He shrugged his shoulders.

"So much for that idea. I'm sorry to have dragged you here on such a fool's errand, Harry. I'll just have to try another tack. But thanks anyway."

"Hold on a moment." Rosen, who had half risen, dropped back into his chair. "It's just a thought, but you might try chess players. Quite a number of the top ones, the grand masters, have had amazing memories. Take Pillsbury, for example—he could memorize anything. Letters or numbers. Incredibly long sequences. Hear them just once and repeat them months later. Backwards, forwards, sideways—you name it. And there've been others. I can't remember the names, but quite a number of them."

Roskill leaned forward.

"You say chess players?" There was a new note of interest in his voice. "Akiba Rubinstein—wasn't he a chess player?"

"Sure he was. One of the greats. But I don't know that his memory was anything special."

"So the Akiba Rubinstein Memorial Tournament would have to be a chess tournament, wouldn't it?"

"I guess so. But listen, I'm not so sure about this chess idea after all. For one thing it doesn't really shorten the odds very much. There are only about five grand masters in the entire U.S. And for another—" He hesitated.

"For another?"

"Well—" Rosen was reluctant to finish. He hated large generalizations. On the other hand, large generalizations were what the Agency paid him handsomely to make.

"Listen. I don't know what you want this individual for. But if you do get lucky and find a chess player to do it, drive with care. Those guys are not your average citizens. They do their thing superlatively. But that's usually it. They tend to strike out in other areas."

"Such as?"

"Well, they're often emotionally underdeveloped. Without the system of social bonds and loyalties that keep the rest of us on the straight and narrow. They often have little sense of responsibility. Odd sets of values. To sum it up, they're unreliable."

"But not," Roskill objected, "necessarily so."

"Of course not. You'll find individuals as sane and sober as you and I. But we're speaking of groups here. As a group I'd say they were bad risks. In fact, if you took one at random, I'd be reluctant to put him in charge of a crap game, much less entrust him with Agency business."

Roskill leaned forward again and smiled.

"I hear what you're saying, Harry, and I'll bear it in mind. But it's true of most of the people we deal with in this business. They're all more or less unreliable. In any case, you've been very helpful, as always, and I'm very grateful to you."

Grateful was not the word for it, he thought, as he saw Rosen out. He couldn't think of the right word, but it seemed possible, for once, that Rosen had earned his money. It seemed just possible, this time, that they had gotten lucky, because the list on his desk—he was absolutely sure of it—contained three names whose reason for traveling to

the Soviet Union had been given as "participation in the Akiba Rubinstein Memorial Tournament."

The stack in Roskill's IN tray the next morning was almost double
the normal height. In addition to the normal flow of paper, there
was a folder several inches thick of press cuttings, a sheaf of records
from Immigration, and a dossier—evidently newly compiled—on the
comings and goings of a certain Arden Wylie. As usual, Records had
been more than thorough.

He contemplated the press cuttings with dismay. But when he attacked it, he discovered that the ever-devoted Solveig had been there
ahead of him; a typewritten index had been prepared and the more interesting items were asterisked and flagged. . . . He really would have
to do something for Solveig: flowers, he told himself, or perhaps even
lunch.

Of the flagged articles, one especially caught his eye. Datelined Dubrovnik, August 10, 1975, it was entitled, "Chess Master Amazes with
Feats of Memory."

Chess masters have long been noted for their phenomenal powers
of concentration and memory. Among the galaxy of stars assembled here for the 15th Annual Invitational Chess Tournament,
which will commence on August 12, perhaps no one possesses
these powers—and particularly the power of memory—to a greater
degree than the American grand master, Arden Wylie.

It was Wylie who, last Friday, less than ten hours after his arrival from the United States, gave an exhibition of simultaneous
blindfold chess against 50 members of the Dubrovnik Chess Club.
In doing so, he surpassed the record established many years ago by
the Argentine master, Miguel Najdorf, and set a new mark which,
in the opinion of knowledgeable observers, will stand until Wylie
himself decides to better it.

In simultaneous blindfold exhibitions, a single competitor, who
is not permitted to see the boards, takes on a number of other
players, each of whom has the board in front of him. The blindfold
player thus faces, in addition to the normal difficulties, the problem of having to remember, at each stage of each game, the exact
position of the pieces. It was computed that in his recent exhibition
Wylie held in his memory control over 3,200 squares, with as
many as 1,600 pieces arrayed upon them, through an average of
40 changes of position. Observers, including this correspondent,

who endeavored to emulate this feat on one board alone generally lost control of the position after six to eight moves.

What made Wylie's feat particularly impressive was the caliber of his opponents. The field contained two grand masters, three international masters, and no player with an FIDE rating of less than 1,800. (Under the FIDE rating system, an approximate scale of equivalences would be: 2,000=expert; 2,200=international master; 2,450=grand master.) Of the 50 games, Wylie won 32, drew 13, and lost only 5.

After the exhibition, which lasted more than 12 hours and during which he lost 2½ pounds in weight, Wylie submitted to further impromptu tests of memory. In one test he was allowed a two-second glimpse of a sequence of 52 letters and numbers; half an hour later, after a number of intervening tests and questions, he repeated the sequence, faultlessly and without hesitation, both in the original and the reverse orders. In another test he was read more than a thousand words from a textbook on biochemistry and repeated them without error, though he confessed to having understood no more than five complete sentences in the entire passage.

Witnesses to the exhibition could not call to mind anyone who could equal or even approach these feats since the days of Pillsbury. Pillsbury, who was also an American grand master . . .

There were several more paragraphs in the same vein, but Roskill had read enough. Providing the security checked out, this was plainly their man. He turned to the dossier on Wylie.

Given the relatively short time at their disposal, Records had assembled an amazing number of facts. Indeed, Roskill reflected, the average U.S. citizen, with his touching faith in constitutional guarantees of the right to privacy, would be dismayed to learn how little in practice these guarantees meant. Almost every significant event in the ordinary American's life was recorded somewhere, and the only real safeguard of privacy—the problem of correlating an embarrassment of information—had largely disappeared with the advent of data banks and computers. Wylie's life—as much of it as Records had thought worth submitting and much more than Wylie would probably have wanted—was spread out on the surface of Roskill's desk. Records had transformed him, almost literally, into an open book.

And a rather intriguing book at that, Roskill thought, for it quickly dispelled the image of withdrawn, owlish intellectualism—crew cuts, pimples, and horn-rimmed glasses—that sprang to mind whenever he thought, which he seldom did, of chess players. Wylie's personality, decidedly, did not conform to that type.

The surface facts were unexceptional. Wylie was thirty-eight years old, single, without close relatives or known romantic attachments. The entry in *Who's Who* described him simply as a chess master, winner of several international tournaments, including the Candidates Tournament of 196–. His address was given as New York City, and his hobbies were listed as: chess. Behind that somewhat monochrome façade, however, there appeared to live someone distinctly offbeat.

The most recent photographs, for instance, offered hints of a character loose and freewheeling. A posed portrait for the cover of *Chess Life* showed Wylie on his favorite battleground, leaning back in his chair waiting for an opponent to make his move. A long, wolfish face stared at the camera, the eyes sharp and watchful, the lips twisting into a smile both humorous and faintly insolent. There was a touch of the maverick in that face, Roskill decided; something almost provocatively self-possessed. *I am who I am,* it seemed to say, *and if you don't like it, you can do the other thing.*

This suggestion of determined individualism was reinforced by the substance of the dossier. There was, for example, the matter of schools. Wylie had attended a surprising number of them, both in the U.S. and abroad, and his removal from most had been involuntary: gambling at one, drinking at another, a too-public relationship with his housemaster's wife at a third—this record topped off by a postal betting fraud, fortunately nipped in the bud, which had hastened his departure from a private school in England.

College, on the other hand, had gone somewhat better. Two almost impeccable years at MIT, where he'd distinguished himself by emulating, on a bet, Oppenheimer's feat of memorizing the log tables to five figures, had been followed by a transfer to Cal Tech and a bachelor's degree in math and physics. Deferring military service, he'd enrolled in a master's program. But then his interest in academics, already diluted by a fascination for bridge and poker, had quickly, it seemed, been preempted entirely by chess. He'd dropped out, moved to New York, taken a part-time job as an elevator operator, and devoted his evenings to sessions at the Manhattan Chess Club with occasional hustling forays —less and less frequent as his reputation spread—to the chess cafés in the Village.

At this point the military had caught up with him. He'd served, surprisingly, in the military police, mostly in Germany. The record stated, among other things, that he'd received a marksman's certificate for pistol shooting, that his IQ had been measured at 183, and that his score for tests involving memory had been off the scale. It also stated that he'd been considered, at one time, for transfer to Military Intelligence, primarily because he was fluent in Russian and German. The transfer had not gone through, however, and he had never risen above the rank of corporal. Nor was this altogether surprising, Roskill thought, for the efficiency reports were unanimous in recording "low motivation" and "tendencies to insubordination." There had also been some question, never satisfactorily resolved, of a possible involvement in some black-market PX scheme.

The dossier concluded with a security evaluation. Wylie was classified "low risk." Apart from an arrest for possession of marijuana in the early sixties—the charge dismissed, when it came to court, on Fourth Amendment grounds—he had no criminal record. Neither did he have any affiliation or recorded contact with the extreme Right or Left. He had not been associated with any protest group. There was no record of his ever marching. He had never joined any political party—he had never joined anything, Roskill guessed, except chess clubs—he had never even registered to vote. His attitude to the political process, in short, suggested that it was a game in which he could summon no interest.

There was no indication, the report further stated, that the subject's sexual proclivities were other than normal. . . . Roskill smiled when he read that. It was a formula, he reflected, whose meaning changed with the times; nowadays it could be stretched to cover a multitude of sins.

Financially, also, the subject was stated to be stable. His reported income in 1976, derived from "chess-related activities," had been $15,660—slightly above the national median. He lived in a furnished studio apartment in the West 80s and paid the rent with clockwork regularity. He held American Express and Mastercharge cards, but nothing was owing on either. He didn't own a car.

Roskill liked the sound of all this . . . Wylie traveled light, evidently: no family, no attachments, no debts—no one to squawk, in other words, if he should happen to disappear. And yet the man was intelligent, obviously, and self-reliant, possessing, if one read between the lines, an undeniable talent for self-preservation. So, with luck, he *wouldn't* disappear. . . . Really, Roskill thought, if one disregarded the consuming interest in chess, what he'd been reading was the profile of the perfect field agent. There was no doubt about it; Wylie was going to be their man.

The schedule from Immigration, however, brought this conclusion immediately into question. It was typical of his luck, Roskill thought, that it should go so far and no further: having found the man, he stumbled forthwith on another problem: Wylie, it seemed, was already in Moscow.

That made things tough. He couldn't, for instance, contact Wylie directly, for there was not a single Agency operative in Moscow whose cover was sufficiently secure. This meant using a cut-off, an intermediary with no traceable connection to the Agency, and also that the cut-off would have to be someone—an ordinary U.S. citizen—already scheduled to be in Moscow by June 10th. Roskill didn't like this idea, didn't like it one bit. One amateur was trouble; two could be murder.

But after half an hour spent considering other possible ways of approaching Ivkov, he was forced to conclude that there weren't any. All the usual ploys—blackmail, body-snatching, or a stealthy approach by an agent whose cover, and person, were readily expendable—were ruled out by the risk. It would have to be Wylie, he decided, there just wasn't anyone else.

The DCI was out when Roskill called, so getting an appointment meant negotiating with Miss Harrison. It was marvelous, Roskill thought, how the secretaries of powerful men invariably assumed their masters' auras; Shakespeare's phrase about the "insolence of office" might have been coined with them in mind.

"I don't know, Mr. Roskill." Harrison's manner was distant and self-important. "The DCI is very tied up with the Senate committee this week . . . I'm not at all sure we can fit you in."

"Look in his book." Roskill was patient. "Tomorrow morning or, at the latest, the afternoon. I need an hour with him and the deputy director. . . . If you can't make a space, I shall have to call him at the Senate and get him to ditch something."

Silence. This was a threat that always worked. Harrison couldn't bear to be bypassed.

"We could fit you in at three," she conceded. "We have the Brits at three-thirty, but they never mind waiting a bit. . . . I'll ask Operations and Research if that's convenient."

"No, Harrison." Roskill was never generous in victory. "Don't ask. Tell."

CHAPTER IV

∎

The office of the Director of Central Intelligence faced east. It occupied —together with Miss Harrison's office, the private bathroom, the reception area, and the private dining room—a substantial part of the top floor of the building, and commanded a sweeping view of the Agency campus, its expanse of parkland dotted with elms and beeches, and the green countryside of Virginia spread out beyond. It was overlooked by no building in the vicinity. Nevertheless, the DCI's desk was set well back from the picture window which faced it, and, though covered with all the usual furniture of office—telephones in several colors, an intercom, a blotter and file trays in tooled Moroccan leather, and a small vase of fresh-cut flowers—it contained no papers or documents whatever.

The file Miss Solveig had prepared for him, having received a suitable addition—in the form of an extra cover bearing the legend "DCI Only"—at the hands of Miss Harrison, reposed in the DCI's lap. He shut it carefully as Roskill and the others filed in and handed it to his secretary.

He was a tall man, thin and sharp-faced, to whose air of assurance and cool efficiency his impeccable neatness and habit of wearing his hair combed back tight against his skull did much to contribute. His eyes, to the extent they were visible behind his thick-lensed spectacles, were flat and lacked animation, seeming to promise intelligence, perhaps, but not much warmth or human understanding. In this they were slightly misleading, for the DCI, the very essence of a political animal, had gotten where he was by virtue of possessing a very acute under-standing of what made his fellows tick. He reminded Roskill of a large, predatory fish.

"You've all read the documents?" He waited until they had seated themselves and Miss Harrison departed. "Then perhaps you, Bob, would begin by giving us your thoughts."

Roskill had spent some time preparing. He knew exactly what action he wanted to take, and he believed he could support it. He was not about to make a formal proposal, however, or parade his arguments for the others to shoot at. What he wanted was a consensus, gently stage-managed by him, in which the others would be implicated. So he began with the negatives.

"My first thought," he said, "was undoubtedly everyone else's—the thing smells. A Soviet research scientist, who claims to be working on their ABM system and who claims to have made a breakthrough which makes immediate development feasible, offers us information. He won't pass documents, however, or microfilm; he wants a meeting. To that meeting, which is to take place in one of the more public spots in the entire Soviet Union, he wants us to send one of our ABM experts, someone who'll be able to understand and remember what he has to say.

"It's not difficult to imagine how the scenario continues. We send our expert. He arrives at the meeting place but, instead of Ivkov, he meets two large policemen who proceed to take him downtown to Dzerzhinski Square and beat the shit out of him until he tells them all he knows about *our* ABM system. Then they put him on trial. He confesses to being a U.S. spy set on by the Agency. The entire Third World calls 'Foul.' The Soviets expel six or eight of our people in Moscow. The press here goes to town on the subject of CIA incompetence, and the Senate subcommittee starts bitching about the size of the Secret Fund." He paused. "Did I leave anything out? Oh, yes." He flashed a grin at the ex-pressionless features of the DCI. "The DCI accepts a job with the Rand Corporation."

Smart, thought Antony Holland, watching Roskill's performance with admiration. Very smart. Appealing direct to the DCI's machismo. Hol-land was Roskill's aid and protégé, very bright and an eager student of Agency politics.

"But let's look at the other side," Operations objected. "The risks are obvious. What about the rewards? Let's assume that Ivkov is on the level. What's he offering? If we believe him, he's offering us a complete, immediately developable ABM package. In that field, where the Soviets are known to be ahead, he's offering parity. Complete parity."

"And yes, Virginia, there is a Santa Claus. . . ." This dry aside from Research produced a thin-lipped smile from the DCI.

Roskill grinned. Things were working out nicely. Research had antagonized Operations, who would now support action whatever the risks. He had always known, of course, that Operations would support him. Action, covert action, was that branch of the Agency's *raison d'être*. They'd lost a lot of ground recently to electronics and the more overt forms of intelligence. These days their desire to prove themselves was almost neurotic. The last remark would commit them absolutely.

"My point is this—" Research moved quickly on to the offensive. "All you say is true only if we make the big assumption. But why should we? I think we should look at the evidence very, very carefully before we embark on what may be no more than a suicidal fishing expedition."

"Right," Roskill nodded. "So let's start with Berenstein. Antony, you talked with the Pentagon. What did they tell you?"

"The Pentagon confirmed. Berenstein is an associate professor at Chicago, specializing in atmospheric physics. His research is funded by Defense and apparently they asked him to zip over to Helsinki and keep his ears open. They know we always cover these things, but the General said they wanted their own man there, too. 'Double coverage,' he called it. That's a football term, and I think it means—" He paused and grinned at them. Holland was young but not diffident. "I think it means they don't trust us."

"What about Ivkov?" the DCI asked.

"Here the vision becomes cloudy." Roskill took over again. "He's in the field; that's certain. But whether he made a breakthrough—whether, indeed, there was a breakthrough—we can't say.

"There are some pointers though. One: if Ivkov is not a very important contributor to the Soviet military effort, why does he alone, of all the Bloc scientists at the conference, need a bodyguard? This Varischenko is listed as an interpreter, but that's obviously a cover because, according to Berenstein, Ivkov's English is almost perfect. There are only two answers. First, Ivkov may be considered a security risk; but in that case why let him go to the conference at all? Alternatively—and to me this is the only explanation that makes sense—he's super important.

"The second pointer comes from Olofson. Unless Ivkov were working directly on the system, Olofson claims, he'd be unlikely to know what the big hang-ups are. But Ivkov told Berenstein enough, apparently, to convince Olofson that he does know."

"Could you perhaps tell us,"—this from Research—"in paraphrase, of course, exactly what Olofson said?"

Roskill grinned. In paraphrase was right. Olofson had talked for the best part of forty minutes before getting to the point.

"Well, it was very technical and I can't pretend to have grasped all the detail, but in essence the big problem, the one that's holding everyone up, is integrating the radar coordinates on the incoming missiles with the targeting instructions for the destruct missiles. In other words, getting a clear fix on a zillion incoming missiles—all of them fitted with devices to jam conventional radar—early enough to zap them before they give birth to n zillion mini-missiles, each armed and loaded for bear. If Ivkov had solved that one, Olofson said, he'd hit the jackpot.

"Olofson also said—and in the light of what we read in the interrogation report this may be worth noting—that in his opinion the most promising approach to solving this problem lay in the application of lasers."

He continued. "There's another thing I'd like to mention. It's perhaps only my intuition, but there's an amateurish, comic-opera flavor to this whole situation which strikes me as uncharacteristic of the KGB. If the whole thing is only a trap, then to my taste it's much too obvious. Open-air meetings in Gorki Park. Passwords. Information passed verbally in huddles over the chess tables. To me that looks like the plan of an amateur, improvised on the spur of the moment, under pressure."

"I don't know about that." Research, the resident expert on the KGB mentality, resented the intrusion into his domain. "The Soviets are sophisticated enough to be unsophisticated on occasion. That line of thinking gets you nowhere. They'll think we'll think, so they'll think, etcetera. It just leads to an infinite regression.

"It's all so inconclusive," he continued, "but what it boils down to is this. The risks are very real and very grave. The rewards are highly speculative."

The DCI leaned forward.

"I'm inclined to agree with Ed," he said. "The risk is horrendous. We're only just beginning to recover from Watergate. Another scandal like that might set us back years."

"I don't think any of us would dispute that, sir. But if the risk could be cut, virtually eliminated—?"

"Then we'd be morally obliged to go ahead," Operations cut in impatiently. "Listen, we can sit here all afternoon worrying about the risks without adding a jot to what Bob said at the outset. The point is this. We're an intelligence-gathering agency. We're offered a prospect of what could be the intelligence coup of the decade. We can't afford to ignore it. Instead of hemming and hawing about whether we should go after it, we should be considering how."

"Then perhaps you'd be good enough to tell us that." The DCI's voice was silky. "It's your province, after all."

"I've an idea that might do it," Roskill came to the rescue. "As I see it, the risk is twofold. One, that the Soviets acquire information about our research. Two, that the Agency suffers a scandal. I think risk number one can be eliminated entirely, and risk number two reduced to perfectly manageable proportions. You see, Ivkov wants us to send someone who'll remember because he will understand what Ivkov has to tell him. That means a research scientist with a direct traceable connection to the U.S. government and hence to us. But what if we send someone who'll simply remember but won't necessarily understand a word?"

"Is that possible?"

"Olofson thinks it is. According to him it's the principle of the solution we need to get at. Once we have the principle, the details are easy to work out. And he says that the principles behind technological discoveries are almost invariably simple to state. One or two pages—a couple of thousand words or symbols—will generally do it. He doesn't expect this to be any different."

"So what you're saying is that we find someone who can do the memorizing; send him; and then if the whole thing turns out to be a trap—?"

"Exactly." Roskill nodded. "If KGB show up at Gorki Park, they capture themselves not a valuable package of information, but merely a private U.S. citizen. A memory man."

"They'd still make a fuss about it."

"Of course they would. But he wouldn't be traceable to us. We'd simply deny it."

"We wouldn't be believed."

"Of course not." The DCI's voice was weary. "The day's long since gone by, Ed, when an Agency statement would be believed even if it were supported by sworn testimony from the Archangel Gabriel. The point is that, without evidence, they can't prove anything. We'd catch shit for a few days, I expect. But then it would die down. I think we could tolerate that."

"The question is," he turned to Roskill, "who are we going to send? It's not everyone who can manage that kind of assignment, I'd imagine."

"No, it's not," Roskill admitted. "We're going to need a memory capacity of rather a high order. But fortunately," he played his ace, "I have a candidate. There are one or two drawbacks, but I think you'll agree that this type of operation is a hell of a sight better than the alternative." He told them about it.

When he had finished, the DCI was silent for a few moments.

"That sounds, in principle, very acceptable," he said at last, "unless, of course, anyone here has another suggestion."

He looked at each of them in turn. Nobody had.

CHAPTER V

Roskill yawned. He was not at his best first thing in the morning. He seemed to have the type of metabolism that took several hours to get into top gear. It did not take kindly to rousing at six-thirty to catch the eight A.M. shuttle to La Guardia, missing breakfast in the process. Now, if Congress really wanted to investigate something worthwhile, it should consider some of the airlines monopolies instead of hassling the Agency about covert operations. The shuttle, for instance. Thirty-four dollars one way. Without breakfast. If they transported cattle that way there'd be a national outcry.

He could have sent Holland, he knew. But this was his operation. He was responsible; and, since it was his neck on the block, he wanted to make all the judgments. It was not that he lacked confidence in Holland. Holland was bright and dependable. But Roskill was twenty years older; and twenty years of experience, he believed, counted a great deal when it came to sizing up people.

The security checks helped, of course. They eliminated some of the negatives, threw out the people who were obvious risks. But they couldn't tell one whether a person was dependable and intelligent, or lacked common sense and might panic in a crisis. Given forty minutes of conversation, he believed that he, on the other hand, could make a very educated guess.

A woman entered, holding a styrofoam cup on which she balanced a hamburger-shaped object wrapped in aluminum foil.

"This is the best I could do, I'm afraid," she said, depositing the cup on the desk in front of him. "They don't serve burgers this early, so I brought an English muffin instead. I hope that's all right."

She glanced at him curiously. A Mr. Hunter from Immigration, her boss had told her, would be borrowing the office for the morning. That happened occasionally. Some kind of investigation, she guessed. Drugs, probably. Well, he certainly wasn't your run-of-the-mill lawyer. More like a diplomat, really. Nice suit. English shoes. Beautiful manners, too. Odd that he'd asked for a hamburger.

Roskill looked up at her, saw her appraising him, and smiled.

"They're not really English, you know."

She looked blank.

"The muffins. We call them English, but you never see them in England. Anyway, it'll do perfectly. Thank you very much."

She turned to leave, when he added, "I'm expecting a Mrs. Crossland. When she arrives, show her right in, would you? Thank you."

When she had left, he opened his briefcase and took another look at the report from Markham.

CROSSLAND, ANNE. Born: Des Moines, Iowa, 12/12/44. Parents—Antony Irving Shipton, Captain U.S. Marine Corps, killed in action, Normandy 6/20/45, and Margaret Maitland McLoskey, both of Des Moines.

There followed two paragraphs of detailed, but essentially uninteresting, information about her education. And then . . .

Subject was married 8/11/68 to Andrew Garfield Crossland, Lieutenant 1st U.S. Air Cavalry. The marriage took place in Hawaii where Crossland was on R & R from Vietnam. Crossland was killed in action, Tay Ninh province, 3/2/69. No children.

Subject has supported herself, since the death of her husband, as a free-lance journalist specializing in subjects relating to the women's rights movement. To the extent they are expressed in her publications, subject's political views, though radical in respect to women's rights, seem moderate, left of center, on other subjects.

Subject is fourth-generation American of English-Scottish descent, has no known family connections outside the U.S. She has never, to the best of our knowledge, visited any of the Soviet-bloc or Chicom countries, had any affiliation with the U.S. Communist Party or any communist front organization, or been closely associated with anyone who had.

Subject has no criminal convictions, and to our knowledge, no personal habits (drugs, alcohol, etc.) that would render her an unusual security risk. There is an outstanding mortgage balance of $32,000 on her house in Queens, NYC, but the mortgage is in good standing and subject appears to have no other significant financial liabilities.

Underneath, in red ink, Markham had written, "Seems clean enough, but I must stress that, given limited time available for clearance, our checks were necessarily cursory."

Roskill grinned. Cursory indeed. Markham, as ever, was protecting his rear. But then, security services were necessarily paranoid, animated by distrust. He himself, knowing rather better than Markham the difficulty and expense of recruiting and establishing deep-cover agents, was not oppressed by any great sense of doubt. There were more than a hundred million adult Americans. Of these, perhaps two or three hundred might be actual KGB agents and a couple of thousand more potentially disloyal. Once one eliminated the obvious risks, as apparently they had in this case, the mathematics of the situation were overwhelmingly favorable. He was not worried, at all, about security. The real problem was different.

Image. That was the problem. Time was when the Agency—when he had joined it, for instance—had been a company of knights in shining armor. Vietnam had changed that. Vietnam, the Bay of Pigs, Chile, Peru, Watergate. . . . The list was too long. Now, in the eyes of the popular press and hence in the eyes of many—too many—of the great unthinking American public, the Agency was just one step up from the Mafia. A band of sinister *fascisti*, fortunately rather incompetent, engaged in a conspiracy to prevent world peace. When one approached the Great American Public these days, one did so diffidently, with an eye on the nearest exit.

There was a knock at the door. The secretary stuck her head in and announced his visitor.

Roskill rose and greeted her, gesturing toward a chair on the other side of the desk. He himself left the desk and sat down opposite her.

Her appearance reassured him. It suggested nothing very radical. She was dressed simply—plain skirt and sweater beneath a light cotton raincoat—but with an air of elegance which, Roskill thought, had less to do with what she wore than with the way she wore it. A silk scarf, possibly from Hermes, was knotted loosely around the grip of her purse.

She was certainly attractive: slim, but full-figured, her face surrounded by a frame of dark brown hair in a style that Roskill recognized as the "wedge" and dominated by two features—the eyes, gray-green, clear and arrestingly candid, and the mouth, full and generous, with lines which suggested its corners turned up much more often than down. It was an intelligent, humorous face, Roskill decided, not the face of someone who would be likely to greet his proposal with a howl of outrage.

"Mrs. Crossland," he began, "I should start by saying that I owe you an apology. My name is indeed Hunter, but I'm not with the Department of Immigration. I'm with the Central Intelligence Agency."

He paused for a reaction. But, although her eyes widened in surprise, she said nothing and waited for him to continue.

"Perhaps you'd like to check my credentials?"

There was an Agency procedure for this. For the time being, Mr. Hunter possessed a convincing, though electronic, identity. When his usefulness was over, he would simply cease to exist.

She shook her head.

"Then, perhaps, I should start by asking you a question. It may seem irrelevant, or fatuous, or simply none of my business. But it would make this all much simpler if you'd answer as honestly as you can. What is your opinion of the function of the Central Intelligence Agency?"

"You mean, what's my opinion of spying?"

"You could put it that way."

She made a face. "Well, I don't like it particularly. But I suppose, if everyone else does it—and apparently they do—we'd be foolish not to ourselves. That's not to say, though, that I think all your activities are justified. Your interference, for example, in the politics of other countries often strikes me as stupid." She smiled. "You do have rather a record, don't you, of backing the wrong horse?"

"But you'd have no objection to a simple intelligence-gathering operation?"

"I'm not sure about that. It would rather depend on what it was."

"O.K. That's fair enough. The reason I wanted to talk to you, went to these elaborate lengths"—he gestured at their surroundings and smiled as though to acknowledge the cowboys-and-Indians quality of the proceedings—"to get in touch with you, and put you to no little inconvenience, for which I truly apologize, is that I need some help and you're ideally placed to give it."

He was careful to speak in the first-person singular. He found people reacted much better to him personally—present, concrete, and not, if he was forced to admit it, entirely without charm—than to the abstract and slightly sinister "we," the Agency.

"Before I explain what I'd like you to do, let me say two things. First, if you've already decided you want nothing to do with it, it would be better to leave now, before we go any further. I may say I'll understand completely if that's what you decide."

He waited for some reaction, but she said nothing.

"Second. I'd like you to treat this whole incident, what I'm about to tell you, my identity, the fact of my having contacted you, and the manner in which it was done, as completely confidential. That's as much for your protection as for ours."

She leaned forward. "It wasn't you, was it." It was a statement rather than a question. "It wasn't you who called yesterday."

"No. It was one of my minions." He smiled to remove the self-importance from his statement.

"I thought not. His voice wasn't the same. His whole manner was more peremptory." She smiled, finally, as if to acknowledge her acceptance of the situation. "I'm sorry. I know that was irrelevant. Please go on."

"You're planning to be in Moscow on June 5th?"

She nodded.

"There's someone there I want to contact. He's an American citizen, and he has absolutely no connection, at present, with the Agency or with any branch of the Federal government. I want to keep it that way. So I don't want to run the risk of using any of our people. What I'd like you to do is to contact him there—it won't be difficult; I expect you'll both be in the same hotel—and make a request of him. That's all."

"That's all?" Her expression seemed to tell him it was a very great deal. "What about risk? I can't believe there is none."

They had reached the big obstacle. He scouted the notion of prevaricating, as he had considered prefacing his request with some patriotic reference to her husband and father. But she was too intelligent for that.

"Yes. I can't pretend there isn't some risk. But primarily it's to the person you'd be contacting. There'd only be danger to you if he were to land in trouble. It's to minimize that possibility that I'm asking you to help."

"That reasoning sounds a bit circular to me."

"Well, perhaps in a way. But not really. You see, most people assume that big governments—we and the Russians—spend all our time watching each other. Now, we'd like to, I'm not denying that, but it's not possible in practice. It would take too much time and money. So what we do is limit ourselves to areas of obvious exposure or danger—diplomats, officials, people who behave suspiciously. We don't bother much with ordinary citizens, because we know that all but a tiny fraction of them are just that. In this case both you and the other person involved are ordinary citizens. You both have perfectly innocent reasons for being in Moscow. And both of you made your plans to go there long before my need of you arose. You're the kind of people, Americans in a strange country, who might be expected to strike up an acquaintance. There'd be no reason for anyone to pay any particular attention to you.

"There's another thing. The danger to your contact will occur only when he carries out the request you make of him. We'll schedule that to happen when you're safely out of the way."

She noticed, with amusement, his shift from the conditional. It was sly, but not oversly. He wasn't lying to her, she thought. Minimizing, perhaps, but not lying. And he wasn't patronizing, either. She appreciated that.

"I think you'd better tell me about it," she said.

"I can see problems," she told him when he had finished. "First. Assume I do as you ask: I approach this man and pass on your request. How does he know it's genuine?"

"I'd thought of that," he replied, "and I don't have any foolproof answer. But tell me this. Suppose someone—a sane and well-balanced person like yourself—approached you and asked you, as a matter of national importance, to meet a man, receive a message, and pass it on to the Agency. You'd be intrigued, wouldn't you?"

"I suppose I would."

"You'd be tempted, wouldn't you, to check the story out?"

"Probably."

"And if it turned out that there was a man, and he did indeed have a message, you'd be convinced and pass it on."

"Yes. I might do all that if—and here's my second problem—if I wasn't too scared."

"Well, you might be scared. But I think you'd also be curious. Most people are, especially about situations like this. He'll be curious, too. At least, that's what I'm banking on. If he's not—" he shrugged, "that's too bad. We don't have any other way. And, besides, I've wasted time and money on situations less promising than this."

She considered this. At length she said, "Speaking of curiosity, there's something *I'm* curious about."

"What?"

"There's been no carrot and no stick. You haven't bribed or threatened. You haven't appealed, very strongly, to my patriotism. You just made me a proposal, discussed it candidly, and left it at that. That surprises me. You people are supposed to be more devious."

He laughed. "Oh, I can be sneaky enough if I want. With you it didn't seem necessary. That's what made it—whatever you decide—so pleasant to talk with you."

She accepted this without comment.

"I suppose you know that I'll do it?"

"I hoped you would, and I'm extremely grateful. I wish," he added, "I could show some of my gratitude by inviting you to lunch. But, after all the trouble you've been put to to keep our meeting a secret, that really wouldn't be very wise."

He really was quite devious, she thought later as she left the building. There'd obviously been quite a lot he hadn't told her. But perhaps that was better. The less she knew, the less she'd worry. She wondered why she'd agreed to do it. Patriotism? Yes, there was something of that. It really did seem, on the face of it, very important. Excitement? That too, perhaps. There'd been little of that in her life of late. Mr. Hunter himself? Yes, that as well. She liked him. And also, she was quite surprised to find, she trusted him.

Roskill left a little later. He took a route which led him via a service elevator and the offices of an insurance agency into John Street. It was the route by which he had entered.

He hailed a cab and gave the address of the Harvard Club. Lunch was what he needed. Lunch and perhaps a quick game or two of backgammon afterwards.

CHAPTER VI

Colonel Yuri Lermontov, chief of the Moscow Section of the Internal Security Division of the KGB, performed, he sometimes thought, much the same function as a priest: he was responsible for the conscience of every member of the Greater Moscow District. It was, as he knew only too well, an impossible task. For in Moscow he faced not only the spirit of irony with which Russians, through the ages, have greeted the actions of their governments, but also a sophistication in whose eyes the very notion of conscience seemed slightly provincial. It was these qualities in his flock that made the problem of the *samizdat* so troublesome.

Samizdat are publications of the literature of the Soviet underground: works of dissident or unorthodox thought which, denied the imprimatur of the State Publishing House, circulate secretly in manuscript. In theory the existence of *samizdat* should have been a great help to Lermontov. The quantities in circulation at any given time, if measured, could furnish an indicator of the state of the district's loyalties; while an individual manuscript, planted by one of his agents, could be used, like a barium meal, to trace a pathway through the intestines of subversion. In practice, however, these advantages were never realized; the real problem with *samizdat* was not that *some* people read them, but that everybody did.

Lermontov, in spite of his profession, was a sanguine and level-headed man. He was not overly concerned, himself, with *samizdat*. There was, he recognized, a great difference between genuine subversion and the playful defiance of government regulation which accounted for the continued and increasing popularity of *samizdat*. Indeed, he thought privately, it was the very existence of the regulations which prompted the defiance. When individuals were faced with a complete orthodoxy of official thought, the reading of banned publications was bound to offer an acceptable way of asserting a small degree of intellectual independence, harmless in itself and psychologically necessary.

This, however, was not the view of his government. Lermontov, a dedicated and hard-working public servant, felt bound to register token recognition of that view. Faced thus with a plethora of information on the readers of *samizdat* which devoured an ever-increasing portion of his organization's time and threatened to swamp his filing system, he had solved the problem, and salved his conscience, by installing a computer into which all such information was regularly fed. The computer was programmed with a list of individuals who, by reason of their occupation, rank in the Party, prominence, or connections, were labeled "Security Sensitive." Since the list was absurdly long and constantly expanding, a ranking of "sensitivity" had been established, each rank numbered, five through one, in an ascending order of importance. In order to protect his sanity, Lermontov had issued instructions that he was to be notified only when the machine, in the course of its daily regurgitations, spat out the name of an individual classified as "Security Sensitive I."

The efficiency with which such systems function depends on how carefully they are administered. Lermontov's attitude toward *samizdat* had communicated itself by degrees, wordlessly, to his subordinates. The information was supplied faithfully to the machine; but the sensitivity ranking was updated with increasing infrequency. Originally it had been done continuously. Now information on changes of security status was allowed to accumulate and was programmed only once every three or four months.

It was for this reason that the name of Alexei Ivkov, although the change in his ranking had occurred some three months previously, was not brought to Lermontov's attention until May 28th.

The computer recorded correlations. Lermontov was not particularly impressed by correlations. The fact that Ivkov was recorded as possessing an unauthorized publication by his colleague Saltonov, relating to the problems facing the modern scientific conscience, was probably not, in itself, significant. Indeed Lermontov, who had browsed through a confiscated copy of the work himself, was not entirely sure why it had been banned, since the reasoning was so obviously faulty. But when the correlations multiplied beyond a certain point, Lermontov was bound to take notice. On June 1st, he received, in different dispatches, the reports from Varischenko and the Resident in Helsinki.

Ivkov, he now recalled, had been the subject of an elaborate program of surveillance he had been called upon to organize for the duration of the scientific conference in Helsinki. He had not been informed of the reasons for this unusual procedure, the "need to know" having applied in this case with unusual stringency. He had simply assumed that Ivkov must be in possession of extremely sensitive information. He had chosen Varischenko for the important, but possibly embarrassing, role of the overt member of the program partly because Varischenko combined a high degree of visibility with a total disregard for the niceties of social behavior. Varischenko, he had believed, would cling like a burr. But Varischenko, it appeared, had let him down.

The report from the Resident had been delicately worded. He had read it at first, in conjunction with Varischenko's overeager self-justification, primarily as a criticism of Varischenko's conduct. Certain phrases of the report, however, suggested that rather more than Varischenko's competence might be at issue. . . . Ivkov had met Berenstein —an apparently impromptu meeting, probably innocent enough. . . . Ivkov had upset a pitcher of beer on Varischenko, who had then left to change his clothes. . . . But "Varischenko, on the basis of his experience in surveillance and observations of Ivkov's subsequent behavior, is convinced that the upsetting of the beer was an accident." There was an omission there, a subtle absence of comment, which spoke volumes. The Resident himself was not so sure. . . . Ivkov had been alone with the American for perhaps four minutes. That again was reassuring, innocent enough.

Berenstein, though, was disturbing. He had gone straight to the U.S. Embassy. Or rather, not straight. He had taken an "erratic and round-about route." Aspects of his behavior had been "consistent with the interpretation that he believed he was being followed and was attempting, in a clumsy and amateurish fashion, to avoid pursuit." Now why would a man behave like that?

If one were willing to make certain assumptions, he knew, the conclusion was only too obvious.

But the assumptions were large and troublesome. Ivkov's previous security record was clean; he had a twenty-year record of successful and vital work for his country; he was important and well connected. Also, very possibly, he was innocent.

Lermontov was not a cynic. The problem of innocence always troubled him. A full-scale security investigation invariably traumatized its subject and left him, were he innocent, with an abiding sense of outrage.

He was reluctant, always, to bring that upon anyone. But he was particularly reluctant to bring it upon someone whose sense of outrage might have sharp practical consequences for him and for his department. Plainly the case called for the utmost discretion.

He reached for the telephone.

"Please get me General Stein."

There was a pause punctuated by a variety of electronic squeaks and buzzes. Why was it, Lermontov wondered, that the technological expertise of his department had never extended to the telephone system. They had cameras that could photograph a page of newsprint readably at a hundred meters, listening devices so efficient and unobtrusive that foreign ambassadors had to resort to soundproofed cubicles in order to have confidential conversations with members of their own staffs. The telephone system, on the other hand, seemed beyond hope.

Presently he heard Stein's voice, barely audible, above the crackling on the line. It seemed to be coming from Siberia, although his superior's office was only two floors above his own.

"Stein speaking. Who is this? Speak louder, please. . . . Oh, Yuri. Good morning. Listen, I can't hear a word you're saying. Can you come up?"

Lermontov went up.

Stein was in a good mood, relaxed and expansive. He insisted Lermontov have a glass of tea and launched into an ironic tirade against the telephone system. "So finally," he concluded, "I spoke to the Chief of Communications for the Greater Moscow District. 'Comrade,' I told him, 'the telephones prevent us from talking to one another.' 'Comrade,' he replied, 'in the Security Service that ought to be a tremendous advantage.'" His big laugh boomed around the room.

"But you didn't come up here to listen to my jokes." He leaned forward. "You have a problem. What is it?"

"General, you recall that I was instructed to place Academician Ivkov under surveillance and protection for the duration of his visit to Helsinki?"

"Yes."

"Would it be possible for you to tell me, in very general terms, of course, why these extraordinary precautions were taken?"

The general frowned and was silent for a moment. Then he said, "To tell the truth, Yuri, I don't know. I understand he is involved in work of a very sensitive nature. I assumed the surveillance was, as you say, primarily for his protection. . . . Why?"

Lermontov told him.

Stein was again silent, resting his chin on his hands and gazing out of the big window into the busy square below. Finally he said, "Listen, when the request for surveillance was made originally, it came through the usual channels. I pointed out that if Ivkov's position were so sensitive as to require the full-time services of five members of my understaffed department, the wisest course might be for him to stay at home. One hour later I received a telephone call . . . it was one of those days when the telephones were working . . . the call was from the Minister of Defense. He told me quite bluntly that Ivkov was going to Helsinki. That it was his decision and that in the matter of surveillance he was requesting not advice, but action. You understand what I'm saying?"

Lermontov nodded.

"So, for the time being, we will do nothing. I shall speak to the Minister, of course, and request his advice. He is fond of taking decisions. Let him take them."

Lermontov rose to leave. "I shall send you copies of the reports from Helsinki, General," he said, "and the computer printout. I assume you will wish to make your request in writing."

"But naturally, my dear Yuri. Naturally, in writing."

CHAPTER VII

∎

Grand Master Wylie surveyed his position. He was a pawn down already; the pawn at Q4 was isolated, probably indefensible. To make matters worse, his remaining knight was badly placed and his entire position was cramped. His opponent would have no difficulty forcing an exchange of rooks, and he would be left with a lost endgame. The defeat would take his score in the tournament below fifty percent. His worst result in years. His share of the prize money would barely cover expenses.

With the air of one suddenly resolving a difficult problem, he got up and extended a hand to his opponent.

"I accept a draw," he announced.

The Australian, Greene, pulled back as though stung. "A draw? You've got to be kidding. You're lost. Screwed. You ought to resign. You bloody Yanks are all alike. No fucking sportsmanship. . . ."

His nasal snarl could be heard all over the hall, disturbing its cathedral-like hush. A sudden clatter of conversation from the spectators was peremptorily stilled by a glare from the tournament director. From the tables adjacent to Wylie's there came a series of urgent and irritated hisses. The tournament director left his seat and made his way toward them.

Wylie shrugged. "The position is obviously drawn. However, if you need the practice . . ." He bent down, gave his king's rook's pawn a contemptuous nudge with his middle finger, advancing it out square, and stopped his clock. Then he strolled away from the table, pausing en route to light a cigarette, and drifted toward the window, where he stood, a study in indifference, gazing out upon the scene below.

Behind him he could hear the remonstrance of the tournament director.

"Perhaps you were provoked, Greene. But I must ask you to control your temper. There are other players here. You are disturbing their concentration. Please continue your game in silence."

More hisses from the nearby tables. Wylie continued his gazing. He allowed fifteen minutes to elapse before he returned to the board.

Greene's move, the product not of thought but of overwhelming anger, had been a blunder. He had realized this even as he was making it; but his hand had touched the piece, and his instincts as a player, not to mention the inhibiting presence of the tournament director, precluded second thoughts. He could only sit, poker-faced, and pray that Wylie would overlook the fact that the rook at B5 could now be taken with impunity.

Wylie did not. He glanced briefly at the pieces, took the rook, and sauntered back to the window, neglecting to stop his clock.

Wylie crossed the hotel lobby, brooding. He had been enormously lucky. Six and a half points, out of a possible twelve so far, instead of five and a half; there was a world of difference. He might possibly make some money. There was Petrosian to come, of course—a draw there would be something. And Stein, another draw, perhaps. And Karpov? Doubtful. He had chances, certainly. But . . .

He was desperately tired. The doubts which, since Amsterdam, had gathered, like rain clouds on a clear day, slowly but perceptibly around him, could not be ignored. Draws. He was hoping for draws. His win over Greene had been a plain swindle. . . . Greene—a player whom in five previous meetings he had crushed offhandedly—had almost defeated him.

He could write it down to fatigue, of course, to that idiotic, fifteen-hour simultaneous he had given too close to the tournament. But at heart he knew better. It was always an effort now. Each time he sat down at the board it took more courage, a greater summoning of will, to peer into the swirling vortex of possibilities the black and white squares and thirty-two pieces could produce. The game, a playground he had lightheartedly inhabited for as long as he could remember, had become strange country, full of pitfalls and dark places. He played safe now, terrified of blunders. He had lost his nerve, and he was losing his talent.

It would take time. He could hang on for a few more years, his results getting worse, his rating slowly dropping. Then the tournament invitations would stop coming. He would be reduced to occasional journalism—at fifteen dollars a hundred—and teaching openings to patzers.

He was, in some ways, a proud man, conscious of belonging to a tiny, specialized aristocracy of the intellect. He had seen some of his peers deteriorate that way, painfully and in public, and he did not wish to follow their example. He did not want to be forced into more swindles, to betray, in insolence or timidity, the game that had dignified his life.

He should face facts. It was over. If he had courage he should play out this tournament and retire, resign honorably. But to what? With what?

That was the big problem. He had some money, but not enough to live on. He was virtually unemployable in any capacity he cared to contemplate. Welfare was unimaginable. So to what? With what?

On reaching his room he took his shoes off and lay down on the bed, hands behind his head, staring up at the ceiling. In this space, roughly square, its paint a drab gray, cracked and peeling in places, he now imagined a chessboard and began to reconstruct the game he had just played, trying to discover just where its pattern had begun to elude him. Perhaps it had been at move thirteen, where his pawn push, an effort to force simplifying exchanges, had ceded to his opponent the long white diagonal to his KR1. Perhaps. . . . His mind, happy to abandon its contemplation of such gloomy imponderables as his future, began to sift the possibilities, sorting them into concrete variations, each to be analyzed separately.

He got up and fetched his board. Ceilings were unsuitable for serious analysis. He had begun to arrange the pieces into the position at Greene's move twelve when he heard footsteps coming to his door and then a knock, barely perceptible, and another, louder.

"Who is it?"

"Is this room forty-two? Is that Mr. Wylie?" The voice was clear and feminine. American.

"Yes to both questions. Come in, please."

He was irritated at the distraction. But when he saw her, the irritation evaporated. She was young, about thirty, he estimated, and quite pretty.

"Mr. Wylie. I hope I'm not disturbing you. I should have called first, I know. But I tried at the desk and they told me the telephones were out of order. They always are here apparently. So I decided to try your room. I hope you don't mind."

"No, I don't mind at all. But what can I do for you, Miss . . . ?"

"Mrs." She was recovering her composure. "Mrs. Anne Crossland. I'm a journalist. Free-lance. I've been commissioned by one of the women's weeklies to do an article on the status of women in Russia. But while I was here I discovered that there was this big chess tournament going on and that Americans were playing. I thought perhaps you might agree to an interview. Chess is very topical now, and I know several papers that might take it.

"By the way," she added, "I should congratulate you. I understand you had a notable victory today."

He smiled wryly. "I had a victory. But it was hardly notable."

"Why?"

"My opponent blundered in a winning position. I was lucky. Very lucky. . . . What sort of interview did you have in mind?"

"Oh! 'The Life-style of a Chess Player'—that sort of thing. Nothing very technical, or very personal for that matter."

Wylie looked at her. The session of analysis was shot, obviously, and the last thing he really wanted to do was talk about himself. But he needed diversion and she really was, when you studied her closely, remarkably attractive. He decided to amuse himself.

"What do you know about chess?"

"Nothing, really. I know the moves, but that's all. I'm not really interested in you as a chess player, but more in your life away from the game. How being a professional chess player affects it."

"But I am a chess player," he objected. "It's my defining characteristic. Chess players don't have life-styles." He motioned her into one of the chairs. "They leave that to TV stars, advertising executives, or even journalists. Chess players play chess. Period. Everything else is a detail. So unless you know something about chess, how can you write intelligently about our lives? There's nothing else to write about.

"Did you know, for example, that the average professional chess player in the U.S. earns less than ten thousand dollars? Did you know that he spends probably seventy-five percent of his time in hotels—mostly cheap hotels? That ninety percent of his meals are eaten in restaurants, also cheap? Or that chess players enjoy, if that is really the word, the lowest marriage rate and the highest divorce rate of any recognized occupation?"

He had begun to enjoy himself. It was amazing, he reflected, how much conviction, a number—any number—could carry. When they came to label the twentieth century they should call it "The Age of Statistics."

"You see," he continued, "it's impossible to understand how we put up with such a life; how grown, intelligent men, who could certainly make more money in other professions, can tolerate this poverty, this lack of recognition, roots, and security, unless you can appreciate something of what the game means to us. And that, too, is probably impossible unless you yourself, however obscurely, have felt its pull."

"You're saying, in effect, that one has to be a junkie to understand junkies?"

"That's not a bad analogy."

"I see. Then I guess I'll have to approach the problem the other way round."

"How do you mean?"

"Approach an understanding of what chess means to you by discovering what you give up for it—the way we do with junkies. As a matter of fact, you told me a good deal about your life-style even while you were claiming to have none."

He smiled. "I see you're not to be discouraged."

She smiled back. "Were you really trying?"

"I guess not. I suppose everyone would like to imagine his life is interesting. I'm no exception. . . . What did you want to know?"

"Well, I suppose I could just ask you my list of twenty invariable questions, call it a day, and depart. But that sort of approach always comes out rather lifeless, I feel. I'd rather—" She hesitated. "If you have the time, and if it wouldn't be too much of a drag, I'd rather spend a couple of hours with you, walking round the city, sightseeing or sitting in the park, and see what comes out of it. I find people are always more interesting when they're just talking. Not answering direct questions."

"Ah, the New Journalism." He smiled. "Of course, you understand what a terrible burden that places on me. I have to just talk and yet I have to be interesting. I could get terribly self-conscious."

"Oh, I imagine you'll manage." Her mouth twitched ironically.

"Well, in that case, I suppose, it wouldn't be *too* much of a drag."

They smiled at one another. Two contestants in a match that had come out even.

They went, naturally, to Gorki Park, where they walked and chatted inconclusively until, through the influence of some obscure psychic pull, they found themselves at the concrete chess tables provided by a thoughtful government for aficionados. The tables were all occupied and surrounded, in many cases, by kibitzers who noisily encouraged and advised the contestants. Wylie wandered to one table and stood over it for a moment, frowning his disapproval of what he saw there.

"You're never far away from it, are you?"

For a moment he looked at her blankly, lost in his intricate imaginary world. Then he collected himself and answered, "No, I guess not.

It's really my whole life, you see. I don't have very much else. I've never wanted it."

"You said I'd never understand you chess players unless I understood the lure of the game. Suppose you try and explain it to me."

He was silent for a while. When he spoke it was not directly in answer to her question. "You know, you've caught me at a good time."

"How so?"

"Well, if there ever has been, in my life, a proper time to make an accounting, it's now. . . . I mean," he explained, "a time to add up what it's all cost and whether it's been worth it."

He was thinking aloud, she sensed, speaking not to her but to himself.

"In a way we are seekers after truth. We play; we like to win; but winning is really subordinate. What we are always really after is an ideal.

"Chess is a problem, you see. Trivial, perhaps, but very intricate and challenging. It's a problem with finite solutions which, in theory at least, can be completely stated. Fortunately for us the problem is so vast that no statement of these solutions is in sight or even, really, imaginable. For example, the number of ways the first twenty moves for both sides can be played is a number so large there is probably no name for it. Approximately, it is one, followed by six, followed by twenty-nine zeros. But the problem *is* finite and we keep on trying. . . . We spend our lives, in effect, charting small areas of the solution."

He looked at her and hesitated. Then, with what seemed to be a deliberate and painful effort, he continued.

"When I was young and confident—a little arrogant even—there seemed no end to the fascination. I thought it would last forever. I knew that the truth, the complete set of solutions, was always in plain sight, open to anyone with the imagination and courage to grasp it. I believed I could go on advancing toward it, making sense of more and more of it, indefinitely. . . . But one gets tired, one's vision becomes cloudy, one's courage falters. One stops searching and becomes concerned merely with winning. And, perhaps because of that, one no longer wins. And then, when the ideal is betrayed, the fascination passes, and one's obsession, if it persists, is with survival. The playfulness is gone, and one begins to count the cost.

"Today, by simply making my opponent angry, I won a game I should have lost. It's not the first time I've done it; but I've realized finally what I've been doing, and I hope it will be the last. For me, it's probably time to start counting." He paused. "The costs are obvious:

no money, no home, no real friends, no family. . . . What troubles me is, when I ask whether it has been worth all that, I just don't know."

To this, she could find no answer. She felt like an intruder on some private scene of grief. And when she recalled how it had come about, she was ashamed.

"All of which is, of course, not for publication. . . ." He broke off, sensing her discomfort. "I'm sorry. I've embarrassed you. I didn't mean to burden you with my problems. Forgive me."

"No, it's the other way round. It's you—" She faltered. "Oh, damn, I've made this so difficult. I feel so . . . so ashamed."

"Ashamed?" He stared at her in amazement. "Why? What have you done?"

"Listen." She was conscious suddenly of where they were. "Let's go over there." She pointed to a deserted bench in the distance shaded by two elm trees. "Away from all these people and I'll tell you."

When she had finished they sat in silence, staring out over the warm greens and yellows, the lengthening shadows of the almost deserted park. She was still angry at herself and the false situation she had stumbled into. At length she turned and touched his arm, lightly and tentatively as if fearing rejection.

"I'm sorry," she said. "I didn't mean things to happen like this. I really am a journalist, and it—the interview thing—seemed such a good way to approach you. I wasn't just wantonly prying."

"It's not important." He shrugged. "You never asked me to make confession; I just did. I must have needed to. I've met people on planes who've done it to me. Just poured out their whole lives as though I were a hole in the ground. And usually," he smiled, "I wasn't in the least interested."

"Oh, I was interested," she insisted. "I just feel uncomfortable having got it under false pretences. . . ." She hesitated. "Will you do it? . . . Can you?"

"I can try." He shrugged. "It sounds important and not very difficult or dangerous. No one's paid much attention to me since I've been here."

"To you, perhaps. But what about to him?"

He considered this.

"I assume he'll take precautions. If it seems unsafe he won't come, or he won't talk. You say I'm to wait until the tournament's over and then go home and call the number you gave me?"

"Yes. Do you think you can remember that long?"

"Oh, God." He rolled his eyes upward. "I'm a freak. Don't you know? I can remember anything. It's forgetting that gives me problems."

He stood up.

"Perhaps we should go. There's almost nobody here."

She caught his arm.

"Why don't we have dinner together?"

"You think that's wise?"

"I don't see why not. We're Americans in a strange city, we strike up a casual acquaintance, we have dinner. What could be more natural?"

He laughed. "I like your idea of casual. I tell you all my problems, and you embroil me in . . . all this."

CHAPTER VIII

Lermontov was unhappy. He had considerable respect for his chief's intelligence, but he sometimes felt Stein was too much of a bureaucrat. The matter of Ivkov was a case in point. It was all very well to issue oblique warnings to the Minister—"naturally, in writing"—but Stein *must* know that they would be disregarded. And surely there was more at stake here than questions of departmental responsibility. It was still a very open question, Lermontov recognized, whether Ivkov was a traitor. But if he were, then surely the case involved nothing less than the security of the Soviet Union.

Lermontov had been fifteen years with the KGB. He had developed instincts, and he trusted them. His instinct now was that Ivkov would bear watching. By itself, of course, the *samizdat* meant nothing. But the *samizdat* and the incidents in Helsinki, taken together, formed a pattern that Stein—and the Minister, too, for that matter—should have found disturbing.

He, of course, agreed with Stein that a full-scale investigation was, at this stage, out of the question. The evidence was insufficient, and, indeed, it had been expressly forbidden. An official surveillance operation was, for the same reason, also out. But an unofficial operation—something very low-key that could conveniently be forgotten or denied if his suspicions proved groundless—that might be a possibility.

He pressed the buzzer of his intercom.

"Send me Lieutenant Pogrebin, please."

Pogrebin was the man he needed. Smart, intuitive, and energetic, he possessed all the attributes of a first-class security officer except, perhaps, the prime one—discipline. He was reluctant to go through channels and not always absolutely scrupulous in following instructions. It was this disregard for the niceties of bureaucratic life that had landed him in his present disfavor. He was doing penance in the Archives Division, or, as it was more familiarly named, "Siberia."

Pogrebin knocked and, without waiting for a reply, entered. He strode up to Lermontov's desk and saluted smartly—a shade too smartly. It seemed to Lermontov that he detected, in the other's demeanor, lingering traces of the spirit of irony that had come close to blighting his career.

Pogrebin was blond, of medium height, with nothing distinctive about him except his movements, which were fluid and athletic, and his eyes, green as a cat's and alive with intelligence and humor.

"Well, Lieutenant, and how are you enjoying your work in Archives?"

"I'm happy, Colonel, to be doing anything to further the work of the department."

"Which means, if I understand you correctly, that you are totally bored, but have finally discovered the value of doing as you are told."

"You understand me perfectly, Colonel." The young man smiled.

"Well, in that case, perhaps we can find something else for you."

"I should appreciate that, Colonel."

"For example, how would you like to spend a week, maybe ten days, taking a vacation?"

"Vacation?" Pogrebin looked blank. "I'm not due. My vacation is from August 15th to 25th. It's in the Division schedule."

"Well. Let us say then that your mother has been taken sick, and you have requested ten days' leave, starting tomorrow, on compassionate grounds."

"Let us say so, Colonel." Pogrebin grinned. "But since my mother is not sick, what is it that you want me to do with my vacation?"

"I should like you to watch someone—

"Listen to me carefully, Grigori Petrovich," Lermontov said sternly. "We have been joking, but now I am serious. I am about to give you a mission, and a precise set of instructions. If you complete it, obeying my instructions to the letter, I shall reinstate you in your former position. If, however, you exceed your instructions or disregard them in any way, there will be no further place for you in this department. You understand?"

Pogrebin nodded.

"Good. Now, in the first place, this mission is unofficial. There will be nothing in writing. You will make your reports verbally and to me only. If a question is ever raised officially about this mission, you know nothing about it. It does not exist.

"In the second place, you will work alone. This will make your job extremely difficult, I know, but I can't help it. If you lose touch with the subject occasionally I shall understand, but, since he has no reason to expect that he will be watched, I don't think you will find him trying to avoid you.

"Thirdly, while your main task is surveillance, it is of no less importance that you remain undetected. Therefore, take care. And, please, no bright ideas. If you think you've been discovered, discontinue at once and report.

"Now to specifics. The man I want you to watch is Academician Alexei Ivkov. He will be staying in Moscow from June 10th—that's three days from now, so you will have three days at least of genuine vacation—to June 17th. I will supply you with a description, photographs, and details of where he is staying. You have a reliable camera? No? A pity." Lermontov shrugged. "I shall have to lend you mine. Take care of it.

"Now, what I am chiefly interested in are his unofficial contacts. He will be attending a conference each morning, so that should take care of him between eight and twelve. In the afternoons he will be free. I want reports—and photographs, if possible—of any persons with whom he has more than casual contact. I leave the interpretation of that to you, but it would include, for example, anyone he talked to for more than two or three minutes. You will make a report to me by telephone, before ten-thirty each evening."

He scribbled the number on a piece of paper and handed it to Pogrebin, who glanced at it offhandedly, crumpled it into a ball, and tossed it across the desk into the wastepaper basket beside Lermontov's chair.

Lermontov sighed. "Grigori Petrovich, there are times when I worry about you. That was not a tactful way of reminding me that your memory is better than mine."

"I'm sorry, Colonel. . . . Was there anything else?"

"Yes. Go back to your desk and write an application for compassionate leave on whatever plausible grounds your imagination can devise. Bring it to me in half an hour and I shall have the photographs ready."

Pogrebin hesitated. "Colonel."

"Yes, what is it?"

"I was just wondering. I made plans for my scheduled vacation in August. Should I cancel them?"

"Certainly not. If you perform this task properly, I'll find a way of getting you off in August. If you mess it up, you'll be getting more vacation than you can possibly find a use for. Now go and write the application."

Anne Crossland, lying awake in the darkness, contemplated the sleeping figure beside her with something approaching affection. He had been surprisingly gentle, unexpectedly tender; he had certainly given her no cause for regret.

And yet she wondered why she had done it, why she had invited, practically dragged, a stranger of barely eight hours' acquaintance into her bed. Physical attraction? Possibly. He was good-looking, in a scruffy sort of way, and his body, entwined with hers, had proved remarkably lithe and trim. But that was not really it. Appearance, in a man, counted for very little with her. Was it perhaps guilt? No. She no longer felt guilty. He had absolved her of that. Indeed, in some subtle and generous way he had absolved her of everything. She had handed on the responsibility; and he had taken it, and released her. Relief, then? That was conceivable. The days since her meeting with Hunter had been filled with a nagging anxiety and tension. Perhaps relief of that tension, when she passed on the mission to him, had sought an accompanying physical release. Possible. But, good God, she had felt horny before without making a grab for the nearest thing in pants.

No. There was something else, some other reason why, when he said goodnight to her and started to turn away, she had taken his hand, grasping it firmly, and drawn him into her room.

He was alone. And she admired him. She admired the objectivity with which he could contemplate the wreckage of his past, the probable emptiness of his future. He made his choices, he accepted his mistakes, he regretted nothing, and he expected nothing. Because of that she had reached out to his loneliness, and had impulsively given him what she had.

He stirred beside her. Gently she reached out and touched the arm stretched out behind him across the sheets.

"You're still awake?" His murmur was drowsy.

"Yes, I'm thinking."

"What about?"

"You, mostly."

"What about me?"

"Well," she giggled, "for one thing I was thinking that you're really fit, considering your occupation."

"Oh," he grunted. "I swim. I have to keep fit. These tournaments require a lot of stamina."

"Chess again. Is everything you do connected with that game?"

"Not absolutely everything." Fully awake now, he turned over to face her.

"Give me one example."

"This, for example." He placed his hand on her stomach and drew the fingertips lightly down, across the delicate intersection of leg and torso and along the inside of her thigh.

She giggled again. "You are fit. But you should sleep. You have to play tomorrow."

In reply he pulled her toward him. He placed his lips on her breast and let his tongue slide lazily over the nipple.

"Mmmmmm . . ." She murmured, "Is this to be rape or seduction?"

"Seduction, if it succeeds. Otherwise rape."

"Seduction then. You're too sleepy for rape." She placed a leg across him and drew him into her.

He awoke later to find her tugging at his shoulder.

"Wake up. It's six o'clock. You have to go back to your room."

"Why? It's still early."

"Well, for one thing, a guide from Intourist will be calling for me soon. I have to go visit a collective. I'll be away two or three days." She paused, hesitating. "Shall I see you when I get back?"

"Do you want to?"

"Yes."

"Then you'll see me."

He struggled into his shirt and pants, stepped into his shoes, and gathered up the rest of his clothes. She stood before him, her body a pale ivory in the morning light. Still holding his clothes with one arm, he stretched out the other and pulled her to him, placing light kisses upon her upturned face.

"Don't kiss my eyelids."

"Why not?"

"I'm superstitious. I heard that if a man kisses your eyelids, you'll never see him again."

He kissed her mouth.

"You'll see me." He released her and turned to leave.

"Take care, chess player," she called after him. "And good luck."

He turned at the door. With his free arm he made an emphatic thumbs-up signal. Then he stepped quickly into the corridor.

CHAPTER IX

Throughout the morning conference, Ivkov's mind wandered. His replies to the Minister's questions were laconic and perfunctory—so much so that at one point the Minister had asked him quite sharply if he were feeling well. He excused himself on the grounds of overwork and strain, remembering, as he did so, that he had just returned from ten days of supposed vacation. Thereafter he had struggled hard to pay attention. Nevertheless his mind wandered, veering away from the business at hand to a series of images in which he himself, interrogators, the bleak cells of the Lubianka Prison, and a wall in one of the prison courtyards —a wall without windows, scarred and pitted with holes—were chillingly juxtaposed.

He had no direct experience of the KGB or the Lubianka. His career since his student days had followed a path much like those of the rockets he worked with, smooth, accelerating, practically vertical. But one could not live through the tail end of Stalin's regime, or survive the intellectual dictatorship of Lysenko, without acquiring disturbing secondhand knowledge of the consequences of political error. He could recall several colleagues who had disappeared—most of them permanently —and the few who had returned described experiences whose vicarious reliving made no great demands on his imagination. There had also been experiences of which they had not spoken, and had not needed to, because their physical debilitation and a certain look they had of humiliation and defeat were eloquent enough.

So he could not quite bring himself to believe, even now, that he had willingly made a decision that might bring him face to face with these nightmares. He kept telling himself that, in spite of Helsinki, he had committed himself to nothing, that he could go home, forget the whole idea, and complete his work in peace.

But he knew he couldn't. He was not naive enough to believe that the Americans would let him alone now that he had permitted them that tantalizing glimpse of knowledge so vital to them. Besides, he had too much pride to permit fear, mere moral weakness, to deflect him from a course he had freely and rationally chosen.

He had never considered himself a brave man—perhaps because the circumstances in which such a judgment could be validly made had never arisen. His work so far had kept him behind the scenes; he had not been associated with any serious failure; his close friends had stayed out of trouble. He had been able to pursue his career successfully and without any serious injury to his self-respect. But he knew that there was in his character an element of inflexibility, of stubborn commitment to his moral convictions, that could endanger the tranquillity he had managed to preserve. For him, integrity was a matter of acting rationally. One considered the circumstances; one made one's judgment; and one acted upon it. To do otherwise was to behave irrationally—to a thinking man, unthinkable. Given this straightforward faith, it would have been safer, he often thought, if his talents had led him into some other field.

The confrontation between his work and his values, when it arose, took him, nevertheless, by surprise. His work was in defense and, although he was well aware that "defense" was a euphemism designed to cover the full range of military activity—what country, after all, had ever established a Ministry of Aggression?—he felt that the missile detection system on which he had been working was, in intention, genuinely defensive. What he had not sufficiently recognized was that a sense of defensive superiority, if it ever becomes complacent enough, can become a license for aggression.

This became clear, from his point of view, only when it was already too late. In solving the practical problems involved in setting up a foolproof, long-range missile detection system he had, in effect, given his country a period of relative invulnerability to U.S. nuclear attack. It would not last long—a year or two at the outside—because the United States was known to be working on the same problem and would catch up in the end, as it always did. But while it lasted, the Russian superiority would be devastating. In the event of a full-scale nuclear war, it had been estimated, the United States would suffer casualties—the precise figure depending upon the weather conditions and the obstinacy of its political leaders—in the range of fifty to seventy-five million, while the Soviet Union would be able to limit its own losses to between eight and ten million. As the strategic planners and military statisticians expressed it in their report to the Politburo: "the risks to the domestic population in case of nuclear attack by the United States have been quantified and fall within acceptable limits."

Half a lifetime devoted to weapons technology had made him familiar with the military mind and its vocabulary. Behind the bland and neutered terminology the thought was clear and obscene. "If you want to start a war, we see no objection."

If there was ever a precise moment when he crossed the line between dissent and treason, it was when he read that sentence. Eight to ten million dead Russians were not acceptable to him. Nor for that matter were seventy-five million dead Americans. Certainly not as the result of attempts to exploit a defensive superiority brought about in large part by his exertions. That was not a responsibility he was willing to bear. But it had settled upon him, willy-nilly, when he had failed to recognize the implications of what he had been doing. His situation reminded him of the old arguments on scientific responsibility he had often used as a student. A gun is not in itself an evil. The evil is the man who uses it to kill. But if you give a gun to a man, knowing he is likely to use it, then you share in the responsibility for his action. It was a logic that had haunted many of the early nuclear physicists. It haunted him now.

The unbearable conviction that he was responsible had been followed rather quickly by the thought that, just as defecting British and American scientists had given his country the atomic secrets that had enabled it to regain defensive parity in the fifties, so he could, in this situation, enable the Americans to catch up. All he need do was give them the results of his work, and the disparity—at this point one of knowledge only —would disappear, and with it the temptations which had been brought to light, like centipedes under an upturned stone, by the report to the Politburo.

Some ideas become compelling as soon as they are conceived. Ivkov was a convinced Marxist and he loved his country. He was terrified for his own safety and the future of his family. He was overcome with reflex convulsions of fear and guilt whenever he considered what he was planning to do. But he knew he could no more stop himself doing it than he could stop himself breathing.

So he could not console himself, as he struggled to avert his mind from the nightmare images to which it kept returning, that he could back out. He could only pray that the Americans would not keep him waiting.

* * *

Pogrebin was not enjoying his little task. He had not expected to. He was doing the work of four or five men and without the necessary equipment. His consolation was that Ivkov's official black Moskvich had been easy to follow through the sparse Moscow traffic; but his own car, Lermontov's private vehicle—he grinned when he remembered how reluctantly Lermontov had parted with it—was not official, and he had encountered the usual problems parking. He had twice lost Ivkov while searching for a space and in each case had succeeded in picking him up again only when the scientist returned to his vehicle. So far—and it was only the first day—seventy-five minutes were not completely accounted for, although fifty of these had presumably been spent in the Lenin Mausoleum from which he had seen Ivkov emerging, and four in a public lavatory. He hoped Lermontov would be understanding.

Ivkov had not wanted the official car. It made him feel conspicuous. He recognized this feeling as the product of a paranoia understandable enough in the circumstances, but it was an additional strain on a nervous system which was bearing, already, too great a load. Besides, the chauffeur was showing an alarming gregariousness. It was he who had suggested visiting the Mausoleum and, once there, he had insisted on joining Ivkov in the line of devotees who filed, mute and awestruck, past the earthly remains of the Old Revolutionary.

"I've visited the old boy hundreds of times before," he said, firmly rejecting Ivkov's suggestion that he must be tired and might like to rest and smoke in the car, "but I never miss an opportunity to pay my respects. After all, if it wasn't for him, God bless him, we wouldn't be where we are today. Now would we?"

In other circumstances Ivkov might have enjoyed the unconscious irony in the remark. But today it jarred him with the reminder of his resolve, provoking twinges of fear and guilt which the stern features of the figure on the sarcophagus, pale and waxlike despite the pink light of the chamber, did nothing to still.

To Ivkov the company of the chauffeur, the old-fashioned simplicity of his political faith, were simply oppressive. When it became clear, from a suggestion that after the Mausoleum they might visit St. Basil's Cathedral and other tourist attractions in the neighborhood, that he considered his function to be as much companion as chauffeur, Ivkov demurred.

"You know, Evgenyi Alexandrovich," he said, as pleasantly as he could manage, "I spend all morning cooped up in meetings, sitting on my backside, opening and shutting my mouth. What I really need is some fresh air, a walk in the park. . . . So why don't you take the rest of the afternoon off? Take the car and drive the wife and kids around a bit. Nobody'll know, and I shall be perfectly happy on my own. You can pick me up at the hotel at eight."

He insisted with the hearty bonhomie of one determined to do a favor, until the old man, though not without considerable misgiving, agreed.

Left alone, Ivkov waited until the tail lights of the Moskvich disappeared around the corner of Gorki Street. Then he strode off in the direction of Kalinin Prospekt. Once there he made his way toward the Metro and disappeared down the flight of steps leading to the ticket counter.

Seventy yards down the street, inching his vehicle along the curb with the air of one unsure of his way, Pogrebin watched Ivkov with dismay.

"I'm going to lose him again," he thought. "By the time I've parked, he'll be in a train, halfway across the city, heading God knows where."

He pulled in to the curb and switched off the ignition. Parking here was almost certainly illegal, but if it came to a confrontation with the police, Lermontov's position would protect him. To help out, he pulled a notebook from his pocket, scribbled a message on one of the sheets, and placed it on the dashboard where it would be clearly visible from the outside. "Out of gas" the message read. Probably the police would take him for a tourist and be understanding. Filling stations were few and far between in Moscow.

He reached the ticket counter two minutes or so after Ivkov. The scientist had disappeared, presumably down one of the passageways leading to the trains. Pogrebin was now in a quandary: was Ivkov going north or south?

While he purchased a ticket, Pogrebin heard in the distance the rumble of an approaching train. He listened intently, his head cocked to one side, trying to distinguish the direction from which the sound was coming. Unfortunately, it seemed to come from both sides at once, causing the whole station to echo and reverberate. As it grew nearer, however, the greater volume of sound appeared to issue from the southbound exit. From the escalator tunnel there came a faint stirring of air, the advance guard, possibly, of the column driven through the subway by the approaching train.

He dashed down the escalator onto the platform. Wrong. It was instantly clear that the train was on the other track.

He scanned the throng on the platform, his eyes moving systematically in a zigzag pattern up the platform. No Ivkov. He turned and ran back up the escalator, taking the steps three at a time, ignoring the angry stares of the people he brushed against in his hurry. Already he could hear the clatter of wheels and the screech of brakes as the train pulled into the other platform.

By the time he reached it the passengers were crowding into the carriages, pushing past the crowd that was simultaneously pushing to get off. It was impossible to tell whether Ivkov was among that mass of bodies. Pogrebin didn't try. He made for the car nearest the escalator and secured himself a place beside the sliding door. Unless Ivkov had detected him, he would be on the train. Pogrebin could only hope that he would be able to spot the scientist when he reached his destination. He prayed the other stops would be less crowded.

When the train pulled into Oktiabrskaia, Ivkov considered staying on it. He felt a tremendous aversion, now that the moment might be approaching, to what he was planning to do. His mind might tell him it was a rational step, morally justified, but his heart still called it treason. He had an impulse to think it over again, to ride on to Kalinin Prospekt and then, if his resolution held firm, to walk back to the park. But this impulse, his reason told him, must be resisted. Above all, guard against panic, he told himself; I doubt if they are watching—they have been given no cause—but in case they are, I must be careful to act naturally. I mustn't, at all costs, look as if I'm trying to avoid being followed.

These instants of reflection, while the train was standing in the station, delayed his exit. The doors started to close. He leaped to his feet and rushed onto the platform, narrowly avoiding the doors and conscious as he stood there, breathing heavily, that he had just done the thing he had warned himself to avoid.

It was then Pogrebin spotted him. But by that time the train was moving and he could only watch, helpless, as the train moved into the tunnel, gathering speed, and the figure of the scientist, still standing on the platform, receded into the distance.

It was a working day for most of Moscow, so there were few people around when Ivkov arrived. Three or four chess tables were occupied by old men, playing and smoking in silence. Their play was observed by a handful of schoolchildren who stood at a respectful distance from the boards and whose whispered comments and gestures were ignored by the players. There was also, seated at a table some distance from the others, a solitary man, middle-aged. He was hunched over the pieces, engaged, to all appearances, in playing a game against himself.

Ivkov wandered over toward the man and sat down on a bench adjacent to the table. His approach was not noticed by the man, who seemed totally absorbed in his game. He would sit for minutes on end, deep in contemplation, then his hand would swoop down on the pieces, making six or eight moves in rapid sequence. When making a capture, he would move the attacking piece with his thumb and forefinger, gathering up the captured piece with his third and fourth fingers in a single expert motion. After each flurry of moves, he replaced the pieces in their original positions and resumed his contemplation. Ivkov decided he was probably analyzing.

He was dressed, Ivkov observed, in a manner distinctly un-Russian: the shoes were of good quality, soft black leather in a casual style that Ivkov recognized as Italian; the denim trousers were clearly Levis—Ivkov could read the label—and the light cotton turtleneck was too fine to be of Russian manufacture. Beside him on the table were a pack of American cigarettes and a disposable butane lighter.

It was several minutes before the man became conscious of Ivkov's scrutiny. He looked up casually and nodded, a movement which contrived both to acknowledge Ivkov's presence and convey disinclination for closer contact. Then the eyes, which had seemed to Ivkov to be looking through or beyond him, traveled back to his face and widened perceptibly.

Ivkov got up.

"Are you American?" he asked.

The man nodded.

In his excitement Ivkov forgot momentarily the formula he had devised for this moment. Then he remembered. The words sounded somehow stilted and foolish.

"It is a pleasure to greet a stranger to our city."

He glanced at the other tables, fearful that the sound of a strange language would draw attention to them. But the old men still smoked and played, and the children had drifted off and were playing tag in the distance, well out of earshot.

"It is a pleasure to be here, when the people are so friendly."

It *was* him.

"My name is Alexei Ivkov." Ivkov sat down. "I, too, am visiting Moscow. Perhaps we two tourists could play a game together."

"It would be a pleasure." Gathering up the pieces, the American started to set up the board. "And while we play, we can talk."

Had anyone asked Pogrebin to state his philosophical beliefs he would certainly have answered that he was a dialectical materialist. Today, however, he found it hard to resist the conclusion that there was indeed a Deity—a malignant one who was devoting His powers to the sole purpose of frustrating Pogrebin. First: seventy-five minutes unaccounted for. Second: Lermontov's car, abandoned and probably in police custody. And now this. . . . He had to force himself to think calmly.

Ivkov had left the train, at the last possible moment, at Oktiabrskaia. Did his impetuous exit mean that Pogrebin had been spotted? He didn't see how; but it was certainly possible. And Pogrebin's orders had specifically stated that if detected he should back off. On the other hand, it was more probable that Ivkov had been daydreaming and had almost missed his stop. Besides which, it was more disgrace than Pogrebin could bear to slink back so soon to Lermontov and confess failure. He would try to find Ivkov, assume that the scientist had not detected him, and maintain that assumption until he was faced with incontrovertible proof to the contrary.

But where was Ivkov? He had spent most of the afternoon, to Pogrebin's exasperated eye, merely wandering about. So unless his exit at Oktiabrskaia had been prompted by some specific business in the neighborhood, it was probable that he would simply continue his wanderings in the park. If, on the other hand, he did have some specific destination in mind, Pogrebin had little or no chance of catching him. The sensible course then—the only one that offered any hope—was to go to the park and hope to reestablish contact without further loss of time.

The northbound train was, of course, delayed. It was a full thirty-five minutes before Pogrebin arrived at the north entrance to the park, and a further fifteen before his search brought him to the chess tables.

Ivkov had begun in a fever of anxiety. It was bad enough that, contrary to his instructions, they had sent someone who had absolutely no understanding of what he was being told; it meant that he had had to waste time giving the American a background briefing before he could get to the point. But what was worse was that they had chosen a chess master whose exploits were only less celebrated, in the Soviet Union, than those of Bobby Fischer. Most likely, he had thought bitterly, the information will be garbled in transmission and I shall be arrested and executed, all for nothing.

Wylie's imperturbability, however, had been calming. Though he understood nothing, he assured Ivkov, he would remember it all. As for his being well known, surely that made for added protection. Nobody would be likely to imagine that someone so highly visible could be engaged in anything not perfectly innocent. Moreover, he pointed out, he had been at the tables for most of the afternoon and, to his knowledge, not a soul had recognized him.

So, with misgivings, Ivkov had told him, reciting in brief conversational snatches the information he had carefully prepared and rehearsed. He was reassured by Wylie's ability to repeat, faultlessly, almost absentmindedly, in the same conversational tone, what he had been told. By the time they were finished Ivkov felt almost confident.

They played two games. In the first Wylie had played mechanically, harmlessly, prolonging the intervals between his moves to give Ivkov the opportunity to speak. In the second game his instincts reasserted themselves. It was swift and brutal. In spite of his nervousness, Ivkov was fascinated. It was almost a pleasure to be beaten with so much distinction. At the end he got up and shook hands.

"I must go now," he said. "Goodbye, Grand Master. It has been a pleasure and an education to meet you."

Wylie acknowledged the compliment with a smile and a slight nod.

This was the moment caught by Pogrebin's camera. The picture, taken at seventy-five meters, was subsequently much enlarged. It showed them shaking hands, Ivkov speaking, Wylie smiling and nodding his head.

PART II

CHAPTER X

Anne Crossland was very happy to be back. Her visit to the collectives had been interesting; she'd gathered a good deal of material for her article, and she was confident the article itself would turn out well. But the satisfaction this confidence would normally have brought her was missing. She'd been spending time thinking, and it had made her worried.

For one thing, Mr. Hunter—if that was really his name—had snowed her. "They don't bother with innocent tourists," he had said, "because all but a tiny fraction of them are just that." It had seemed fine at the time. But she'd been back home then, safe in his office, lulled by his charm and easy authority, not thinking very well. Here it was different. Now his assurance, his offhanded juggling with the probabilities of detection, seemed less convincing.

For the fact was she'd been watched, these past few days; she'd been an object of open suspicion. The interpreter had never left her side. Her questions, and the answers to them, had been garbled and probably censored in translation. She'd been permitted to take very few photographs and forbidden, a lot of the time, even to carry her camera. The farmers had been nervous and on their guard with her, their conversation sullen and monosyllabic. It had changed her image of Russia, had her visit to the collective. It was a society, she now thought, inhabited by paranoids and animated by distrust. It was certainly not a place where there was any such thing as an innocent tourist.

And if she'd been watched, so obviously, at the collective, then presumably she'd been watched, though less obviously, before. And if that were true, then so had *he*. So she was worried about him. More than worried. The mission she'd passed on to him, she now realized, was quite appallingly dangerous.

And not just to him. She was ashamed to admit it, but now that she analyzed her feelings, her concern for herself was just as great. For she'd made a mistake: she'd ignored Hunter's instructions.

"Be sure to tell Wylie," Hunter had emphasized, "not to make contact until you've had time to get clear. That way the risk to you is minimized." That also had seemed fine at the time. But it had been impossible, in practice, for her to ask Wylie to take a risk she was unwilling to take herself. So she hadn't told him. So he'd probably made the contact already. And if something had gone wrong . . .

It was stupid, in that case, to get in touch with him. But he was expecting her. She wanted to see him if only to be able to lay her doubts to rest.

It was one-thirty when she reached the hotel. She knew that play in the tournament began each day at ten. He would probably not be finished yet. She would leave a message for him at the desk and then get something to eat. By the time she returned he would probably be back.

"Mrs. Crossland. Room forty-nine," she told the desk clerk. "Oh, and can you give me a pencil and some paper? I'd like to leave a message for Mr. Wylie. He's in room forty-two."

He reached under the counter and produced a message pad and a pencil. She was about to write when he stopped her.

"Did you say room forty-two?"

"Yes."

"Grand Master Wylie?"

"Yes." Her voice carried a note of irritation. God, these Russians were so slow!

"I'm sorry. I'd forgotten. He's not here."

"That's why I'm writing a message."

"No. You misunderstand me. Grand Master Wylie has checked out."

"Checked out?" She stared at him. "When?"

"Yesterday morning."

"There must be a mistake. Grand Master Wylie is playing in the Rubinstein Tournament. It doesn't end for several days yet."

He shook his head. "No. He checked out. I was here at the time."

"Did he leave any messages?"

"I don't think so."

"Would you make sure, please?" She made no effort to control the impatience in her voice. It was better to express that than the panic she was feeling.

With a sigh he turned to the box behind him, making a small performance of examining the message slips it contained.

"No. No messages."

"Did he say where he was going then? I'd arranged to meet him, you see. I'm a journalist, and I wanted to interview him for an article."

"No."

He watched her retreat with a sardonic smile. An interview? That was a new name for it. He'd heard it called lots of things, but never that. He was grateful once again for his friendship with the chambermaid on the fourth floor.

Relax. Don't panic. Stay calm, and try to think clearly. Anne Crossland, sitting at a small table in the corner of the hotel dining room, repeated these instructions to herself over and over, like a mantra, until she realized that the words were producing in her exactly the state of mind she was trying to avoid. A ham sandwich lay half-eaten on the plate in front of her. She was no longer hungry.

Something was wrong. Either he had been discovered and arrested, or he had panicked. These seemed the only alternatives, but neither made much sense. An arrest, surely, would have created so much stir that the desk clerk would hardly have forgotten it. On the other hand, Wylie had taken her request so calmly. He would not have panicked without good reason. Then, perhaps, he *had* been arrested. The desk clerk could have been ordered to keep quiet about it, perhaps to take note of people asking for Wylie. No. That was absurd. The clerk had been too genuinely indifferent. She must not start assuming that everyone in sight worked for the KGB.

But then, why no message? Why leave her dangling, with no word of explanation or reassurance? To avoid risk perhaps? To protect her? But didn't he understand that she would worry about him, and herself, too? . . . It occurred to her then, with hurt and a sudden anger, that perhaps he had not thought of her at all.

What should she do? Try and trace him. That could draw suspicion on herself if he were in trouble. It would establish too firm a connection between them. But the connection was established firmly enough anyway. And she had told the desk clerk she would enquire at the tournament. It might look more suspicious if she didn't.

There she went again. Suspecting everybody. But it was impossible not to. She was in the dark; out in the open. She felt like a rabbit in a field full of foxes. She *had* to trace him. She would enquire at the tournament. If they had no news of him, she'd take the first plane home.

CHAPTER XI

Lermontov, contemplating the stack of photographs, sighed. He was beginning to think it was pointless. Three and a half days had gone by, and they were no further forward. More to the point, six hours were already unaccounted for . . . six hours. Enough time for Ivkov, had he been so inclined, to pass on every secret in his possession.

The six hours were not Pogrebin's fault. Pogrebin had done as well as could be expected in the circumstances. It was unreasonable to hope —though Lermontov, of course, had hoped—that one man alone, however skillful and devoted, could tail someone for three and a half days and not lose contact sometimes, even when the subject made no attempt at evasion.

And that seemed to be the main point. Ivkov had not tried to shake Pogrebin. He'd not even seemed to suspect Pogrebin was there. There'd been a monotonous sameness about his behavior for which innocence, Lermontov recognized, his own intuition notwithstanding, was the best explanation. Each afternoon he'd gone to play chess at the park; each evening he'd eaten alone at the hotel and gone to bed. The only exceptions to this pattern had been the afternoon he'd spent at the movies and the dinner he'd attended one evening at the house of his friend, the Minister of Defense. Even his disappearances—visits to the Mausoleum and the like—had seemed natural. Probably he was what he seemed to be: a man, away from home, harmlessly whiling away a few empty hours.

In setting Pogrebin to follow Ivkov, Lermontov had been acting on a number of assumptions, some reasonable, others less so. It was reasonable to assume, for example, if Ivkov's contact with Berenstein had been deliberate, that it was only a preliminary; they had simply not had enough time alone for it to be anything else. It was also reasonable to assume that the follow-up contact, if it ever took place, would happen in Moscow. Security at the Lenin Research Establishment, where Ivkov both worked and lived, was far too stringent to permit a contact there. But these assumptions, however reasonable in themselves, made sense only if one were willing to assume that Ivkov had decided to turn traitor. And Lermontov recognized that, if one discounted intuition, the evidence for this assumption was really very shaky. It turned on whether Berenstein had really been trying to avoid surveillance, that afternoon in Helsinki, or had simply been wandering around. It was easy to make a mistake about something like that. Paranoia was an occupational hazard in security work. He wondered if he had fallen victim to it himself.

It was possible. He would bear it in mind. Nevertheless, he wasn't willing, yet, to discount his intuition. He turned again to the photographs.

There were twenty-six. Some were duplicates, shots of the same conversation taken at different angles. Most of them involved Ivkov's chess opponents or onlookers. Two were of protracted, though apparently desultory, conversations he had had in the street. One of these involved a child whose age, Lermontov guessed, could not be more than twelve. He could imagine the sardonic amusement with which Pogrebin had taken *that*.

They would all have to be checked, fed into the computer and matched against the thousands stored in that creature's extensive memory. But there were only two that seemed at all interesting.

The man in these pictures did not look Russian. It was partly his haircut but mainly his clothes—the Levis and, especially, the shoes. Lermontov knew that Levis were common enough in Moscow. It was illegal, but foreign tourists were frequently offered exorbitant sums for faded and tattered denims whose original value could not have been more than a few roubles. Somehow these shapeless and, to his taste, raffish garments had acquired among the youth of Moscow a perverse social prestige, so by themselves, the Levis meant nothing. Together with the shoes, however, they acquired significance. The shoes were good, stylish, and well made. There was nothing Russian about the shoes; and no Russian, Lermontov would have been willing to bet, would wear shoes like that with a T-shirt and a pair of worn-out Levis. The combination implied a casual affluence that could only be foreign.

He would have them checked. He would have them all checked. But first there was the need for discretion. He took a pair of scissors and started to cut away all traces of Ivkov from the first picture.

The whole pile took him five minutes. When he had finished, he took what remained of the photographs, attached a note to them, and placed them on his secretary's desk. Then he took the discarded cuttings and fed them through the shredder.

It was close to six before he got word from the computer. Negative. No one in the photographs was in the files. The two pictures that had aroused his interest, however, were clipped together and had a note attached to them.

"Subject of the attached," he read, "closely resembles the American chess master Arden Wylie. Subject is currently in Moscow for the Rubinstein Memorial Tournament. We have no file on him."

Something stirred in Lermontov's memory. He retrieved his copy of *Izvestia* from the wastebasket and turned to the section dealing with cultural activities. There it was. "American Withdraws from Rubinstein Tournament." He had noticed the headline before, but had not bothered to read the article. He did so now.

The American grand master, Arden Wylie, yesterday withdrew from the Akiba Rubinstein Memorial Tournament on grounds of ill-health. In his letter to the tournament director, Wylie, who is scheduled to fly home this morning, stated that he had suffered a recurrence of the stomach ailment which afflicted him earlier in the year, and wished to consult doctors in the United States. Observers had noticed, however, that the quality of Wylie's play here was well below its usual level. In the early rounds he lost to Bronstein and, unexpectedly, to his fellow countryman, Pal Benko. On Monday he was lucky to defeat the Australian master, Allen Greene, when the latter blundered in a winning position. Facing matches with Petrosian and Karpov in the next two rounds, Wylie may have withdrawn, observers speculate, to avoid the humiliation of further defeats.

Lermontov took a pad of paper. At the top he printed IVKOV. Below it to the right he printed BERENSTEIN. He connected the names with an arrow pointing in both directions. On the left he put WYLIE and connected it with a similar arrow to IVKOV. After a moment's thought he added, below BERENSTEIN, the word PENTAGON and connected them with another arrow. To complete the circle he drew two more arrows, one leading from PENTAGON, the other from WYLIE. The space between these arrows he left blank.

He tore off the sheet and, folding it in half, placed it in his pocket. Then he went upstairs to see Stein.

General Stein looked at the diagram on his desk and frowned. Then he got up abruptly and went over to a metal cabinet in the corner. From it he withdrew a gray folder which he handed, without a word, to Lermontov. Lermontov opened it and began reading. It was Stein's memo to the Minister, worded with his usual circumspection. Underneath, in ink, was written:

I commend your department for its diligence. However, Academician Ivkov is well known to me personally and may be regarded as completely trustworthy. He is working on a project of the highest importance and is not to be harassed or disturbed in any way. Should any further "evidence" come to light, take no action before consulting me in person.

The signature was the Minister's.

Sticking his neck out, Lermontov thought. Aloud, he said, "Don't the photographs constitute further evidence?"

Stein pursed his lips. "In a way, Yuri. In a way they do. But consider two things. One, how did we get them? And two, are they enough?"

Lermontov said nothing.

"You know," Stein continued, "technically you have disobeyed instructions. Personally, I think you were right. But I can hardly go and admit this to the Minister unless I can also prove to him that the action was justified.

"Your nice little circle, now," he pointed to the diagram. "It looks good; but what does it amount to? These arrows that seem so significant, what do they represent? . . . Assumptions. Merely assumptions. Ivkov met Berenstein. Perhaps they talked espionage. Perhaps they just talked about women." He shrugged. "We don't know.

"It gets worse," he continued. "Your circle isn't complete. There's nothing to suggest a connection between Wylie and any United States government agency. . . . I can't take this to the Minister. It's not enough."

"Wylie's sudden departure," Lermontov objected. "This picture was taken on Monday. On Tuesday, that is to say, at the very earliest opportunity, Wylie withdrew from the tournament and went home. That raises questions, don't you think?"

"Questions, certainly. But what else do we have here but questions, and more questions? Where do we see any answers? I'm afraid it's still not enough."

Lermontov shrugged. Taking the diagram from Stein's desk, he rose to leave.

"Yuri, listen." Stein waved him back into his chair. "Your intuition is exceptional, I know. It's also true that, in any other case, I would recommend an investigation. But this case is different. For your sake and mine, I can't go to the Minister armed with nothing more than this scrap of paper and Colonel Lermontov's intuition."

"What do you need then?"

"Close the circle. Show me a connection between Wylie and the U.S. government, and I'll go to the Minister at once."

Lermontov considered this.

"General," he said at last, "I may never be able to do that. Wylie may be an occasional, a one-time agent. If not, he probably works through a cut-off. Maybe several. In any case he is in New York by now. By the time we trace him it may be too late. If he already has information from Ivkov, it's certainly too late—"

"You're forgetting one thing"—Stein cut him off—"the Minister. The Minister is an intelligent man. He knows the risks, and he is willing to trust Ivkov. If there were the slightest doubt, would he be so willing? Would you?"

Lermontov was silent. He had little contact with ministers. He assumed they were fallible, like everyone else, but there was no point in putting that opinion on record, his friendship with Stein notwithstanding.

"So why don't we relax," Stein continued. "It's the Minister's decision. We have it from him in writing."

"As you say, General." Lermontov rose. Before he left he saluted. It was not a thing he normally did.

Oh, certainly, he thought bitterly as he descended the stairs, no need to worry about anything. Our security is not endangered. The Minister is an intelligent man, and we have it from him in writing.

CHAPTER XII

Roskill did not normally read the chess column of the *New York Times*. As the Ivkov operation developed, however, he began to feel he had acquired a proprietary interest in Wylie—on whom he had bestowed the code name "Murphy"—and he found himself following Wylie's progress in the tournament with an almost paternal concern.

"I see our boy lost again," he would say to Miss Solveig as she brought him the first of the ten or twelve cups of coffee he consumed each day. Or, "Murphy seems to be leading at adjournment. Hang in there, boy!"

He knew nothing about chess, beyond the moves. But once, moved by idle curiosity or the desire to fathom the workings of a mind that was now working for the Agency, he had taken the paper home and played through one of the games. It had not been enlightening. He could discern no pattern in its ebb and flow; and the exclamation points and question marks with which the moves were sometimes annotated had seemed to him frankly baffling. There was some pattern to it all, no doubt, but it was too deep for him.

By Thursday, June 15th, his interest in chess was flagging, superseded by his more pressing concern for the outcome of the operation. It was little more than a reflex that made him turn, that morning, to the arts and entertainment pages. What he read there thoroughly spoiled his day.

His first reaction was for Anne Crossland. Assuming that Murphy had made contact, became nervous for some reason, and bolted, where did that leave her? Hanging, he concluded, in limbo, her fate dependent upon whether Murphy's nervousness was justified. Then he remembered the dates. The report was datelined Wednesday. Murphy had left Moscow, therefore, on Tuesday. Which meant that he had been in the U.S. for at least one whole day. But they had heard nothing from him. Which could mean either that Murphy had refused to do it, or that he was alarmingly casual. Or it *could* mean that something had gone wrong.

"Solveig!"

She entered briskly, startled by this peremptory departure from normal courtesy.

"Murphy's disappeared. I want passenger manifests for all direct flights from Moscow to the United States in the last forty-eight hours. Failing that, try Immigration. He may not have taken a direct flight. Also, get on to the FBI and get them to put Murphy on the Immigration blacklist. That's a request from the DCI. Make it urgent. If he's not already here, we can have him held when he tries to enter."

If something had gone wrong, Murphy could be in danger. The sooner they got him off the streets and safe in Langley, the better for him. New York was crawling with KGB men—most of them protected by UN passports. If the Russians were on to him, he wouldn't last a day in New York.

But suppose he couldn't be traced at this end? That was the problem. Then they would have to start in Moscow. That presented difficulties. They could hardly start calling the airlines there without attracting interest and increasing the risk to Murphy—and the girl. But finding him quickly was paramount. If it came to it, they would just have to take that risk.

His plan had not originally called for any direct involvement by the Station in Moscow, though the Station Chief had been kept informed. That was for the protection of the principals and, not least, the Agency itself. Send Murphy trotting off to the Embassy directly after his contact with Ivkov and you created a trail of evidence for all the world to see. Minimize the links to the Agency by having Murphy make his report in the U.S. and you minimized the risk of detection and the stink that would ensue if detection, against all the odds, did occur. It had involved relying a good deal on the intelligence of Murphy and the girl. He felt good about the girl. She had her head screwed on. But Murphy was something else. He knew nothing about Murphy. Now he recalled with misgiving what Rosen had said about chess players. Eccentric, he had called them; eccentric and unreliable.

It was late afternoon before the situation was clarified. Wylie was missing; he'd not entered the country by any direct flight nor, to Immigration's knowledge, by any other means. They would have to start looking in Moscow.

Roskill's telegram to Preston in Moscow was composed in a hurry. It requested Preston to make discreet inquiries as to how Murphy had left the USSR and where he seemed to be headed. When he drafted it, Roskill neglected to attach any security classification. Perhaps he assumed Miss Solveig would do so. Or perhaps he just forgot. When the cable was forwarded to the State Department for transmission, the clerk who relayed it sent it *"en clair."* He then compounded his error by hitting a wrong key when typing the word "Murphy." As received—and within a few hours the message was not only in Preston's IN-tray but on the desk of Colonel Lermontov at KGB headquarters in Dzerzhinski Square—the name "Murphy" had been transformed into "Morphy."

Lermontov initially did not pay much attention to it. He had received it in the first place only because Preston, described in the Diplomatic List as "Counselor, Economic Affairs," was an individual as to whose true place in the scheme of things the KGB had doubts. Normally, it might have aroused Lermontov's interest. Now he put it to one side. He would think about it later. For the present he had other axes to grind.

He had not been deterred by Stein's refusal to act upon his hunch, nor by the knowledge that, if his hunch were correct, the damage had perhaps already been done. It was the function of a security service, not only to prevent leaks, but, if they occurred, to plug them and assess the damage. Obtaining information about Wylie would not, he had concluded, compromise Stein or himself. He had, therefore, set about obtaining it. The results had been interesting.

For one thing, Wylie had not been sick. Or, if he had, his stomach ailment had not been serious enough to interfere, in the days prior to his departure, with either his eating habits or his sex life. For another, if Wylie had indeed traveled home to consult his doctor, the route he had taken had been extremely roundabout. Originally booked from Moscow to Paris and thence to New York, he had apparently changed planes in Paris and flown instead to Geneva.

This information puzzled Lermontov. Plainly Wylie had not gone home to see his doctors, for he had not gone home at all. If he were working for the CIA, on the other hand, common sense would surely dictate that he hurry back to the protection of his employers. But he had not done so. And the irritating thing was that they had lost track of him in Geneva. In the meantime, the investigation was spreading out alarmingly, and it was still unauthorized. Lermontov wondered if he could take the risk of starting a search in Switzerland. For one thing, it would mean involving the Resident in Bern. There would be complaints, telegrams to Stein, requests for authorization. . . .

He sighed. Perhaps he should drop it for the time being. One could beat one's brains out against a problem for only just so long. He needed a change of problem. Then perhaps his subconscious might come up with something—the intuitive sideways leap—of which mere reasoning had so far proved incapable.

He turned again to the intercepted cable. Who was this Morphy whose disappearance so interested the State Department? A diplomat, perhaps, or a businessman, who'd been scheduled to return to the United States and had failed to show up. Stopped off in Europe, probably, without bothering to inform his superiors.

He fetched his copy of the Diplomatic List and turned idly to the section covering the United States. It filled ten pages and contained several hundred names. It was ridiculous, he thought angrily, to permit so many Americans, each one a potential spy, to wander about his city. Then he remembered what Stein had once said on the subject, and he smiled. The Soviet Embassy in Washington, Stein had pointed out, employed more than five hundred Soviet citizens. That was one race the Soviet Union was definitely winning.

The Economic Affairs Section listed a staff of ten. None of them was named Morphy, Murphy, or any conceivable variant. The same was true of the Consular Section, the Political Section, the USIA. . . . Wearily he picked through the entire list, not forgetting to check also the personnel of U.S. consulates in other cities. No Morphys or Murphys there at all.

The list of visiting U.S. businessmen, in whom Preston's Economic Affairs Section might legitimately be interested, yielded the same result. He approached the problem from another angle: suppose Preston were CIA, that his stated position was a cover—there was some evidence to support that assumption—then might not Morphy be a code name? . . . But if Preston were CIA, why had the cable not been sent in cipher?

He couldn't guess. In any case it was eight o'clock. Time to go home. He'd had enough of imponderables for one day.

He scribbled a note requesting the file on Preston and further research into the identity of this mysterious Morphy. Then he went home. Unanswered questions. Stein objected to unanswered questions. So did he. But it sometimes seemed to him that their work consisted of little else.

An hour later he was in the bath. He lay there, musing, watching the curls of steam rise from the surface of the water, while the ripples flowed gently around his chest and lapped against his chin. Presently a name floated into his consciousness and lodged there against the recalcitrant Morphy, like a piece of driftwood caught under a stone. The name was Paul . . . Paul Morphy. Where had he heard that name before? . . . It was a few seconds before he remembered. Paul Morphy? Of course! Paul Morphy had been the greatest American chess player.

CHAPTER XIII

The Minister's office was on the sixth floor of the Kremlin, overlooking Red Square. The room was rectangular, long and spacious, with a high ceiling and, along the exterior wall, three sets of double-glass doors which gave out onto a balcony running the full length of the room. It was an office, Lermontov reflected, that could easily have accommodated Stein, himself, and half of his department.

The decorations were in a style that had probably not changed much since the days of the last Czar. Three crystal chandeliers hung from the ceiling by heavy black chains. The curtains surrounding each set of glass doors were a rich burgundy velvet, held in place with thick silk cords, and hemmed at the bottom with gold tassels. The furniture was equally opulent. At one end of the room, the Minister's desk, heavy mahogany with a surface of Moroccan leather, was flanked by two straight-backed, Empire-style chairs. Their legs, Lermontov noticed, were shorter than those of the Minister's own chair, so that he and Stein were lower than the Minister and were forced to look up at him. At the far end, a sofa, upholstered in red leather to match the curtains, was surrounded by armchairs, similarly upholstered. In between, in the center of the room, there was nothing but a heavy French carpet whose thick pile protected the polished hardwood floor and helped preserve the silence that hung over the room, making Lermontov, in spite of himself, inclined to whisper when he spoke.

There was little in the room, Lermontov noticed, to indicate the arrival of the twentieth century. Only the telephones on the Minister's desk, the portrait of Brezhnev on the wall behind it, and the glass display case in the corner which contained a model of the latest nuclear submarine. Individuals come and go, the room seemed to be telling him, but the State remains. And the instruments of State are always roughly the same. The thought somewhat depressed him.

It had been difficult, in spite of the new evidence, to persuade Stein to request this meeting. But now that he had, Lermontov was glad to see, he was arguing the case with force and conviction.

"Our point is this, Minister," he was saying, "we are faced with a set of facts, heavily circumstantial, certainly, and far from complete, that throw grave suspicion on Alexei Ivkov. We recognize that this suspicion may prove to be unfounded, but if Ivkov is in any position whatever to inflict significant damage on the national security, then, in our opinion, it must be acted upon. The question we ask you, therefore, is simply this: is Ivkov in that position?"

The Minister, lounging in his chair with an air of confidence he was far from feeling, eyed the two stiff-backed KGB officers with distaste. An uncomfortable note had crept into this meeting. Their behavior, of course, was impeccable: formal, courteous, deferential. But it was impossible not to notice that command of the conversation had passed, in the previous fifteen minutes, from him to them. At first *he* had asked the questions, raised the objections, made them justify their position. Now *they* were doing it to him.

They were confident, he thought, and so they should be. Their position was solid. But his? What about his? . . . His mind flicked rapidly over the facts.

First: Stein's original memo, noting the dangers in permitting Ivkov to visit Helsinki. Second: the phone call in which he had quashed Stein's objections—a call which Stein, hardened politician that he was, might easily have recorded. Third: Stein's follow-up report, with his own damning comment at the foot of it.

He sighed heavily.

"Yes," he said finally, "he is in that position."

"In that case," Stein pursued, "have we your permission to begin a formal investigation?"

The Minister ignored the question. He was not ready to swallow that pill. Instead he made an attempt to regain the initiative.

"The evidence, as you readily concede, is entirely circumstantial. I would also add that it relies, to an extent which disturbs me, on intuition. So let me ask you again: what makes you so sure that Preston is CIA and that Morphy is a code name for Wylie?"

Stein looked at Lermontov. It was his intuition; let him defend it.

"In the case of Preston"—Lermontov was ready—"we have indications which admittedly fall short of proof. He's too old for his rank. His educational background is not in economics. He never represents the United States in any negotiations where detailed knowledge of the issues is required. He has frequent contacts with journalists whose expertise is not economic, but political. Though there is nothing directly incriminating about it, this is a profile of a man who is not what he claims to be. And, if he is not what he claims to be, what is he?

"In the case of Morphy, Wylie, beyond the interesting coincidence that both are names of chess players, we have the following facts. First, our inquiries at the hotel revealed that two persons asked for Wylie after his departure. One was an American journalist, a woman, who did not seem to have been aware that Wylie had left and who stated that she wished to interview him for a magazine article. She may be insignificant, but the facts are that she had met Wylie on a previous occasion and apparently spent the night with him. When she discovered that he had left the country, which she did by inquiring at the chess tournament, she, too, cut her trip short and flew to Paris.

"The other inquiry was made on the morning following the receipt by the U.S. Embassy of the cable to Preston inquiring after Morphy. This was made by an unidentified man who telephoned to ask the time of Wylie's departure. The desk clerk is not certain—it is sometimes difficult to tell over the telephone—but he believes the caller had a foreign accent."

He paused. "Now it becomes a matter of timing. Wylie left the hotel at nine A.M. It takes approximately forty minutes to get to the airport—say one hour, to allow for hold-ups. Check-in time for international flights is one hour prior to departure. It happens that between eleven and eleven-thirty A.M. there are three scheduled flights to Western Europe. They are Lufthansa departing to Stuttgart at eleven-oh-five, Air France departing to Paris at eleven-twenty, and Sabena to Brussels at eleven-thirty. We have established that each of these airlines, within an hour of the telephone call to the hotel, received a call from an unidentified man asking if a certain Arthur Willey—he spelled out the name —had left Moscow on its flight. When all three airlines responded in the negative, the caller said that he was uncertain of the spelling and were there perhaps any names on the manifest that sounded like Willey. The Air France clerk replied that the manifest for the Paris flight listed an A. Wylie. The Air France clerk is French and he thought the caller was Russian. The Sabena clerk is Russian and he thought the caller was not.

"So it boils down to this. Preston may or may not be CIA; but he is requested to trace a certain Mr. Morphy. Morphy may or may not be

Wylie; but, if he is a real person, we can find no record of his having entered or left the country in the last month. Wylie, on the other hand, left on Tuesday. And somebody, somebody probably not Russian, has probably been trying to trace him."

The Minister frowned.

"You displayed the extraordinary diligence I've come to expect from your department. Nevertheless, I'm still unwilling to authorize an investigation, which would disturb Academician Ivkov and undoubtedly interfere with his work, for something this vague and circumstantial."

His concern was only partly for Ivkov, though he still believed him innocent. His own position was in jeopardy. Everything had been informal so far, and if he could head them off it would remain so. But a formal investigation, whatever the outcome, would place on the record documents which, from his point of view, were better left in obscurity. Stein and Lermontov had exceeded their authority. A formal investigation which failed to incriminate Ivkov would leave that fact on the record also, and leave them without anything to justify their actions. If he could only shake them, they'd no doubt realize it was in everyone's interest to forget the whole thing, permanently.

"It is circumstantial," Lermontov pressed forward his attack, "but that's why we should question Academician Ivkov. We've gone as far as we can with circumstances. We've established a pattern which is definitely suspicious. Compatible, let's say, with the assumption of guilt. Difficult, at any rate, to explain otherwise. So we must talk with Ivkov, if only to permit him to exonerate himself. It's unfortunate. But the situation demands it. Justice demands it."

Demands? the Minister thought. First it was requests. Now it was demands. He tended to doubt the sincerity of Lermontov's concern for justice. But one thing was rapidly becoming clear. They were convinced, themselves. They'd go ahead now, with or without his authorization. They'd go ahead, and if they were wrong they'd hang themselves. If they were right, on the other hand, they'd hang him.

But Lermontov was not finished.

"There's another fact we must consider. Wylie has gone, but not to the United States. This may mean, as you pointed out previously, that he has nothing to do with the CIA and that our suspicions are false. But make the other assumption. Suppose Preston is CIA and Wylie is Morphy. Suppose Wylie has information obtained from Ivkov. The Preston cable then tells us that the CIA doesn't have it yet. Why otherwise would they be looking for Wylie? Now, they'll have traced him to Geneva as we have. But we lost him there. And the odds are they will, too. And that means we have a chance to get to him first. In other words, the situation may be retrievable."

"I don't follow you. If all your suppositions are correct—which I doubt—then Wylie is working for the CIA and will eventually get in touch with them. The odds are heavily against us being able to find him before he does."

"Well, we've all agreed that if Wylie is CIA, then the most logical course would be for him to report immediately. Apparently he hasn't. So it may be that he was working for them. But not any longer."

"If not for them, for whom?"

"Perhaps he's working for himself."

The Minister sat up abruptly.

"This is absurd." He brought his hand down on the desk with a smack. "You've stretched the chain of assumption so far that even you don't know where it's leading. What you're telling me now is pure speculation."

"Up to a point. Yes." Lermontov's voice was level. "But if Wylie has his own reasons for not contacting the CIA, it still means we may be able to reach him first."

"Well, in that case I assume you've taken steps to trace him. Do that. Bring him back. Interrogate him. Then we'll know the truth of this matter. I don't see the need to involve Ivkov until we've established more of the facts."

Lermontov began to lose patience. Didn't the Minister understand, at least, the danger to his own position? Didn't he see that the time for protecting friends was long past?

"We've lost Wylie. Finding him will be a major undertaking—expensive, difficult, time-consuming. It will mean taking agents away from their normal duties, risking their cover, disturbing, in fact, our entire intelligence-gathering operation in Western Europe. We'd rather not do this unless we know we have to. And we can find this out simply by talking to Ivkov. I'm afraid I don't understand your reluctance to let us." The tone of his voice as he spoke the last sentence was flat, almost hostile. It indicated, perhaps, that he understood very well.

The Minister considered. It was a powerful argument. The KGB was represented at the highest level in the Party. Its influence far exceeded his own. Refuse permission, these officers were telling him, and we'll get it anyway. And in a way that will bring you in conflict with our entire organization. It was a conflict he *had* to avoid.

"If I agree to your questioning Ivkov, what methods of interrogation do you propose to employ?"

"Only those necessary to obtain the truth." Stein's answer was as smooth as cream.

Only those necessary to obtain the truth. The Minister could imagine what they were.

"That's exactly why I'm reluctant to permit it." He turned to Lermontov. "You see, Colonel, I don't believe it would be entirely cynical to observe that your department's investigations—its methods of arriving at the truth—have a remarkable tendency to find what they're looking for. Do you follow me?"

His eyes held Lermontov's. There was a long moment of silence before Lermontov looked away. He nodded.

"Now, in normal circumstances, that would not, perhaps, be important. But in this case, let me remind you once again, we are dealing with a man whose work is of vital concern to the defense of this country. If anything occurs to impair"—he paused to emphasize the next word—"unnecessarily, his ability to continue that work, there will be the gravest possible consequences to the individuals concerned. And that is why, in this case, I shall expect to see external corroboration for any self-incriminating statement made by Academician Ivkov. His unsupported confession will not be enough. . . . Do you understand me?"

He was ignoring Stein. Stein was a bureaucrat. Left to himself, Stein would have capitulated long ago. This other one was different; he was playing in earnest. Or rather, he wasn't playing, because to him it wasn't a game. The Minister rather admired him. He would go a long way, would Colonel Lermontov—or he would go nowhere at all.

This time Lermontov held his gaze steadily.

"I understand fully, Comrade Minister," he replied. "May I assume, then, that we now have your permission?"

"Yes," the Minister told him. "You do."

During this exchange Stein had removed from his briefcase a typewritten memo. It contained a summary of the case against Ivkov and authorized his interrogation. He placed it in front of the Minister. Then, removing from the top pocket of his uniform jacket a large red fountain pen, he uncapped it and handed it to the Minister.

"We shall need your signature on this document, Minister. It is the usual procedure."

His tone was deferential: it contained, almost, a note of apology. But the words conveyed a statement, not a request.

Assume, Stein thought. It was a word he'd heard too often in the preceding three-quarters of an hour. Lermontov could assume what he wanted. He himself liked things in writing.

CHAPTER XIV

Ivkov was in bed reading when he heard the knock at his door. Three evenly spaced raps, not loud, but definite, even peremptory. He got up and started to search for his bathrobe.

"Who is it?"

"Academician Ivkov?"

"One minute, please, while I put something on."

There were two men standing in the corridor. Before he had time to say anything they had brushed past him into the room. Mildly surprised, he shut the door and turned to look at them.

They were dressed identically in black trench raincoats, blue serge suits, gray shirts, black, heavy-soled shoes—civilian clothes which nevertheless had about them more than a suggestion of uniform. Their military aspect was enhanced by their closely cropped hair and a certain brisk economical quality in their movements. He recognized them as the type that mingled, quietly but not altogether unobtrusively, with the State dignitaries at public functions. In this case, he knew, with an intuitive certainty which excluded all possibility of doubt, who they were and why they had come.

The taller of the two reached into the inside pocket of his jacket and produced a wallet which he flipped open and extended for Ivkov's inspection.

"You are Academician Alexei Ivkov?"

"Yes."

Ivkov inspected the identity card contained in a cellophane flap of the wallet. It identified the holder as Andrei Leontiev, Lieutenant, KGB.

Oddly, he felt no reaction, no rush of adrenaline or fear. It was as if, at this moment before disaster—and he knew it was that—his mind had slipped its mooring in his body and had floated away free to regard the situation from a distance, objectively, as though it were happening to someone else. He knew he should act surprised, or indignant, or even curious; but he was not much of an actor at the best of times. Now it was totally beyond him.

"Yes, Lieutenant. What is it you want?"

"You are requested to accompany us."

"Where?"

"Dzerzhinski Square." The tone of voice suggested that the question was foolish.

"By whom requested?"

"By Colonel Lermontov, Chief of Internal Security for the Greater Moscow District."

"May I know why?"

"We were not told that."

"Well, I presume I am permitted to dress myself first?"

"Certainly."

He started toward the bathroom. The smaller KGB man moved to follow him. Ivkov turned angrily to Leontiev.

"May I not get dressed by myself? I don't need assistance, you know."

"Our instructions were specific." Leontiev was imperturbable. "We are to conduct you to Colonel Lermontov, by force if necessary, and we are to accompany you at all times until then."

There was no way out of the bathroom but back into the bedroom. They would know that. Their reluctance to leave him alone there meant that they anticipated the possibility of his trying to kill himself. Which meant, in turn, that it was serious. He'd understood that from the start, of course, but the loss of privacy brought it home to him more sharply than anything else. Five minutes before he had been Academician Ivkov, an eminent and respected scientist; now he was a suspected felon, a person without rights.

He dressed quickly, not looking at the KGB man who propped himself against the wash basin, following his movements with an alert, impersonal gaze. When he had finished, he relieved himself in the urinal next to the wash basin. He was not sure when he would get another opportunity.

They escorted him downstairs, through the lobby, to the waiting car outside, flanking him on either side, but walking a pace or so behind as though to convey, to anyone who might be watching, the impression that he was leading and they were following. It was a piece of tact for which he felt grateful; though it amazed him that he could preserve, in such circumstances, any concern for appearances. Nevertheless he felt oddly reassured.

His sense of reassurance persisted, increased even, when he met Lermontov. Lermontov's gray eyes were alive with intelligence, but his manner was relaxed and affable, devoid of any suggestion of menace. He started by apologizing to Ivkov for the inconvenience he had caused him, and then offered him cigarettes and coffee. He seemed so friendly that Ivkov, for the first time since he had answered the knock at his door, permitted himself a flicker of hope. They are unsure of themselves, he told himself, otherwise they would not be so polite. And if that is so, then, with care, I may yet survive.

He was glad he had spent the afternoon relaxing. His mind was alert now. He felt ready, even eager, to begin the battle.

Lermontov, on the other hand, was in no hurry. He had learned that the art of interrogation consisted essentially in manipulating the subject's emotions. You created a state of fear—he had handpicked the men he had sent to fetch Ivkov—you stimulated a rush of adrenaline through the subject's system. Then you permitted him to relax, to grow hopeful, to become confident. Then you terrified him again. And so, by alternating states of alarm and relief, you led him, through bewilderment and desperation, into despair.

"There is a book by Saltonov," he began, "you have read it, perhaps, called *Science and Conscience*." He produced a thick manuscript, bound in blue cardboard, and laid it on the desk.

"Yes, I've read it. Someone lent me a copy. I forget who."

No unnecessary lies, Ivkov told himself. Stick to the truth wherever possible. And don't talk too much.

"What did you think of it?"

"The argument is not new, and it rests, obviously, on a mistaken premise."

"Which is?"

"Well, Saltonov argues that science has released a destructive power so great that scientists can no longer be responsible simply to governments. Since the survival of the entire human race is at stake, their responsibility is to humanity at large and not just to a single nation or political system. The same thought occurred to Einstein and the scientists who worked on the American bomb. In their case, perhaps, it was justified, since Hiroshima and Nagasaki occurred soon afterwards; but . . ."

"But in Saltonov's case?"

"Saltonov's mistake, obviously, is his assumption that all political systems are morally equal and equally indifferent to the interests of mankind."

"And they are not?"

Ivkov began to grow impatient. How long were they to conduct this discussion of elementary civics?

"Obviously not. The capitalist system serves the interests of a limited class of property owners: the Marxist-Leninist system serves the interests of all the people."

"And that is what you believe?"

"Don't you?"

Lermontov eyed him thoughtfully.

"We should neither of us be here," he said at length, "if I did not."

"Do you mind telling me then, Colonel, exactly why we are here? I can hardly believe that you went to the trouble of interrupting my afternoon, and your own, just for the sake of discussing proscribed literature."

"No." Lermontov's voice hardened. His eyes went cold. "I interrupted your afternoon for the sake of discussing treason."

Ivkov felt a constriction at his throat. His collar was too tight. He noticed that his hands had started to tremble, and he placed them along the arms of his chair.

"Am I . . ." His voice was thick and he paused to clear his throat. "Am I to assume, then, that I am suspected of treason?"

Lermontov shook his head.

"No. That is not correct. What we are going to discuss here is not suspicion: it is fact."

He paused. "This is how we will do it. We will start at the beginning. I will take you through the facts. I will ask you questions. And you"—his forefinger stabbed the air, pointing like a pistol between Ivkov's eyes—"you will answer."

"What was the subject of your conversation with Berenstein?"

"We discussed his specialty, atmospheric physics."

"What else?"

"Other general scientific subjects of a non-military nature."

"Why do you say that?"

"What?"

"Why do you emphasize that the subjects were of a non-military nature?"

"Come now, Colonel, I am not stupid. I am a research scientist employed on a defense project. You drag me here to question me on the subject, as you put it, of my treason. What else would my supposed treason consist of, if not of passing military secrets?"

"You knew Berenstein was connected with the U.S. Department of Defense."

"No. I didn't. But I'm not surprised."

"Why not?"

"Probably more than half of the scientists there were connected with the military in some way or other. Look at me, for example. I am. Why not Berenstein?"

"Didn't you think it might look suspicious that you deliberately engineered a meeting with Berenstein if, as you say, the probability was that he was working for the U.S. Defense Department?"

"No."

"Why not?"

"For one thing it had never occurred to me, until a few minutes ago, that my loyalty was open to suspicion. For another, it is not correct to say that I deliberately engineered that meeting."

"How did it come to take place then?"

"Spontaneously. We were both bored. We decided to leave the seminar and have a drink together."

"Where were you sitting in the seminar, relative to Berenstein, that is?"

"A few seats apart."

"Our reports indicate that, in fact, you were at least twenty seats apart and several rows forward. My question is, how did your spontaneous impulse communicate itself?"

"I suppose I must have suggested it."

"In other words, it took place at your initiative?"

"Yes. If you insist on putting it that way."

"Why did you apply to attend the conference?"

"I was tired. I'd been working under immense pressure. I needed a rest, a change of scenery. I knew the conference was coming up, so I applied. It seemed a good way of combining business with pleasure."

"What business?"

"Colonel, you must know as well as I do that we send people to these conferences to keep their ears open. To see what they can pick up. Since it's essentially your line of business, I'm surprised you asked me that question."

"What pleasure then?"

"Change. As I said. One becomes stale if one never strays outside one's own field."

"But you stated you were bored at the seminar where you met Berenstein. Why was that?"

"It concerned the behavior of certain subatomic particles: It was beyond me. Too far outside my field."

"Atmospheric physics is closer?"

"No, but . . ."

"So you are saying that because the subject of the seminar was too far outside your field you arranged a meeting with an American defense scientist to discuss another subject equally far outside your field?"

"That's a ridiculous way of putting it. I was bored. Berenstein appeared to be bored. I suggested we have a drink. Our conversation just happened to be about atmospheric physics. I didn't plan it that way."

"I see. You didn't plan it. You happened to be bored. You happened to meet Berenstein. You happened to spill beer on your interpreter, with the consequence that he left you alone for several minutes with Berenstein. And I suppose it just happened that Berenstein afterwards decided to visit the U.S. Embassy. Just as it just happened that he went halfway around the city, using three different means of transportation, to arrive at a destination which was a five-minute taxi ride from the hotel. Do you really expect me to believe that?"

"I can explain my own actions. I can't pretend to explain Berenstein's. I'm not responsible for his behavior."

"I repeat. Do you really expect me to believe that?"

"Yes."

"Then it appears, my friend, that in the opinion of each other, we are both of us stupid."

CHAPTER XV

It was dusk. Outside the streetlights had come on. A suspicion of chill had entered the air, and the crowds of office workers, recently released from their labors, were walking or pedaling briskly, hurrying to the warmth and protection of their homes.

Ivkov was too hot. It may have been the lights. Or perhaps the room had been deliberately overheated. In any case his shirt, damp with sweat, was sticking to his back: his pants, clinging to his thighs and the backs of his legs, had begun to prickle and irritate the skin. He had been sitting too long. His muscles were tired. He shifted position constantly, sitting first upright, then slumped, moving his weight from one side to the other; but the relief he achieved was always temporary, diminishing each time until finally he was conscious of his body only as a continuous ache.

"What was the subject of your conversation with Berenstein?"

After two hours Lermontov had summoned assistance, a slim, athletic-looking young man, with clean features and short blond hair, behind whose powder-blue eyes Ivkov could see nothing but a kind of terrifying blankness.

"What was the subject of your conversation with Berenstein?"

They questioned him in relays; Lermontov first, pointing the way, the other following, pouncing, with a paranoid logic, on minor inconsistencies or slips of memory.

"What was the subject of your conversation with Berenstein?"

They made him repeat his answers over and over until their sameness wearied him and he began to feel the urge to contradict himself—for the sake of variety or to placate them.

Occasionally they seemed placated. A subject would seem exhausted and they would move on to another, only to return, after a few minutes, to the first, relentlessly hurling at him the identical questions, forcing him to rack his brains to recall, and return to them, the identical answers. It was primarily a question, he began to realize, not of intelligence—though that was certainly needed—but of stamina. There were two of them, more if necessary. He was alone.

It was the loneliness which, after the fifth hour, began to torment him —the loneliness and the constant uncertainty. They would retire to a corner, whispering together and sometimes smiling, like two doctors discussing a patient, establishing between them a bond from which, irrationally, he felt excluded. When they returned to him he would long to share in their smiles, to be part of their intimacy, but their eyes would be cold, their voices sharp and hectoring.

Moreover he still did not know, after all this time, the precise extent of their case against him. They fed him facts grudgingly, like children teasing a dog, giving him morsels just large enough to tantalize, too small for him to get his teeth into. Often, when they left a topic to return to an earlier one, he would begin to hope that he had measured the extent of their knowledge. But always they would confound this hope with a new detail, another small link in the chain of evidence against him.

He had quickly realized, however, that the evidence against him was incomplete and largely circumstantial. They would hardly be putting themselves to this trouble otherwise. They knew of his meetings with Berenstein and Wylie. They knew that, after those meetings, both Berenstein and Wylie had behaved oddly. Berenstein, in particular, had acted like an irresponsible fool, which he no doubt was—he, thought Ivkov savagely, should be sitting here now—but they did not seem to know what had been said in these conversations, and they were not even really sure what they were looking for. Unless they found that out, he might hold them off.

At length they seemed to grow tired. There was a lull in the questioning. They slouched in their seats, still looking at him with the same controlled hostility, but apparently at an impasse, unable to go forward. Ivkov felt a renewal of hope. Perhaps . . . perhaps, after all, he had won. He pulled himself upright in his chair.

"You know, Colonel, at the beginning of this . . ." His weary gesture included the overflowing ashtrays, the coffee cups, the stale air, the dark stains at the armpits of their unbuttoned tunics, the tape recorder on the desk with its spool now turning aimlessly, the loose end of the tape flapping insistently against the body of the machine—the whole sad debris of their spent emotion. "At the beginning of this, you claimed possession of the fact of my treason. It's obvious we speak a different language. I, after all, am a scientist. You"—he searched for an acceptable euphemism—"you are a policeman. To me, a fact is something impossible to doubt in the context of available evidence. To me, what you have are not facts. They are assumptions—unpleasant assumptions, unjustified by the evidence, generated by the prejudices of your regrettable profession. You are the victim of your own habits of mind."

For the first time in more than five hours Lermontov looked at him with something other than hostility. There was pain in his eyes, and a look of sadness, almost of compassion, came over his features.

"The victim, me?" he asked softly, shaking his head. "You're wrong. If there is a victim here, it's you."

They took Ivkov away then down several flights of stairs to a cell in the basement of the building. They took away his tie and his belt, his watch, his penknife, and his lighter. They made him remove the laces from his shoes; they took those away. They took away his spectacles, his jacket, and his shirt.

The cell was small, about four feet by eight, and it smelled of urine. The walls and floor were of rough concrete, unpainted. There was a small window high on the wall opposite the door. It was protected by a grille of thick iron bars and was, in any case, too narrow to squeeze through. Beneath it was a small cot, of wooden construction with no springs, covered by a thin mattress. The mattress was stained and also smelled of urine. There was no other furniture. Overhead, from a short strand of flex, too high for him to reach, hung a single light bulb. It was burning when they locked him into the cell, but after one or two minutes it went out.

It was cold in the cell without his jacket and shirt; and, although his body and mind ached for rest, he could not sleep. His shivering kept him awake. Besides which, he had a strong need to urinate.

Presently he heard voices and footsteps coming down the passage toward him. Before they reached him they stopped. He heard a key turn in the lock of the next cell. Another poor devil, he thought, dragged out in the middle of the night to answer their interminable questions. But the thought comforted him. He felt a slim bond form between himself and the anonymous unfortunate next door. Tomorrow, he thought, when I get a chance I must try and make contact with him.

Then he heard voices again. Apparently the connecting walls were not that thick, for the voices in the next cell were clearly audible. One said, "I will ask you just this last time." And another, much higher, seemingly on the verge of hysteria, "I don't know." Then the first voice again, "Very well." To which the answer was somewhere between a word and a sob. Ivkov was not sure what the word was. It might have been "please."

For perhaps a minute there was silence. Then a cry, recognizably human at first, but rising higher and higher until it lost all human quality and became a scream that might have been uttered by an animal at the limits of torment and pain. It died away finally in a gasp of relief, followed by harsh, sobbing gulps.

Then the first voice, "Now, I will ask you again." It was level and impersonal, the voice of someone dealing with a recalcitrant child.

Silence.

Then the scream again, longer this time and less human still. And the sobbing: broken, racking gasps, not so much uttered as torn from the chest of the sufferer.

Ivkov could not tell how much longer it went on. Before the third time he pressed his hands over his ears, and when this did not shut out the sound he pulled the top of the mattress down over his head. Even so, he still seemed to hear it, muffled and far off, so faint he could not tell, finally, whether it was real or his imagination.

Lermontov stopped the machine. He pressed the rewind button and stood for a moment, lost in thought, his face gray and haggard, watching the rotation of the spools and the tape peeling rapidly off the smaller spool. Just before it ran out he shut off the machine again, pulled down the lid, and fastened it shut.

"If this is going to work," he whispered, "that ought to be enough. Come"—he gathered the machine under his arm—"we will leave him alone for half an hour to think things over. Then we'll try him again."

This time the footsteps came to Ivkov's door. He heard the key turn in the lock, and, as it did so, the light came on. Lermontov entered. He was followed by a man in a thin cotton jacket that might once have been white but was now gray and stained around the cuffs and down the front with spots of blackish brown. He had a stethoscope around his neck, and he carried a small black case. Behind him came Lermontov's assistant carrying a small but obviously heavy machine, whose most noticeable features were a cranking handle and two leads, each of which terminated in a metal clip. It looked to Ivkov like an ordinary portable generator.

The assistant went out again and returned carrying a wooden bench, on which were placed two heavy leather straps, each of them, Ivkov judged, about six feet long. He set the bench next to Ivkov's cot, throwing the straps onto the floor, and placed the machine on it. He left one of the leads on the surface of the bench and took the other in his left hand, taking care to hold it by the insulation. Bending over the bench, he held the terminal of one lead about a centimeter away from the other. Then he cranked the handle, once, slowly. There was a sudden crackle. An arc of fierce blue and white light danced and flickered across the space between the terminals.

He straightened up.

"It seems to work," he said.

Lermontov did not reply. Instead, he turned to the other man and nodded. The man motioned Ivkov to sit on the bed and started to examine him with the stethoscope, tapping his chest with the last three fingers of his right hand in a deliberate even rhythm which reminded Ivkov bizarrely of the knocks hours earlier—it seemed like half a century—that had started this ordeal.

When the examination was over the man said: "The heart is in excellent condition. Blood pressure is acceptable. The pulse is high. But that is understandable in the circumstances."

"Can he stand it?" Lermontov asked.

The other shrugged.

"He won't die, if that's what you mean."

Lermontov nodded. The other men left. Lermontov came over to the cot and stood over Ivkov, gazing at him with the same troubled expression he had been wearing when Ivkov had last spoken to him. At length he sat down beside Ivkov and placed his hand on Ivkov's shoulder.

"Melodrama," he said. "Bad theater." He wrinkled his nose. "But it achieves something. It shows you what they are going to do."

Ivkov nodded.

"You'll tell them eventually. You know that, don't you?"

Ivkov said nothing.

"There's no question of your courage," Lermontov continued, "but it has limits. Everybody's has. And the further your limits are, the more painful it is to reach them. But who does courage help? Not your accomplice. He's gone. Safe. In fact, his safety was achieved at your expense. So forget him. Think of yourself now. Help yourself."

Ivkov turned to look at him.

"If I could tell you what you want," he said at last, "don't you think that by now I'd have done it?"

Lermontov shook his head.

"You still hope to save yourself," he said. "But it's no use. You're dead already. Back there you accused me of forcing the facts to fit my assumptions. I'm not a scientist with your rigorous standards of proof, that's true. But when I know something, I know it." He tapped his chest. "In here. And, in your case, I *know*.

"Let me ask you, then. And, before you answer, consider what I have just told you and consider all this." He gestured toward the paraphernalia on the bench. "What was the real subject of your conversation with Berenstein?"

Ivkov looked at him. They were down to it at last. They wouldn't draw back now. And he was probably right, this strange intuitive colonel with the sad gray face and the sharp intelligent eyes. He'd probably tell them. So why not now?

He couldn't do it. The words were his death sentence and he couldn't utter them. Instead he said, in the voice, flat and lifeless, of a child repeating a well-learned lesson, "We discussed atmospheric physics and other scientific subjects of a nonmilitary nature."

Lermontov got up.

"Shit," he said wearily. "Oh, shit."

He went over to the door and summoned the others.

"Remember," he told them, "if this man dies before he tells us what we need, I am in a lot of trouble. And that means you," he pointed a finger at each of them, "and you, too." He started to leave.

Ivkov watched his departure with dismay. Although Lermontov was evidently his prime accuser, he felt in some obscure way as if he was being deserted, was losing his last recognizably human contact.

"Wait!" he said. "Aren't you going to stay? Don't you want to watch?" He put into his voice all the contempt he could manage.

Lermontov looked back over his shoulder.

"No," he said. "It makes me sick."

They made Ivkov lie down. Then they lashed his ankles to the cot with one of the leather straps and with the other they bound his arms and shoulders. When he was secure, the assistant came and stood over him.

"You really shouldn't be doing this," he said.

With a sudden movement he reached down and slipped his fingers under the waistband of Ivkov's trousers, dragged them and the underpants to Ivkov's knees. Ivkov squirmed in humiliation. He felt his bowels loosen and was terrified he would lose control of them.

The assistant moved to the bench and picked up the two leads. He fastened one to Ivkov's chest, just below the right nipple. The other he attached to Ivkov's penis, locking the clip to a fold of skin just below the glans. The tiny metal teeth bit into Ivkov's flesh. He flinched and shivered.

"When I crank this handle," said the assistant, placing his hand upon it, "a current will pass between the terminals, through the most sensitive parts of your body. But, of course, you know that already. You're a scientist. You know all about electricity. What you don't know, or otherwise we wouldn't be doing this, is about pain."

With a swift movement he cranked the handle.

Ivkov's body arched and bucked against the restraint of the straps. His face contorted. His mouth was forced open. The breath was forced from his body in a high-pitched, wordless shriek. His head flapped frantically from side to side as if trying to ward off the pain. But it possessed him utterly, mastering him in waves that mounted higher and higher, each one forcing him to a new pinnacle of torment. Then it stopped.

The assistant leaned over him.

"Now you know," he said softly. "So tell me. What was the subject of your conversation with Berenstein?"

Ivkov raised his head. He stared uncomprehendingly at the face pushed close to his. Then he vomited.

It took them five more minutes. At one point he fainted, but the relief was pitifully short. Later he defecated, the stench mingling in his nostrils with the smell of his own charred flesh. It caused him no humiliation. It meant nothing to him. Only the pain was real.

In five minutes they broke him, changed him from a human being into a crawling, blubbering object, smeared with shit and vomit—their possession, their slave.

It was over. He sat in Lermontov's office waiting for them to finish typing his confession, smoking one of Lermontov's cigarettes, and sipping from a plastic tumbler the shot of vodka Lermontov had poured from a bottle he kept locked in a lower drawer of his desk. Chills of nausea and panic still trembled through his body. He made no effort to control his shaking. It was a luxury. The cigarette and the vodka were luxuries. After the pain everything was a luxury.

Lermontov watched him over the desk. His tunic was unbuttoned and hung loosely at his sides. He supported his chin between his hands and his elbows on the desk as though, without that solid and official prop, he would fold up altogether.

"Tell me," he said at length, "what made you do it? Saltonov?"

"No." Ivkov dismissed the suggestion with an irritated wave of his head. "He wrote nothing I didn't already believe."

"Then you think the system is wrong?"

"I don't know. Perhaps the system is all right. But the system is operated by people."

He had been about to say "people like you." But, reaching inside himself for the hatred he had expected to find there, he was surprised to find nothing. Lermontov was no wanton sadist. He had acted, obviously, with reluctance and distaste. And the action was no doubt justified, in his eyes, by reference to the noble and glorious idea. . . . What was it, then, about noble and glorious ideas that made intelligent and well-meaning men descend so inevitably to actions such as this? The notion of sacrifice, perhaps; self-sacrifice. We expend ourselves today for the glory tomorrow. Why was it that the glory was always tomorrow?

"I think," he said finally, "that the people are not ready for the system. And tell me truthfully, seeing what you must have seen . . . tell me truthfully. Do you?"

Lermontov screwed up his face. "I don't know," he said sadly. "Sometimes it's hard."

A secretary entered with a sheaf of typewritten pages which he handed to Lermontov. He read them carefully and then pushed them across the desk to Ivkov.

Ivkov glanced through them. He didn't much care what they said. The first page was entitled "Statement of Academician Alexei Ivkov dated June 17, 1976." The last paragraph of the last page read:

I, Alexei Grigorovich Ivkov, acknowledge that the statement contained in the preceding paragraphs is true, and that the said statement was freely and willingly given.

There were spaces for his signature and those of witnesses.

When he had finished reading, Lermontov passed him a pen, and he signed the statement. Then, without looking at him, Lermontov pressed a buzzer, and a guard came and took Ivkov away.

CHAPTER XVI

"Five . . . hundred . . . thousand . . . dollars!"

For once, Roskill noted, the DCI's calm had deserted him; each word was a yelp of pain and disbelief.

"Half a *million* dollars? . . . He can't be serious."

The DCI turned to the others, inviting some gesture of reassurance, some murmur of assent.

No one spoke.

"What are we coming to, for Christ's sake." The voice was now plaintive. "A nation of mercenaries, or what? . . . The man's an American, isn't he? You'd think he'd be happy to help us. But is he? . . . Hell no. He just sticks his hand out . . . who checked him, anyway?"

"Markham did," Roskill said. "Very thoroughly. I'm sure he's perfectly clean. It's not disloyalty we're facing here—just plain old-fashioned greed."

And not too surprising, at that, he thought, because agents as a breed —regulars and casuals alike—did have their hands out most of the time. They were human, after all, members of a species not noted for altruism. And he preferred them that way because old-fashioned greed he could understand and manipulate; patriotism, though less expensive, was unpredictable.

The DCI's outrage was an act, of course, put on to give himself time to think. He had as much faith in patriotism, Roskill imagined, as he did in the Tooth Fairy. Still, he was overdoing it a bit. They were none

of them children, for Christ's sake, they were professionals; they'd long
since shed their illusions. . . . Except Rosen, perhaps. But Rosen
didn't count. If he hadn't actually sold them his soul, he'd mortgaged it
to the limit. They didn't need to worry about him.

"He's crazy." The DCI reverted to his theme. "He disregards instructions, endangers his associate, jeopardizes the entire operation, and he
thinks we're going to pat him on the head and hand him a check for
half a million? The man must be out of his mind."

Roskill was silent. If the DCI wanted to squawk, it was best to let
him. It might even be therapeutic. And the DCI's emotion, though
largely simulated, did have some justification. Money—at least in sums
as large as the one under discussion—was a sore subject with the DCI,
for he spent a good part of his time heading off raids on the Agency's
coffers. Half a million wouldn't empty them, of course, but it would
make a sizable dent in the slush fund. Too many dents like that and the
DCI would be back in front of the Budget Committee, sticking his own
hand out. That was always painful. For the Budget Committee, a bunch
of grandstanding Senators with constituencies to impress, was apt to
make it an occasion for reviewing the recent history of the Agency's operations. Perhaps the DCI was entitled to squawk a little. . . . It
couldn't be much fun, Roskill thought, to be always apologizing for the
Bay of Pigs.

But the DCI, evidently, had done squawking. He stared, almost
accusingly, at Roskill.

"A check for half a million."

Roskill nodded. "He wants a wire transfer, actually, to a numbered
account in Zürich. And I'd imagine he'd be willing to skip the pat on
the head. . . . But yes, in effect, that's exactly what he thinks."

"Then perhaps we should ask him to think again."

"Perhaps."

The word was noncommittal, but Roskill's tone was tinged with
doubt. The DCI gazed at him thoughtfully for a moment before continuing.

"O.K.," he switched his gaze to each of them in turn, "let's hear
some bright ideas. What are you going to do about this?"

There was no immediate reply. The Section heads looked at their feet
or out of the window. The DCI's "you" had included them all, but they
chose to interpret it narrowly. This was not their problem. They would
help all they could, naturally, with the nuts and bolts, but they were not
about to hazard any "bright ideas." They had seen "bright ideas" come
and go, in their time, and history, by and large, had not been kind to
them; the authors, in most cases, were no longer with the Agency. As

the silence grew awkward, their eyes, wandering over the room along routes which, apparently random, nevertheless managed to avoid the DCI altogether, came to rest upon Roskill.

Rosen shifted uncomfortably in his chair. He wasn't sure why Roskill had asked him to the meeting, unless to implicate him in the choice of Wylie, but in any case he didn't like it. It made him nervous, brought him too close to the action, forcing upon his attention things he could easily guess at but would rather not know. He preferred to sit on the sidelines, filing his reports and banking his retainer.

He, too, glanced over at Roskill.

I warned you, he thought. *When you get around to recalling whose bright idea he was, let's hope you remember that, too.*

"I see." Roskill gave a sour grin. "No doubt, apparently, about who's elected. . . . Well, then, as I see it, we have three options. And for a start, I think we should look carefully at the arguments for paying."

He paused, waiting for the DCI's reaction. There was none.

"Oh, agreed, half a million seems totally outrageous," he went on. "But take a look at the return. The R and D savings, for instance. Defense has blown almost a hundred million on this project already, according to Olofson, and they're not even close. He thinks that figure could double before they're through. If he's right, we're talking a twenty thousand percent return on our investment. Not bad numbers, I'd say, by anyone's reckoning."

They received this in silence. He could almost hear them doing the mental arithmetic. The argument was sound, he reflected, but it wouldn't persuade them. For one thing, the R and D savings would benefit Defense, while the cost would fall on the Agency; the Agency was not known for that kind of generosity. Besides, they now regarded the information as theirs, and they'd never taken kindly to paying ransom. Beyond which, it was simply the number; they compared it with the kind of money they were making, and it sent them into shock; it was simply too much for them to swallow.

"Of course," he resumed, "the numbers are really irrelevant. We *need* that system. We can't afford to sit around until Defense stumbles onto it. If we do, we could end up a permanent second in the strategic arms race. . . . Now don't misunderstand me; I hate the idea of paying. I'd like to take Wylie and string him up by the thumbs. But that's not the point. The point is we need what he's selling and paying is the sure way to get it. I think it's the rational thing to do."

"It's rational, if we grant you your premise," the DCI countered. "But I'm not sure that we should. You're assuming, because he made us an offer, that he has what he claims to be selling. But how do we know that he does? . . . I'm as willing as anybody to invest in the nation's security, but I *would* like to think I'd be getting something for my money—something more, that is, than egg all over my face."

"I'm sure he has it. How else do you explain his offer? How else do you explain his behavior, come to that? How come he quit and bolted before his tournament was half-over? . . . I think he made the contact, realized what he'd been handed—a stick of pure dynamite—and decided he'd be a lot safer the hell away from Moscow. Then later, when he got to thinking about it, it struck him he had something he could sell. I think that, or something pretty close to it, is the only reasonable explanation for his actions. . . . Of course," he turned to Rosen, "I'm not the expert on psychology around here, but as I understand it, chess would be this guy's life—number one on his scale of values. It would have to be something fairly compelling, wouldn't it, to drag him away from the tournament?"

"Money, perhaps?" the DCI murmured. "That seems to rank pretty high on his scale of values." He, too, turned to Rosen. "What do you make of this, Harry? Can you shed some light on Mr. Wylie's obscure mental processes?"

"Well . . ." Rosen hesitated. "I tend to agree with Roskill. It would take something compelling to drag him away from his tournament—compelling to him, that is. The question is, though, what would he see as compelling? We're dealing here with a professional chess player, anything but your normal average citizen. Compelling, for him, may simply mean that the lights were too bright, or his chair was uncomfortable, or his hotel room faced the wrong way. It could be he was losing and couldn't handle it. . . . I'm sorry. I know this isn't much help. It could be almost anything."

It wasn't entirely cowardice. If his studies of the human psyche had taught him anything, he thought, it was that people's motives—specific motives in specific situations, were largely inscrutable. Nevertheless, he avoided Roskill's eyes.

"There's also the money." Roskill ignored the defection. He had hoped for Rosen's support—it was why he'd asked him to the meeting—but if he couldn't have it, he'd soldier along without it. In any case, he wasn't irrevocably committed to paying. He thought it was the best of their options, and he'd argue it as long as there seemed to be hope of persuading them, but he wouldn't bleed for it. This was one of the principles on which he'd based his career: if he had any choice, he wouldn't bleed for anything.

"The money?"

"How did he know what to ask for? . . . He didn't know what he'd be getting from Ivkov, so unless he talked to him and got a pretty clear idea what it was, how would he know how much we might be willing to pay?"

"I'm not sure that he does," the DCI observed dryly. "He knew we were anxious to get it, whatever it was. The figure he came up with could just have been a guess, based on that knowledge and an exaggerated notion of the Agency's resources. . . . There are several possibilities. Let's say the woman contacts him in Moscow, for example; at first he agrees to do it, but later he gets nervous and backs out. Then he gets a bright idea: he knows he's supposed to have received information; why not pretend to have it, leave Moscow in a hurry to lend the story some credibility, and then offer to sell us what we already expect him to have?"

Roskill started to object, but the DCI cut him off.

"You don't buy that? Nor do I necessarily. It fits the facts, though, and it's no more speculative than your own theory. And that's the point, isn't it? We're so short on facts here we're forced to speculate. And I don't feel like backing anyone's speculations—yours or mine—with half a million of the Agency's money.

"And there's something else to consider; Wylie isn't the only unknown; there's also Ivkov. Wylie may very well have got something from him, but it may not be worth a nickel. Because we don't know anything about Ivkov, either. We have indications, of course: unconfirmed reports, tentative identifications—the usual crap—but nothing positive. When we ask ourselves what we really know about this alleged Soviet scientist, the answer is, frankly, zip. That's something we mustn't lose sight of."

He paused and turned away, swiveling his chair and tilting it back in an abrupt movement that removed Roskill and the others from his field of vision. For perhaps half a minute he sat in silence, staring up at the ceiling while they waited. Then he turned back to Roskill.

"We won't pay," he said. "We can't. It's too thin."

"O.K.," Roskill capitulated. "Option number two: we try our luck with the Swiss. According to Wylie, the information is in a bank in Zürich and the bank has instructions to release it to us against payment. Suppose we go to the Swiss and tell them that what he deposited belongs to Uncle Sam. Could they make the bank hand it over?"

"It's been tried." The DCI shook his head. "The Swiss are obsessive about their banking regulations. They'd tell us to go to hell."

"Which brings us to option number three. . . ." It was the one Roskill liked least, but the one, he'd always recognized, most likely to appeal to the others. "We find Wylie. We bring him home. And we threaten to kick the shit out of him unless he comes through with the information. . . . There are a couple of problems with that one though. One: we don't know where he is. Two: we have a time limit. Unless we pay within a week, Wylie says, the offer is withdrawn and he'll make a deal somewhere else. He also warned us against trying to find him in the meantime. In other words, he expects us to try and find him; we have a week to do it in, and we'd better not be caught trying."

"Make a deal elsewhere? . . . He's bluffing, surely." This from the Swiss Section head. "The U.S. is his only market."

"Not necessarily. We may be the only country, apart from the Soviets, with the resources to develop an ABM system. But if Wylie knows what he's selling—and I wouldn't mind betting he does—he's bound to realize that the market is practically unlimited. Almost anyone could buy with the idea of reselling to us. . . . If that happens, Wylie's original offer will look like the deal of the century. Imagine what the price will be if the PLO are the sellers . . . or the Libyans. Those guys would make OPEC look like a charity."

They received this in silence.

"We're not paying," the DCI said at last. "That's been decided. . . . So you'd better set about finding him. How do you plan to begin?"

There was an edge to that "you," Roskill thought. Though he'd approved the operation himself, the DCI had no doubt, apparently, about who was responsible. This was not particularly surprising. The DCI was a politician; politicians behaved like that.

"We might as well start in Switzerland." Roskill shrugged. "He went there to do his banking apparently. There's no record of his leaving, or entering the States."

"What about the call?"

"We traced that to New York City. A call box on Second Avenue. But I'm sure he didn't make it. He got someone to do it for him, probably."

"How so?"

"Well, whoever made it was pretty relaxed about a trace. I stalled, of course, pretended not to have a pen handy, made him repeat the message to make sure I had it down right—that sort of thing. It didn't faze him a bit. Now our friend Wylie is something of a thinker—that much is obvious whichever way you figure it. If *he'd* been on the other end, I wouldn't have had that much time. In fact, I wouldn't be surprised if he'd sent us the message that way deliberately, hoping we would trace—and go blundering off on a false trail.

"And besides, look at things from his point of view. He hopes to stay out of sight for a week, and he's already assumed we'll be after him. Why make life easy for us by coming back here?"

"So where does that leave us?"

"I think," Roskill said, "it leaves us with passports. Switzerland's a small place, with a good police force. He's going to feel very exposed there. In his shoes, I'd go somewhere bigger, easier to get lost in—Italy, maybe, or France. But that means crossing a frontier. And for that, unless he's into mountaineering or taking very large risks, he has to show a passport. But he can't show *his* passport, so he'll have to get a fake. That's not easy, not if you don't know where to look; he'll have to feel his way carefully. We, on the other hand, do know where to look. So we'll be there before him, and when he starts making inquiries, we'll nail him."

"So that's the way it is," Roskill said. "We catch him. DCI's orders. And that means cables to Weston in Geneva and Faraday in Bern. This is top priority, tell them; they're to drop everything that can be dropped until it's over. . . . Use the FBI for liaison with Interpol and Swiss Immigration. You'll have to invent some kind of criminal record for him, of course."

"Will do," Holland nodded. "In six to eight hours, he'll have every cop in Europe on his ass. You know," he grinned, "he may be sorry he started this."

"His problem," Roskill growled. "The man wants to play; he mustn't bitch if he loses."

You'd better move, chess player, he thought. *And you'd better move fast. Because the game is going to get serious.*

And because of that, he thought, he was looking forward to it.

CHAPTER XVII

Now that she was safe, Anne Crossland was angry. It was not something she'd had time for before—she'd been too frightened. Indeed, her memory of the past two days—the time it had taken her to get clear after she learned of Wylie's disappearance—had been dominated by fear, was still obscured by the shadow fear had thrown over it.

Wylie had gone—so she'd learned at the tournament—he'd withdrawn, on grounds of ill-health, and flown home. And that had left her with questions. And, beyond the questions, with fear. Why had he gone? Had he simply ducked out, realizing, as she had done, the dangers involved? Or had he—this was the possibility that troubled her most—had he kept the assignation and then been alerted to some *real* danger that demanded his retreat? She hadn't known. The only fact she'd had, the only real certainty, was that they—Wylie, Hunter, the rest of them—had slunk out and left her in the most total, helpless isolation she'd ever known in her life.

The greatest terrors are those the mind creates for itself. She'd realized that. But it hadn't helped. It hadn't prevented her from reading hostility and suspicion in the faces of the officials at Intourist when they learned of her decision to cut her tour short, although what she had seen was probably only bureaucratic irritation at the prospect of more paperwork. It hadn't prevented her from feeling certain that she was being followed, her last day in Moscow, although she knew also that, in a large crowded city, that particular form of paranoia was the easiest to develop and the hardest to shake. And it hadn't prevented her, either—

although reason told her that if they suspected her they'd hardly leave her at liberty so long—from lying awake all night in her hotel room, starting at every footfall in the passage outside, expecting at any moment the knock at her door, the cold official invitation to disaster.

The greatest terrors are those the mind creates for itself. She knew it. They must have known it, too. And still they had left her in the dark, without a message, or any word of reassurance or comfort. Why? For her protection, of course. She could almost hear Hunter say it. It was the smooth and convincing answer: convincing, because, of course, it made perfect sense: smooth, because it came too easily, looked too open, made her suspect, in fact, that sense and openness were simply strategies they selected from the wide range of options available.

So now that she was safe, she was angry. She wanted to tell Hunter that. And she wanted to know what had happened. They'd been willing to trust her before. So now they could trust her with that. They owed her that much, at least.

So she called him, using the number he'd given her for Wylie. And someone had answered. But it hadn't been Hunter. Mr. Hunter was busy, it appeared. He was in conference and couldn't be disturbed. If she would leave a number, he'd call her back. In the evening probably, sometime before eight.

But it was now eight-thirty and he still hadn't called. And she realized that she hadn't really expected him to, had been sitting, in fact, by the telephone, with that intuitive sense of hopelessness with which one waits for news that is never going to arrive.

Well, she would call him again, then, if only to confirm her suspicions.

Almost before she heard it ring, the number was answered. A voice, female and supercilious, obviously recorded, regretted that the number she had dialed was not in service at that time. She was advised to check her listing or call the operator for assistance.

She called the operator. Yes, the operator confirmed, the number had been disconnected. When? The operator had no information on that point. She had little sympathy, her voice implied, with people who neglected to pay their phone bills.

The operator at the Agency switchboard was more courteous, but no more helpful. Sorry, but there was no Mr. Hunter listed in her directory. Was the caller sure that had been the name? . . . The caller had dialed that afternoon and received an answer? What number had she dialed? . . . Strange, but the prefix to that number was not an Agency prefix. . . . Was there perhaps someone else who could help her? If she could say what the call was in regard to, perhaps the operator could transfer her to the appropriate department. . . . She couldn't say? In that case the operator was sorry, but there was nothing more she could do to help.

They were sorry. They'd used her, risked her, and terrified her. And they were sorry. Somehow it didn't seem enough.

But there was nothing she could do. She thought of making a scandal, writing a story about what had happened, letting the facts speak for themselves. But there were no facts. There wasn't a single piece of corroboration for anything she could write. No editor would print it. No self-respecting journalist would even submit it. Besides, writing it could do harm, damage the innocents, the odd stray bodies who, like herself, had been caught up in the thing. If there were any innocents, besides herself.

Wylie perhaps? He'd seemed innocent enough. And she'd liked him—more than liked him. She was reluctant to believe he'd been in it from the start. But perhaps he had. She wondered, at any rate, if she'd ever see him again. Would he emerge finally from that nether world into which he'd disappeared? Perhaps he would. And then again . . . It was pointless to wonder. She could wonder all she wanted, inventing as many possibilities as time and her imagination would permit. She had plenty of imagination, its scope marvelously enlarged now by what she'd seen; and there'd be plenty of time, probably. And probably, most probably, she would never know.

CHAPTER XVIII

∎

Wylie sat at a sidewalk table of the Café de la Paix in Geneva, surrounded by maps, railroad schedules, and the remains of his breakfast.

The morning was clear and brilliant. The street, still wet from the recent passage of a road sweeper and sparkling in the sunshine, murmured with just enough activity to have filled him, in normal times, with a comfortable sense of his own indolence. Breakfast, moreover, had been excellent: croissants, crisp and golden, with sweet butter and black cherry jam; orange juice and coffee. Nevertheless he was unhappy. He'd been reviewing his position—since his return from Zürich he'd been doing little else—and the conclusion disturbed him. Incontestably, he had blundered.

For one thing, he shouldn't still be in Switzerland. He'd had to come, of course, to make the visit to his bank: to collect the few thousand of European winnings he'd managed to squirrel away there, and to arrange for the extraordinary services required by his impending transaction with the CIA—services that only the Swiss banking system, with its passion for anonymity and healthy unconcern for the origins of its deposits, could be trusted to provide. But he should have done that first, before sending the demand to Hunter. As it was he'd wasted the two days' start he should have had on them.

That was serious, but it wasn't his major mistake. His major mistake, he now realized, had been to do the thing at all.

It had seemed straightforward at the time. He'd wanted a new life, a chance to taste pleasures the years spent hunched over chessboards, chainsmoking and figuring, had denied him, but he lacked the money for it. *They* had money; what they lacked was information. What more natural, then, than an exchange? The notion had seemed to combine the simplicity and neatness of genuine inspiration.

It was only afterwards, when he was already committed, that doubts began to gather. He'd understood, naturally, that the CIA would not be overjoyed to part with half a million dollars for property it had expected to receive gratis, but the only alternative to paying, so far as he could see, was to track him down among the several hundred million inhabitants of Western Europe. He'd assumed, complacently reviewing the mathematics of the situation, that their chances of doing this were infinitesimal. This assumption, he now saw, was dangerously wrong.

He'd believed, for a start, that he would be dealing with the CIA alone. Although that organization was large, he'd figured, with tentacles reaching out into any country he might run to, its resources for conducting a manhunt outside the U.S. would be relatively slender. And that probably was true, but the CIA would get help. It wouldn't take too much imagination to concoct a story that would bring the police, the secret services, and the immigration authorities of every West European country into the hunt. . . . The Swiss, for instance; their police—formidably efficient and energetic, no doubt, like everything else in that clockwork country—were probably looking for him now.

So he should get out, go someplace bigger, someplace that would make him less conspicuous. But whenever he thought about how, he ran into the problem of his passport.

His passport was the albatross around his neck. It prevented him from using the airlines, from crossing the frontier, from cashing the few hundred dollars he still had in traveler's checks. It restricted his choice of hotels, though he'd have been unlikely, in any case, to have used a hotel where they'd ask to see it. It prevented him from renting a car, so whenever he needed to move around he was forced to risk himself in bus terminals and railway stations, precisely the places they'd be most likely to watch. And he needed to keep moving, for the longer he stayed in one place the more likely he was to be noticed. So he needed a new passport and a new driver's license. In fact, he needed a whole new identity.

The conclusion was elementary, but it didn't take him very far. He hadn't the faintest idea how to set about getting a new passport.

Ironically, the very lawfulness of his previous existence presented the major obstacle. With a criminal past he might have known, if not where to go, at least where to start looking. There was an underworld network, he imagined, where any contact might be able to point him in the right direction. And there, at least, he could have made the initial approach with reasonable confidence that, whatever else, the contact would not immediately turn round and head for the nearest policeman. . . . As it was, he was stuck in the most law-abiding country in Europe, surrounded by several hundred thousand complete strangers, any of whom, selected at random, would be more than likely to do just that.

The hours he'd spent pondering the problem had, however, yielded nothing more practical than an advertising slogan remembered from his previous existence—*let your fingers do the walking*. As inspiration this had struck him as being about level with the one that had landed him in this mess. . . . Assuming the Geneva phone book *had* yellow pages, there was still the small problem of where to start looking—under "Passports, Forged," perhaps, or under "Documents, Phony"?

So he'd shelved the passport problem, pending further brainwaves. He was now considering the alternative—how to get out of Switzerland *without* using a passport.

Italy was his best bet, he decided. He spoke the language well—or well enough to pass for a native if the conversation remained elementary. And Italy had a long frontier with Switzerland with few towns along it. It was reasonable to assume that in the stretches between roads or towns the obstacle would be nothing more than a chain-link fence, irregularly patrolled, with outposts several miles apart—easy to reconnoiter in the daytime, not difficult to get across at night. And once he was there, Italy offered another advantage: the police had their hands full with political disturbances and terrorism; besides which, they were notoriously inefficient.

But the stretch of frontier that seemed at first so promising revealed, on closer inspection, a new set of problems. Names like Monte Rosa, Mont Cervin, Gornergrat, followed by numbers denoting altitude in meters, reminded him that nature, herself, protected the border more effectively than frontier guards with carbines could ever hope to. No doubt there *were* routes, winding precipitously through rock and ice, but for them he would need a guide. That brought him back to the question of trust. It was as risky to ask a stranger to smuggle him across the frontier as to ask for directions to the nearest dealer in forged documents. Either course involved extending a lot of trust. In his present situation that would be madness.

So he turned his attention, instead, to the other end of the map . . . Locarno. That seemed to offer a better chance. Italy was on the far side of the lake and the lake was narrow at that point—only four or five kilometers by the look of it. He might be able to steal a boat. In any case, the lake offered opportunities for improvisation. Moreover, though the town was smaller than ideal, it would expose him less than tiny Alpine villages like Visp or Zermatt.

He was exposed everywhere, of course. And he would have to go by train. That would be risky, but less risky than staying another day in Geneva. Perhaps he should go to Locarno?

There was, of course, one final possibility: go to the CIA and throw himself on their mercy. He could reasonably hope that, once they had the information, they might forgive him his previous trespasses. It was an alternative, he thought, that at one time had had much to recommend it. But there was now one fatal objection. . . . He no longer had the information.

He still couldn't believe that he'd forgotten it. But he had. Somewhere between Gorki Park and the Bahnhofstrasse in Zürich it had buried itself in some fold of his unconscious, and now it obstinately refused to come out. The irony was so pointed he was tempted to ascribe the occurrence to some malicious Grand Design. . . . Why, for God's sake? Why had his memory, that freakishly perfect storage and retrieval system, which dealt so effortlessly with so much trivia, chosen this maddeningly inopportune moment to break down? He had waited too long, perhaps, before trying to write the information down. No, not perhaps; certainly. Because he'd discovered the lapse too late, discovered it only, in fact, when he was already in a cubicle outside the vault of his bank, intending to seal the information in an envelope and give it to Monsieur Laplace to hold until the money was paid over. He'd settled into a chair, taken a sheet of bank stationery, uncapped his ballpoint, and confidently plugged into the appropriate memory circuit. . . .

No response.

System malfunction. The panic that had seized him then still lived in his memory. Helplessness. The total frozen terror that paralyzes the prisoner when the hangman approaches with the blindfold. *Get a hold of yourself. Relax. Take a deep breath. It's temporary; wait for it to pass.*

But it hadn't.

Frantic then, he'd tried thinking himself back into the original situation. He'd forced himself to visualize the circumstances of his conversation with Ivkov—the park, the chess tables, the anxious elfin features of the Russian, the children playing, even the moves of the two aimless games they'd had—but nothing had come. In half an hour of trancelike concentration, he'd succeeded in recalling every circumstance of the trip to Moscow—except that conversation. Of *that* every syllable had disappeared.

It would come back, of course. Somewhere, sometime, the short circuit would mend itself and the conversation would return to him, clear and in sequence, as if it had never been away. But in the meantime . . .

In the meantime he was up the creek without a paddle—wasn't he? Because the message to the CIA had gone out and couldn't be recalled. So now if he threw himself on their mercy, they wouldn't believe him. How could they, when he'd also made that lunatic threat to market the information somewhere else? They'd think he was lying, playing games with them. And if they thought that . . . he didn't like to imagine the games they'd play with him.

So there were no real choices. He would have to keep on running—this way or that—until his memory returned or some other solution occurred to him. And there was no longer a time limit. Because if the week he'd originally given them ran out and they decided to pay, they'd receive for their money only the schoolboy formula which, with the flippancy of despair, he'd left with the bank: $E=mc^2$—one of the great thoughts, perhaps, but hardly, at this point, worth half a million dollars. When they discovered it, their rage could be murderous.

So there were no real choices. It was the devil or the deep blue sea. So it might as well be the deep blue sea. Or, in this case, the deep blue lake. Locarno. He might as well head for Locarno.

As soon as his visitor had left, Carl Zeitler reached for the phone. Midway through dialing, however, he stopped and replaced the receiver. There were some calls it was safer not to make from the Ministry.

He was known in most of the city's better restaurants, so he went to lunch at a small café away from the lake. He'd been there, by chance, once before and at the time had vowed never to go back, but today the Pot au Feu offered one decided attraction: he was unlikely to meet anyone he knew there.

On the way he stopped at a pay phone. The call was brief, and anyone who overheard it—by chance or by design—could not have made much of it. . . . "Larry? This is Victor. Same time, same place?" . . . But Weston would now leave his office, where the phones might very well be bugged, and go to his club, where they almost certainly wouldn't be.

When he arrived at the Pot au Feu, Zeitler was pleased, but not surprised, to find it almost empty. He selected a table near the phone booth, noting with satisfaction that no other table was within earshot. It was a little paranoid, perhaps, to take so many precautions, but they cost him nothing; it was a more dangerous form of insanity not to.

He ordered *raclette*—boiled potatoes covered with melted Gruyère cheese—salad, and half a bottle of Muscadet. He wasn't particularly fond of *raclette,* but it was the safest choice, more difficult to overcook than anything else on the menu. Overcooking, he recalled, was the specialty of the house.

When he had given his order, he went to the phone.

"Monsieur Weston, s'il vous plait."

A slight delay while Weston was summoned, then:

"Weston içi. Qui est là?"

Zeitler winced. German was his main language, but still it hurt to hear French mangled.

"Larry. This is Victor." His own English was impeccable. "Remember that request you made of me recently? Well, I have news for you."

"You've found him?"

"Not yet. Though, if he's still around, I imagine it won't be long. . . . The question is, however, how much longer will he be around?"

"I don't get you."

"I had a call this morning from a friend—a colleague, perhaps I should say—in a related line of business. I think you know him. He deals, rather too closely I've often thought, with your main competition. . . . He wanted to know what progress we were making with your request."

"So?"

"He shouldn't have known about your request. It doesn't involve his department. And even if he'd heard about it—by chance, let us say—he wouldn't normally have been interested. Not interested enough, at any rate, to go to the trouble of inquiring about it in person. . . . Now do you see what I'm getting at?"

There was silence at the other end, then a low whistle.

"You mean he's inquiring on behalf of the competition?"

"I don't see any other explanation. . . . This individual you asked me to help you recruit—they must be hoping to recruit him, too."

A pause.

"I thought you would want to know."

"You can say that again! . . . Listen. What did you tell him?"

"The truth. At present it's harmless enough. I told him that the search was progressing, but no final outcome was yet in sight. . . . He asked me to keep him posted on any developments. He stressed the word 'any.' "

"I see. . . . Look. You couldn't just later that request, could you?"

"Later it?" American slang was amusing but almost impossible to keep up with.

"Forget about it . . . ignore it. . . ."

"Impossible, I'm afraid. It wasn't exactly a request, you see, and he gets his paycheck from the same source I do, only his is much larger than mine. But . . ." he hesitated, "I can do this. If there *are* any developments, I can call you first, give you an hour or two's start. But that's the best I can do. . . . Unless, of course, you wish to assume the burden of supporting me and my family. I have two children, as you know, and a very expensive wife."

"No. I don't think so." Weston chuckled. "But listen. Thanks for calling. I really appreciate it. Perhaps you'll let me buy you a good dinner one of these days?"

Zeitler hung up and went back to his table. In his absence the waiter had brought his lunch. The *raclette,* already congealing on the plate, was cold; the wine, on the other hand, was not. The salad was nowhere to be seen.

A good dinner, he thought. Yes, I'll certainly allow you to buy me that.

Weston read over the telegram, signed it, and handed it back to his secretary. This, he thought, is where the shit hits the fan. He hated confrontations with the KGB: people got hurt; cover, that might have taken years to establish, got blown; the Swiss got upset and all his sources in the government clammed up. It was wasteful and destructive. He hoped it was worth it.

He permitted himself a moment of sympathy for the object of all this attention. One individual. An amateur. Against the two largest outfits in the world. The poor misguided bastard. He didn't stand a chance.

CHAPTER XIX

"I'm sorry, Colonel. They're really all I can spare."

Lermontov sighed. The KGB establishment in Bern, he knew, was the largest in Europe. It had formidable outposts in Geneva and Zürich. In addition, there were no doubt sizable contingents of "illegals"—agents without diplomatic or consular cover—in the other cities. Beyond which, if the capitalist press could be believed, KGB officers infested the Palais des Nations and the UN agencies like termites. Then why was it, he wondered, that for the recovery of the most vital information to have leaked out of Russia in decades he was having so much trouble getting help?

He had brought twenty men with him to Switzerland. He'd requested three times as many, but as Stein had reasonably pointed out, the problems of providing visas and cover at short notice for sixty agents were forbidding. The Swiss were hospitable people, but capable of putting two and two together; they could hardly be expected to tolerate an invasion. As consolation, Stein had agreed to send people to France and Italy to cover the borders there. For the rest, Lermontov would have to call upon the agents already *in situ*. There were plenty of them, and they would all be at his service.

In theory this was consolation enough, and indeed Stein had obtained a directive, addressed to the Resident in Bern, instructing him to render Lermontov "every possible assistance." The problem was the word "possible"; there was more than one interpretation of it. The Resident, for example, construed it as "every assistance short of disturbing the normal course of business." Which meant, as he had just explained to Lermontov, precisely three men.

"You see, Colonel," the Resident continued, "it's a question of cover. The Americans, as you say, are in this, too. They will soon realize that they have company, and they will note which men we use. Then, of course, those people will be blown, totally useless for other work."

It was a fair point. But the logic, Lermontov thought, compelled one to wonder about the three men whom the Resident, in his generosity, felt able to spare. Since they were evidently expendable, might it not be reasonable to suppose that they would prove totally useless for any work? But there was no future in arguing, he decided. He could cable Stein, of course, and ask him to send the Resident a forceful clarification of that infuriatingly ambiguous "possible." But Stein was in the First Chief Directorate, while the Resident belonged to the Third, so Stein would have to go through the Resident's superior. And that, given the KGB's history of interdepartmental squabbles, was likely to take time. There wasn't that much time.

"I understand," he said wearily, "though it seems to me that your argument should apply with equal force to the Americans."

At this, the Ambassador intervened.

"The Americans," he complained, "are what worries me about this."

The Ambassador was a career diplomat; intelligence was a tool of his trade. But he disliked the men who gathered it, and he disliked their methods. He resented the fact that more than half the people attached to his mission belonged to an organization that behaved as if he didn't really exist, and he resented particularly the present influx of "tourists," led by this Colonel Lermontov, who were placing such a strain on the resources—and credibility—of his consulate in Geneva. He had insisted on being present at the meeting, and he'd been somewhat taken aback when the Resident had readily agreed.

"I don't know what you want this man for," he continued, "and I don't want to know. What I do know is that he's an American citizen on Swiss territory, and what you are discussing here, in plain terms, is kidnapping. I find this very disturbing. Our relations with the Swiss are vital and delicate, if only because Bern is the center of our intelligence-gathering operation in Western Europe." He cast a sour look at the Resident. "So I must demand that you proceed very carefully and, in particular, that you refrain from any action that might give the Americans grounds for complaining to the Swiss. The Swiss are very sensitive about their neutrality. Do you understand what I'm saying?"

Lermontov nodded. He knew what the Ambassador meant: do what you have to do, but don't get caught, and don't expect any help if you do. He got this kind of double-talk whenever he needed to operate on foreign territory. Relations were always delicate. There was always a need to proceed carefully. . . . He didn't plan to pay any attention; he didn't have time, and he didn't have the people. So what he'd told the people he did have would no doubt have appalled the Ambassador: "Find Wylie. I don't care how. Bring him back, if you can; if you can't, kill him."

This meeting, it was clear, was a waste of his time. The three men the Resident had offered, however competent, were insignificant in relation to his needs. It was just lucky that Wylie seemed, inexplicably, to have stayed in Geneva—at least he'd been registered at a hotel there on the 16th, and that was one day after they'd set a watch on the airports and the terminals. He'd moved from the hotel, of course, before they'd caught up with him. But if he'd left Geneva, it had not been by any orthodox form of transportation. So there was at least a reasonable chance he was still there, or somewhere in Switzerland, and if that were the case, then somebody would surely nail him. The problem was that that somebody might very well be the Americans. The Ambassador was right about one thing at least: the Americans were certainly the most disturbing element in the situation.

The Ambassador was staring at him, he noticed; he evidently expected a reply. But Lermontov was in no mood to prolong the discussion; he had no more interest in their problems than they did in his. He got to his feet.

"I have to get back to Geneva," he told the Resident. "Please have the men you offered me report to the consulate by six this evening. They should be armed, but not, obviously, with Soviet weapons."

He turned to the Ambassador.

"I'll do my best not to complicate your task here. But . . ." His shrug removed the need to complete the sentence.

No one could have described the Pension du Lac de Genève as luxurious. To Wylie, however, whose present notions of luxury had nothing to do with bathrooms or color television, it offered compensations. It was located in a part of town not popular with tourists; it was not listed in any of Wylie's guidebooks, and its proprietor, Kurt Dietrich, had about him an air of sly avarice which struck Wylie as encouraging. Here is a man, he had told himself when checking in, who with proper encouragement may be able to help with the passport problem. He had decided to sound Dietrich out when an opportunity presented itself. Later, however, he abandoned the idea in favor of going to Locarno.

It was perhaps unfortunate that he did. Kurt Dietrich would have been able to help. He was always willing to help, if one made it worth his time. He was a man of few loyalties, and those he had were all connected, in one way or another, with cash. For the right price he would certainly have helped Wylie. But Wylie never asked him. It was Lermontov who did.

The call came through just after Wylie had left for breakfast. The caller's name was Hassler. He was from the Ministry of the Interior, he explained to Dietrich; they were trying to trace a man named Arden Wylie, an American: about six feet in height, of medium build, with dark hair and brown eyes. Age? About forty. He was traveling alone, probably under an assumed name. Had any American of that description checked into the Pension?

American tourists were not frequent visitors to the Pension du Lac. Dietrich remembered the man who had checked in late the previous evening, his agonized struggle with the recalcitrance of French vowel sounds, perfectly well. The description fitted; and given what he had just been told, the fact that his guest had signed the register as Marvin Anderson did not impress Dietrich as being any real evidence that he was not Arden Wylie.

Kurt Dietrich was not fond of the police, and so far as he was concerned, the Ministry of the Interior was just the police going under another name, but he was not in principle opposed to helping them. In cases like this, however, he never did anything without first examining the situation from all angles, to discover whether there might not be something in it for him. The possibilities here were obvious, but nothing was to be gained from showing his hand too soon. No, he told the caller. No one of that description was registered at the Pension. But yes, he promised, if anyone did, he would certainly call back. He made a note of the number.

He was conscious, as he did so, that something about the conversation was out of place. For one thing it was unlike the police to telephone. Usually when they wanted someone, they sent a couple of flatfoots around to make inquiries in person. But it was not that. It was something else, some small significant fact, trapped, like a grain of sand in an oyster shell, in his subconscious. He thought about it for a while, but nothing came. He shrugged. It might come to him later. Meanwhile he had things to do. He reached into the pigeonhole behind him and took down the key to Anderson's room.

It seemed there was nothing in it to help him. Anderson had left nothing lying around—not even his shaving kit. It looked, also, as though he were prepared to make a sudden departure, for his suitcase, packed and ready, stood by the door. Dietrich was not surprised to find it locked.

He fiddled for a while with the combination, hoping—for it was an elementary, three-digit lock—that he might strike it lucky. After a while he gave it up. There were a thousand combinations available and checking them all would take too long. As he put the case where he'd found it, however, his eye fell on the strip of metal which reinforced the edge of the lid. There, in the center, directly above the lock he'd just examined, was a small metal disc engraved with two initials. The initials were A.W.

Wylie, returning from breakfast an hour later, was surprised and a little irritated to find himself engaged in conversation by the proprietor of his pension. Was he enjoying his stay in Geneva? Was this his first visit? Where did he live in the United States? The questions, at first casual, began at length to reveal a curiosity that seemed more than idle.

"Do you plan to stay long in Geneva?"

"No. Actually, I've had a change of plan. My business here is finished, and I've decided I owe myself a visit to some of your famous mountains. I have to leave shortly for the station, so I'd be grateful if you'd make up my bill."

The bill was already made up. At the Pension du Lac, the bill was always made up.

"Which of the mountains do you plan to visit?"

"The Bernese Oberland, I think—Jungfrau and perhaps the Eiger." Wylie studied the bill for a second, then reached into his pocket and pulled out his wallet. Dietrich, following his movements with sharp, beady eyes, noted that it was very well lined.

"Thank you. And have a pleasant journey." He handed the change to Wylie.

"Mr. Wylie." The voice was curt, peremptory.

Wylie, at the foot of the stairs, turned instinctively. Then he froze. *You idiot,* he cursed himself, *you total idiot!*

"Mr. Wylie." The voice insisted. Wylie looked around the lobby. No one else was there. He turned back to Dietrich, struggling to keep the panic out of his face.

"My name is Anderson," he said. His voice contained a note of mild surprise.

"Is it?" Dietrich came across the lobby and stopped in front of him, a shade closer than normal courtesy would permit. "Is it?" He shrugged. "Possibly it is. But I've had an inquiry, under the name of Arden Wylie, for someone who fits your description. If it's not you, then the coincidence that your suitcase happens to bear the initials A.W. is rather remarkable, don't you think?" He paused. His voice was soft, but his eyes, small and shrewd, never left Wylie's face. "Of course, if your name really is Anderson, you'll be able to show me a passport to confirm it?"

Wylie said nothing.

"You can't? I thought not. Perhaps you'd care to explain. You see, in this country, we don't like foreigners who go around using false names. It makes us uncomfortable. I'm wondering if I should go to the police about it."

Go to the police? . . . Wylie's thoughts churned. Then it hadn't been the police inquiring. The CIA then? That must be it. Probably they were on their way right now. But perhaps not. If it were them—and it must be—they'd have warned him not to alert me.

"Go, by all means." He kept his voice level. "The explanation is perfectly innocent. It's really a matter . . ." he improvised, ". . . it's really a matter of commercial competition. The call you had was from a rival company. I'm trying to conclude a deal, you see. It involves bidding on a large contract. I don't want the competition to know I'm in Geneva."

It was weak, he knew. And Dietrich didn't buy it. There was skepticism all over his face.

"It involves a good deal of money," Wylie tried again. "A good deal. It would be worth a lot to me—" He corrected himself: "—to my company to prevent them from getting that information. Do you understand the situation?"

"I think so." Dietrich understood perfectly. "Exactly how much would it be worth?"

"A hundred dollars?"

Dietrich said nothing.

"Perhaps two?"

"Make it three"—Dietrich grinned suddenly—"and you have a deal."

Three hundred. It was a lot. But Wylie had an idea. If his assessment of Dietrich were correct, it could be worth it.

"O.K. Let me run upstairs and get my luggage. I'll have the money for you when I come down."

Dietrich let him go. He couldn't leave without coming through the lobby. There was no danger of his sneaking off without paying.

Upstairs, Wylie sat down, pulled out a felt-tipped pen and opened the railroad timetables. He flipped to the schedule for Geneva to Brig, turned down the corner of the page, and circled a departure from Geneva and its time of arrival at Brig. Then he turned to the schedule for the branch line from Brig to Visp, and marked the departure of a connection there. He contemplated doing the same on the Visp–Zermatt schedule, but decided against it. No need to be obvious.

Putting the schedule under his arm, he picked up his suitcase and hurried downstairs.

He paid Dietrich in twenties, taking them out of his wallet and counting them deliberately into the outstretched palm. In order to do so, he placed the railroad schedule on the counter. When he had finished he gave Dietrich a quick handshake and picked up the suitcase.

"I'm relying on you," he said.

"Don't worry about it." Dietrich winked. "I never even saw you."

He noticed the schedule when Wylie was running down the steps, but he didn't call after him.

Dietrich picked up the telephone. He was not calling the Ministry of the Interior, for—he was almost certain—the Ministry had not called him. He remembered now what it was that had been odd about that call. It was the number they had given him. It was a Geneva number. But the Ministry was in Bern. It was possible, of course, that they had an office in Geneva, but, if that were so, it would be downtown. And the downtown district code was not the code of the number he'd been given.

"Operator. Does the Ministry of the Interior have offices in Geneva? . . . Can you give me the number then? . . . I'm afraid I don't know which number I need. Can you give me all of them?"

There were three, and he'd been right. The number he had was not among them.

He dialed again.

"Mr. Hassler, please. . . . Mr. Hassler. My name is Dietrich of the Pension du Lac. You called recently about a man named Wylie. I told you he hadn't checked in, but I wasn't here last night. Apparently someone answering his description checked in late, using the name Anderson. . . . No, he isn't here now. I'm afraid he's checked out. But, listen, I think I know where he's headed. . . . No, I wouldn't feel comfortable about doing that. To be frank, I've no way of knowing that you're authorized to have this information. I mean, you say you're from the Ministry of the Interior, but how do I know you are? Your number isn't listed with them. . . . If I were to see some identification I'd feel better. . . . You'll be right around. Good. I'll be waiting for you."

He was pleased with himself. It was always worth exploring the angles. One paycheck was good. But two were better.

He almost smiled when the two Russians entered the Pension. Ministry of the Interior indeed. He could hardly contain his contempt. If they dressed like that at the Ministry of the Interior, then he was the president of Crédit Suisse.

Lermontov was in no mood for finesse. "Ask him," he said to Pogrebin, whom he had brought with him to Geneva, not only because he was now idle but also because his French was excellent.

"We are the gentlemen you called just now. I believe you had a Mr. Wylie staying here and can tell us where he is going?"

"I think so, yes."

"Will you tell us, please."

Dietrich was silent. Then he said, "Did I understand you gentlemen to say that you were from the Ministry of the Interior?" He smiled faintly.

"A section of it, yes."

"May I perhaps see some identification?"

Pogrebin was prepared for this. Without speaking, he took out his wallet and handed it to Dietrich.

Dietrich opened it. There was no identification in it, but tucked behind the cellophane window where Pogrebin normally carried his I.D. card was a fifty-franc note.

Dietrich handed it back.

"It doesn't seem to be in order," he said.

Lermontov was getting impatient. It was frustrating to listen to all this chatter and not have the slightest idea what was being said. He nudged Pogrebin.

"What is he saying?"

"He wants more."

"Give it to him, then."

Pogrebin took another fifty francs out of his pocket and placed it inside the window. He handed the wallet to Dietrich.

"I think it is in order now."

Dietrich made no move to take it from him.

"Impersonating public officials is a serious offense in this country," he said. "Offering bribes is worse. If you're going to do it, I think you should do it properly."

Lermontov's lack of French did not prevent him from understanding this exchange. He was frustrated and, above all, weary: weary of diplomatic obstructionism and bureaucratic red tape, weary of traipsing round this foreign and ugly city, weary, finally, of this petit bourgeois and his obsession with money. He looked around him, and whispered something to Pogrebin.

Pogrebin took a step toward the counter. Never taking his eyes off Dietrich's face, he aimed a left at Dietrich's nose. Dietrich's hands flew up to ward it off. The right caught him square in the solar plexus. He doubled up, gasping for breath.

Pogrebin was over the counter in an instant. Grabbing Dietrich by the collar, he pulled him upright.

"Where has he gone?"

The words came to Dietrich through a world of pain. Still gasping and retching, his eyes screwed up in an effort to contain the agony, he nodded capitulation.

Pogrebin yanked him back onto the counter stool and released him, standing over him in an attitude not threatening but alert, his weight balanced evenly on the balls of his feet, arms by his sides, hands lightly clenched.

"O.K.," he said, "so tell us."

"He said . . ." Dietrich was still gasping and holding his gut. "He said he was going to the Bernese Oberland. But he forgot this." He reached under the counter.

"No." Pogrebin caught Dietrich's wrist and yanked it behind his back, forcing Dietrich's face to the counter. "Tell me what you want and *I'll* get it." He was glad to see that Lermontov had moved to monitor the entrance. If the little pig played any more tricks, it might be necessary to break his arm.

"It's the schedule," Dietrich grunted, "the railroad schedule."

Pogrebin flung him back against the wall. "If you move again," he warned, "I'm going to hurt you."

He reached under the counter and found the schedule. He placed it on the counter. Then, still not taking his eyes off Dietrich, he reached in again and groped around. Presently his fingers found what they were looking for. It was a carving knife.

"Listen, you." He held the knife at Dietrich's belly. "You'd better explain yourself fast. Because if you don't, I'm going to bury this where it belongs."

Dietrich's face was a dirty putty color. Small beads of perspiration had gathered in the stubble around his mouth and chin.

"Look in the schedule," he quavered. "The Geneva–Brig page is marked and the Brig–Visp schedule, too. It's his schedule. He left it by mistake. He's going to the mountains, but not to Jungfrau. I think he's going to Zermatt."

—

Pogrebin looked at him. He could be lying. But he probably wasn't. Fear was mastering him now, as greed had done before. In any case, they couldn't risk prolonging the situation.

Picking up the schedule, he quickly verified what Dietrich had told him. Then he turned back to Dietrich.

"Do you know who we are?" he asked softly.

Dietrich nodded.

"Good. Now if we find you have lied or tried to contact the police, we will come back and kill you. Do you understand that?" Pogrebin tossed the knife across the lobby.

Dietrich nodded again.

"Good."

Pogrebin made as if to turn, then, pivoting on his left foot and pushing off with his right, his whole body leaning into the blow, he drove his fist into Dietrich's belly.

CHAPTER XX

Wylie's instinct, when confronted by Dietrich, had been to run—as fast and as far as he could. He had offered money without thinking, hoping to buy himself as much lead as possible. But, as soon as the offer was made, he'd seen it was pointless; Dietrich had already given him, gratis, the only thing he had worth buying—the knowledge that the CIA was closing in. Beyond this he had nothing to sell. He could hardly have done much to prevent Wylie from leaving, and, once Wylie had left, he would have been able to tell the CIA nothing beyond the fact that Wylie was still somewhere around in the city. They knew *that* already. Besides which, Dietrich, had his silence been worth the buying, could not be trusted to keep it.

So Wylie had been on the point of putting his money back in his pocket and telling Dietrich to shove his silence up his ass. Then a thought had struck him. Perhaps Dietrich's greed, his obvious unreliability, could be turned to good account.

Part of the problem, surely, was that the pursuers had no faces. This added another item to the list of their advantages, and the list was far too long already. If Wylie could identify them, even some of them, the odds against him would be substantially reduced. This was where Dietrich could help. If Dietrich could find anything to tell the CIA, he'd undoubtedly tell it. Undoubtedly, he would also want to be paid. And this meant he'd want to talk to them in person. So if Dietrich had looked at the schedule—and Wylie had taken pains to ensure that he would—the chances were that the CIA would shortly be arriving at the

Pension. With any luck at all, they might also leave with a totally mistaken idea of Wylie's intentions.

So, on leaving the Pension, Wylie took a cab, but he told the driver simply to circle the block and pull into the curb about thirty yards before the entrance to the Pension, on the same side of the street. He explained that he was waiting for someone, who might be a little while, so the driver should keep the motor running.

He was taking a risk. If they spotted him, they might nail him there and then. But he banked on their being much too intent on getting to Dietrich to take much interest in the surroundings. If he sat well back in the car, the chances were against their seeing him. But with luck he'd get a good look at them. If he did, it would be well worth the three hundred dollars.

For fifteen minutes he waited, the meter clicking inexorably, the driver contriving, with shrugs and grimaces, to express the conviction that the passenger had lost his mind and that this was O.K. because, one way or other, it was all money in the bank. A couple with two small children arrived, checked into the Pension, and departed. Otherwise there was no activity.

He was beginning to wonder which he had overestimated—Dietrich's greed or his intelligence—when the taxicab, a green Citroën DS, pulled up beside the entrance. A man got out and held the door open for another who, without pausing or looking about him, walked briskly into the Pension, offering little more than a glimpse of his sideview before it disappeared. Wylie's impression was of a beige raincoat and black hair, streaked with gray.

The other man was facing Wylie. He was shorter than his companion, stockily built, but with movements which suggested the economy and grace of an athlete. His hair was blond, and very short. His face had a Slavic look, the cheekbones high, the jaw broad and squarish, the features all slightly flattened. It was a peasant's face, Wylie thought, and without particular distinction. It reminded him, in its fuzzy, unfinished quality, of a snapshot slightly out of focus. In normal circumstances it was not a face he would have noticed or remembered. But the circumstances were not normal; he was sure he would not forget it.

Slamming the taxi door, the man leaned in at the front window and said something to the driver. Then he turned and moved to join his companion in the Pension. The taxi waited.

When they emerged, about five minutes later, Wylie was able to get a better look at the first one. He was thin, almost gaunt, his face a wedge in which the most noticeable features were the nose, thin and high-bridged, and the eyes, set deep in the head and close together. The man's movements were quick, almost impatient. Even at a distance, he seemed charged with intelligence and a barely controlled, predatory energy.

There was no doubt at all that these were the men he had waited for. Everything fitted: they'd arrived on schedule, they had no luggage, and they hadn't, obviously, been expecting to stay.

He leaned forward to the taxi driver. "I'll give you twenty francs on top of the regular fare and tip if you can stay behind that cab," he said. "But I don't want to be seen. If they look back at all, turn off and take me to the station. But don't worry, in that case, I'll still give you the twenty."

But they didn't look back. They were accustomed to thinking of themselves as hunters, not as quarry. Besides which, there was something else to occupy their attention.

"So we go to Zermatt?"

Lermontov did not reply immediately. His eyes were fixed on the schedule as though upon some recalcitrant suspect from whom he hoped, by the silent intensity of his stare, to extract a confession.

"I don't know," he said at last. "It doesn't really make sense. He obviously knows someone is after him. Otherwise he wouldn't keep on hopping around. But if he goes to Zermatt, he's in a box. It's in a valley, mountains on three sides, and only one way in—by rail. He can cross the border by going over the mountains, but for that he'll need a guide. In the meantime he's in a tiny village, incredibly easy to trace. We'd find him in no time. If he's smart he'll know that." He shook his head. "Let me put it this way. It's not what I'd do in his position.

"And we can't even be sure he's planning to go by rail. It's too much of a coincidence, his forgetting this little book. I wouldn't expect him to be that careless. So I don't even think we can afford to put extra people at the station. Not when it means taking them away from somewhere else."

He toyed absently with the schedule, turning it over in his hands. It was paperbound, quarto-sized, about half an inch thick and bound in sections which, glued together, formed a flat spine. There was a break in the spine, he noticed, which appeared to have been made by someone forcing the pages apart to make the book stay open.

He took it between the palms of his hands and placed the spine upon the seat beside him. Pulling his hands apart quickly, he let it fall open. The point at which it did corresponded to the crease along the spine.

The schedules that lay exposed were not Geneva–Brig, or Brig–Visp. One was Geneva–Schwyz; the other was Zürich–Schwyz–Locarno.

Locarno. That made more sense. Lermontov, too, had been studying his maps. He sat up.

"Listen," he said, "we'll go back to the Consulate. I'll cable Turin and get them to send people to Breuil and Macugnaga—just in case he does try the Zermatt frontier. You go on to the station. Wait for me there. But buy a ticket. In case I'm held up, you go on first by yourself. I'll follow you later."

"Follow me where?"

"Why, Locarno, of course." Lermontov looked at him in surprise. "We're going to Locarno."

For several minutes, Wylie's taxi followed the Citroën. The pursuit was inspired, Wylie knew, largely by hope. He'd already gained the important point, which was to see what they looked like, and there was little else to be gained. Unless they went to the station. That would be significant. If they went there it would probably mean that they'd swallowed his bait. With luck they might also lead him to some of their colleagues.

Of the two hopes the first was the more important to him. For three days now he'd been passive, reacting, without any plan of his own, to the threats of his opponents. It was the kind of defensive game he hated, the kind he almost always lost. But now, after so much running and hiding, looking back over his shoulder for pursuers he couldn't recognize but must always assume to be there, he'd regained the initiative. And he'd had a partial success. He was encouraged by that. But he wanted more. He needed to know if his success had been complete.

When the Citroën pulled in at the entrance to an office building, he thought, at first, it hadn't. But only the taller of the men emerged and, slamming the car door behind him, dashed into the building. When the Citroën slid away from the curbside and merged back into the traffic, the taxi was still behind it.

Wylie's driver was enjoying himself. The twenty francs were an incentive, certainly; but more appealing was the conviction that he was actually involved in something he'd been sure only happened in the movies. A man had jumped into his cab and said, "Follow that car!" It would be something to tell his kids when he got home.

He glanced back at his passenger. Now that they were moving again, he'd leaned back in his seat, relaxing a little. But his eyes were still following the Citroën up ahead.

"Tell me," he said, "are we the good guys or the bad guys?"

"What was that?"

The driver repeated his question.

"Oh," Wylie gave him a tight smile, "the good guys, of course."

"I thought so." The driver grinned back at him. "You know why?"

"No."

"That building where the thin one got out. You know what's in there?"

"What?"

"One of those diplomatic missions. Consulates, I think they call them. And who does it belong to?"

"Who?"

"As if you didn't know." The driver chuckled at the idea. "The Russians, of course. That's who."

The Russians . . . For a moment he couldn't think; he was conscious only of physical reactions: the long sucking breath, the stumble in the rhythm of his heartbeat, the slither of fear in his gut. His eyes remained fixed on the traffic ahead of them, but distinguished nothing, made no sense out of the shapes and colors. His mind raced, but, like an engine slipping gears, refused to move.

"Trouble. Sheer trouble, those bastards. I don't know why we go on dealing with them." The driver, still cheerfully conversational, brought him back to himself. He managed a grunt of assent.

Trouble. The word mocked him with its inadequacy. The odds against him had just doubled. That was bad enough. But that was the least of it. What was worse was that stakes had now been raised out of sight. Trouble was what he'd catch if the CIA got hold of him. But if the Russians did, the word was not trouble. The word for that was murder.

How had they known? Who had told them? His thoughts flew back to the little man in Gorki Park, his earnestness and courage. They'd got on to him undoubtedly. But how? And what had they done to him? It didn't bear thinking about. But he thought about it anyway.

Then he remembered Anne. He hadn't considered her. He'd left her in the lurch, realizing she might be hurt and frightened, but not seeing any alternative. He could hardly have involved her in his plans. And besides, he'd never dreamed that his departure would leave her in danger —or any more danger than she was already in.

Perhaps it hadn't. Perhaps she'd gotten clear. He hoped to God she had. But there was nothing he could do now to change anything. And he couldn't afford the luxury of guilt. The past was irrevocable. He must think of the future, his own future—and, specifically, how to prolong it.

The taxi slowed down. Ahead the Citroën had slowed, too, its tail-lights winking, preparing to make a turn.

"He's turning into the station," the driver told him. "You want me to turn in, too?"

"No. Let's pull in here. We're plenty close enough."

He paid the driver, adding a ten, out of gratitude for the man's un-questioning compliance with his various instructions, to the twenty he'd previously promised.

"Thanks a lot. You did well to stay with him in all that traffic. You've been a great help."

"American, huh?" The driver pocketed the money.

Wylie nodded.

"CIA, then?"

"Yes."

"I thought so. Well," he put the car in gear, "good hunting."

Wylie looked at his watch. Eleven-thirty. The train left at one-fifteen. The blond Russian was at the station—with any number of his col-leagues. Americans too, possibly. Well, he'd run that gauntlet when he came to it. But there was no sense in hanging around. He still had things to do.

When he'd gotten his haircut, he went to a clothing store. It was time to abandon his Levis and acquire a little respectability. There was no point in trying for a complete disguise. He was an amateur and would probably only succeed in making himself more conspicuous. So no false mustaches or makeup. Just the haircut, a change of clothes, a pair of glasses, and maybe a hat. They'd be trying to identify him from photo-graphs, he thought, and that probably wasn't easy.

He chose a medium gray summer-weight suit, cut in the French style, with a white shirt and an English Paisley tie. He decided to keep his loafers; they were black and fitted in well with the rest. But he aban-doned the idea of a hat. Hats were too obvious, particularly if you weren't used to wearing them. He didn't like them anyway.

He also bought sunglasses, wire-rimmed, the lenses very faintly tinted. They wouldn't alter his appearance much, but on the other hand, they wouldn't draw attention to themselves. If one were looking for dis-guises, he thought, one would expect Polaroids or heavy black aviator shades which obscured the whole face. His glasses would not deceive a second glance; but then, his whole object was to avoid inviting second glances.

He wore his new clothes out of the shop, getting the assistant to wrap up his sportcoat and Levis in a package which he put in his suitcase. It was then twelve-thirty. He had one other purchase to make.

He chose a hunting knife. The blade, about four inches long, folded into the handle but locked when open. He tested the edge by drawing it gently across the ball of his thumb. It lifted a thin sliver of skin. The point, he noted, was also wickedly sharp.

It was not much, but it would have to do. He'd have preferred a gun, obviously, a small automatic for choice. With a silencer. But this was Switzerland. Without the proper connections he had no more chance of being able to buy a gun than he had of buying a new passport, or, for that matter, a Sherman tank. So the knife would have to do. He didn't place much reliance on it. He'd be much better off to avoid any situation where he might need it. But, even in his inexpert hands, it was better than nothing.

CHAPTER XXI

Pogrebin was prowling the station. It had not, he concluded, been designed to make life easy. Although there was a central hallway from which the trains departed, the ticket counters were in a separate arcade, not visible from the platforms, and surrounded by shops and restaurants. To make matters worse, there were several side entrances into the main departure hall. All in all, he thought, they would need a dozen men to cover it properly. They had been able to spare two.

He noticed that Yasnegin was seated at one of the tables outside the coffee shop. It was a good vantage point, commanding a view of the whole ticket counter. Yasnegin was sipping a coffee and playing at reading the local newspaper. He looked bored.

Pogrebin walked up to the ticket counter and purchased a one-way, second-class ticket to Locarno. Then he made his way to the coffee shop and sat down at a table two or three away from his colleague. He didn't look in Yasnegin's direction.

Yasnegin called the waitress. She came over with his check. He paid her and left, leaving one or two small coins on the table as a tip. He also left the newspaper.

Five minutes went by. Pogrebin's waitress brought the *café au lait* he had ordered. He smiled at her.

"The gentleman who just left," he said, "seems to have abandoned his newspaper. Perhaps I could have a look at it?"

She shrugged and went to get it for him. Returning, she dropped it on the table in front of him. Her manner indicated that she thought he was carrying thrift to the point of stinginess.

He glanced through the pages as though skimming the headlines. It was on the third page, a single word, faintly marked in pencil. The word was "nyet."

Wylie worried about tickets. They might let him on the train without one, allowing him to purchase it from the conductor, or they might not. It was better not to risk it. But that meant braving the ticket counter. That was the place he would watch were he in their position. He'd be exposed there, standing in line, possibly, while his flimsy disguise was subject to the kind of scrutiny it could not bear. He looked at his watch. One o'clock. Fifteen more minutes. Unless he could think of something soon he'd have to chance it without a ticket.

He looked about. The street seemed quiet enough; the passersby seemed like ordinary citizens, coming and going, absorbed in the national preoccupation with making money. Even the kids were at it, he thought, noticing a youth of fourteen or fifteen, dressed in a porter's uniform, apparently waiting to assist passengers out of arriving taxis and help them with their baggage. He was idle, temporarily, leaning against a wall, his hands in his pockets.

Wylie went up and proffered his suitcase.

"Which platform for Locarno?" he asked.

"Number ten." The youth took the suitcase. "You want this on the train?"

Wylie nodded.

"Which compartment?"

"I don't have my ticket yet."

"Better go get it, then."

"Listen," Wylie said. "I need to make a phone call. Could you get me a ticket if I gave you the money?"

"Sure." The youth grinned. "Cost you a franc, though."

"No problem." Wylie handed him a fifty-franc bill. "I want a second-class ticket all the way to Locarno. Will that be enough?"

"Plenty." The boy grinned again. "Meet you at the platform in five minutes."

"Make it ten and meet me back here. O.K.?"

The boy nodded and left at a trot. He was still grinning. Wylie felt certain that the price he paid for his ticket would include, on top of the promised franc, a hefty scalper's commission. He didn't care. It was cheap at the price. He was also sure that the boy would be back with the ticket, and that his suitcase would be on the train. If there was one thing the Swiss were strict about, it was petty crime.

Chuck Todd had been at the station since twelve. Prior to that he had been at the airport. He'd be relieved at three. Then he'd have three hours off—time to take a shower and grab a bite to eat—before doing his final stint for the day at the bus depot.

The schedule had been worked out by Weston. Put a man to watch a place all day, he figured, even a place as large as a railway station and sooner or later he'll be noticed. Put him there for two or three hours and, if he behaves intelligently, probably he won't be spotted. So he rotated his people, including the specials Roskill had sent in, every three hours. It took time, money, and ingenuity to provide agents with good cover, and, like the KGB Resident, Weston had no wish to see half his people blown.

This was the reason the latest instructions from Roskill were so disturbing. Roskill had told him, in effect, to start a war. To track down, harass, kill, if necessary, the Russian agents who were looking for Wylie. In one way it made sense, of course; but the likely repercussions made him wince. The Swiss would not be amused to find their nice neat country littered with dead or broken bodies. And the Russians . . . ? He had no appetite for a game of hardball with them.

So his own instructions to Todd and the rest of them had been more guarded. "If you see any of our friends in your travels," he had said, "and a good opportunity offers, you can later them. But mark this. No fuck-ups. I.D. must, repeat must, be positive; I want no brawling in public."

It had been a long morning for Chuck Todd, but he wasn't bored. The target had failed to show, but there was something else to sustain his interest. Prior to taking up his post he had called the coordinator. Had Davidson, coming off duty, anything positive to report? Apparently Davidson had—a possible hostile who had been at the station when Davidson arrived and was still there when he left. Height? Six foot, give or take an inch. Weight? A hundred and ninety or thereabouts. Hair? Brown. Eyes? Maybe blue. Build? Medium—chunky. Dress? A navy blue raincoat, belted; gray pants; a blue and white striped shirt; navy blue tie; heavy brown shoes. Arms? None visible, obviously.

He had not been difficult to spot. His very restlessness, the way he moved by turns through the ticket hall, to the telephones, to the newsstand, to the coffee shop, and back always to the main departure hall, formed a pattern for which aimlessness was not a reasonable explanation. After all, thought Todd, no one is that aimless for six hours at a stretch. Identification, he decided, was definitely positive.

It was ten after one before he got the opportunity he was looking for. The man in the blue raincoat was making for the men's room. Not surprising, after so many cups of coffee.

Todd followed. The station was not particularly crowded. Conceivably the men's room could be empty. If not, well, Todd would be glad of the opportunity to take a leak himself. He went down the steps.

The men's room was brightly lit and immaculately clean, smelling faintly, but not offensively, of disinfectant. Todd noted with satisfaction that, save for the Russian, it was apparently empty. At the foot of the stairs, Todd paused and listened for footsteps coming down the steps behind him. There were none.

The man in the blue raincoat was standing at the nearest urinal. His feet were planted slightly apart and he was bending forward, buttoning his fly. At the sound of Todd's footsteps behind him, he glanced over his right shoulder.

Something in Todd's manner must have alerted him—something intent and stealthy in the way Todd moved, or something too purposeful in the set of Todd's features. He slid abruptly to his left, turning, and in the same motion reaching down toward his belt. As he did so, Todd turned sideways, leaned slightly back, and launched himself into the air. His right foot shot out, the leg straightening and locking with an explosive jerk.

The blow caught the man's right arm midway between the elbow and the shoulder, snapping the bone like a pencil and hurling the man to the floor. The automatic clattered onto the tiles, skidding under the wash basins to the man's left. Instinctively he started to reach for it with his good arm, ignoring the pain that flooded through his system.

He almost made it. Todd had landed off balance and wasted seconds recovering and turning. The man's fingers were closing around the butt of the automatic when the toe of Todd's shoe crashed into the bridge of his nose.

Todd straightened up. One of the cubicles to his right, he now noticed, was locked. From within, a man's voice, registering simultaneously alarm and indignation, protested.

"What's happening out there? What the hell's going on?"

Todd did not enlighten him. Ignoring the man sprawled beneath the wash basins and the weapon beside him, he hurried up the steps. He was happy about the gun. It would give the man a lot of explaining to do.

* * *

Pogrebin had seen his colleague, Druzhnin, enter the men's room and had noticed another man follow a few seconds later. He hadn't thought anything of it until the second man had emerged hurriedly, paused for a moment at the top of the stairs as if to collect himself, and then walked away with an air that was distinctly too casual. . . . *Shit,* Pogrebin thought. Trouble.

His suspicions were confirmed, half a minute later, when a middle-aged Swiss, white-faced and hysterical, erupted from the top of the stairs yelling, "Police! Help! Police! Murder!"

He was in a quandary. Obviously he could not go to the help of Druzhnin; he had a train to catch. In any case, Druzhnin's misfortune would entail police inquiries in which it would be foolish to become involved. On the other hand, his own departure would leave the entire station to Yasnegin, who could not be expected to handle it alone. He looked at the station clock. He might just have time to telephone and catch the train.

His sprint to the telephone kiosk coincided with Wylie's emergence from the side entrance close to the gate of platform ten. Wylie didn't know the cause of the disturbance which had sent half the station hurrying to the semihysterical man at the entrance to the men's room, but it seemed heaven-sent. He walked briskly to the gate, looking neither right nor left, tendered his ticket to the inspector, and made his way to car number three, compartment five, where he found his suitcase, as he had expected, neatly stowed in the rack above the seat reserved for him. He congratulated himself. Things had gone very smoothly.

CHAPTER XXII

Pogrebin made the train with seconds to spare. It was lucky he'd got through to Lermontov immediately. Wylie, he'd been able to report, had not, to his knowledge, arrived at the station; but there'd been trouble. He'd explained the need to replace Druzhnin.

He settled back into his seat, relaxing to the rhythm of the wheels as the train gathered speed through the suburbs and headed for the open country. He wished he'd brought something to read. He liked trains, and the Swiss countryside was said to be beautiful; but the journey was several hours, and it would be nice to have something to do besides stare out the window.

His had not been the only late arrival apparently. Passengers, lugging baggage, were moving up and down the corridor outside his compartment, looking for their seats. Others were just walking to and fro, impelled, perhaps, by the same restlessness that had begun to afflict him. He decided to walk around, too. Sitting bored him. Besides, he had inadvertently bought his seat in a nonsmoking compartment, and he needed a cigarette.

He was standing in the corridor, leaning against the window frame, inhaling the first puff of a caporal, and contemplating with disdain the bourgeois conformity of the rows of little boxlike houses, each with its own enclosed patch of garden, when he felt a tap on his shoulder. A voice, low and nasal, speaking with a complete disregard for the purity of French vowel sounds, muttered, *"Excusez-moi."* He flattened himself against the window. Americans. It was amazing how much they traveled and how utterly incapable they were of pronouncing correctly any language—including their own.

He glanced incuriously at the retreating back. As he did so the man turned his head to peer into one of the compartments, giving Pogrebin a glimpse of his profile. The face seemed familiar; and, now that he considered it, so did the clothes. Pogrebin's eyes, trained in the procedures of precise observation, began noting details. Beige suit, cream or yellow shirt, dark brown ankle boots. The description corresponded in every detail with the one he had given Lermontov over the telephone. He was looking at the man who had attacked Druzhnin.

Chuck Todd was feeling pleased with himself. Weston had instructed them to take every suitable opportunity to later the KGB. The man in the men's room, he reflected with satisfaction, had been very effectively latered. If he were not dead—he'd be out of commission for a very long time. Besides which, when the police were through with him, he'd be irrevocably blown.

And that was not all. After dealing with the Russian, he'd proceeded, as quickly as he could, to put distance between himself and the outraged Swiss in the cubicle. He'd therefore crossed to the other side of the departure hall, toward platform ten. In doing so, he was practically certain, he had spotted Wylie boarding the train.

There had been no time to purchase a ticket, but the inspector had agreed to let him board and pay on the journey. He planned to get off at the first stop and put a call through to Weston. Weston would then have men waiting at every subsequent stop down the line. Before he made that call, however, he wanted to locate the man he had spotted and make sure that the I.D. was positive. He was confident, as he walked down the train, peering with what seemed to be casual interest into each compartment, that it would be. Wylie was practically in the bag. And he, Chuck Todd, would be the man responsible.

When he came to compartment five, car three, his sense of satisfaction turned to triumph. There in the corner, reading a newspaper through faintly tinted spectacles, was the man for whom thirty-five U.S. agents—and God knows how many Russians—had been scouring the country for the past seventy-two hours.

Wylie glanced up as Todd looked in, giving Todd a quick but thorough inspection before turning back to his paper. He's on the alert, Todd thought. He can't know who I am, but he's keeping his eyes open. I'd better stay out of sight. I don't want to risk spooking him. He stationed himself at the end of the car in the small corridor which, running at right angles to the main corridor, led to the exit. He would be close enough to hear if anyone left Wylie's compartment. He lit a cigarette and prepared to wait.

Pogrebin eased his way down the corridor, each step deliberate and delicate, as though he were walking on eggs. Avoid tangling with the Americans, Lermontov had told them. The task is to find our target. We can't afford any losses. That was all very well, but Pogrebin, following a car or so behind Todd, had also looked into compartment five, car number three. Now that the target was in sight, he couldn't run the risk of interference from the American.

Reaching the end of the car, he paused, and peered around the corner. Todd was leaning against the door frame, his back to Pogrebin, gazing out at the strip of green countryside that went reeling past the window at eighty miles per hour.

Pogrebin glanced quickly behind him. People had settled down now. There was no one in sight. He pulled the automatic out of the holster at his belt, checking to make sure the safety was on. Transferring the weapon from his right hand to his left, he gripped it by the barrel, turning the butt outwards.

Two quick steps brought him level with the American. The butt hammered into Todd's skull behind his left ear. As it hit, Pogrebin's right arm shot out to encircle and support the sagging body.

He slipped the gun back into his coat pocket. There would be blood on the butt, and he'd have preferred not to get it on his clothing; but he needed his left hand free. Bracing himself against the door frame he reached for the handle.

The muscles of his right arm were trembling under the dead weight of Todd's body. He twisted the handle and pushed. The door gave, then, meeting the fierce pressure of the slipstream, resisted. Wedging Todd's body between his own and the door, he withdrew his right arm and placed both hands on the door frame. A pause to gather himself. . . . Now! He thrust forward, driving with his legs and right shoulder.

The door gave. Todd pitched out headlong. His body struck the embankment and bounced down toward the fence at the bottom, a limp bundle of flailing arms and legs. He was dead before he hit the fence.

Panting and trembling, Pogrebin leaned against the door frame. So much for that one. Now for the target. Looking down, he noticed a curl of smoke rising from around his feet. The American's cigarette. He placed his heel upon it and, with a quick twist, ground it out.

There was no doubt about it. The man had seen him. The green cat's eyes had traveled, expressionless, over the occupants of the compartment, rested on him for an instant, narrowing, and flicked away again. The inspection had lasted little more than a second, but he was sure it had been enough. On his part there was no question. The cropped blond hair, the regular but curiously unfocused features—they belonged to the man from the Pension.

He was surprised how calm he was. It was as though his body, more prescient than his mind, had expected and prepared for this. His hands were free from tremor; his pulse, though perceptibly quicker, was steady. He was grateful for it, grateful to know that his nerves and muscles, now that he might need to call on them, would not betray him.

And he *would* need to call on them. He saw, on reflection, that there was no alternative. He could not allow himself to be followed to Locarno. He needed freedom of maneuver there, and he would not get it if the town were crawling with Russians.

There was also the more immediate danger. The Russians simply wanted him dead. They would seize any opportunity to kill him. He had no knowledge of the range of means at their disposal, but he could guess at some and they chilled him. He was not necessarily safe in a crowd, where a knife point or needle might find him. Nor was he safe in the open, against a sniper's silent, telescopic accuracy. Least of all was he safe now, in this swaying and rattling coffin, surrounded by the comfortable indifference of the traveling Swiss. He would rather be locked in a closet with a cobra.

So it was up to him to be his own salvation. And sooner, rather than later. At least he had one weapon at his disposal: he was almost certain, for his part, that he had let no flicker of recognition escape him.

He got up and picked his way around the feet of his dozing fellow passengers, his mind beginning to form the outlines of a plan.

Pogrebin was stationed in the main corridor of the car, a few compartments down from Wylie. When the door slid open, he glanced over his shoulder. Wylie emerged into the corridor and walked up the car, away from Pogrebin, without looking back. Pogrebin watched him walk toward the next car and stop, before he reached it, to turn and enter the washroom adjacent to the last compartment.

Pogrebin considered his options. . . . The corridor was empty; there was still some time before they were due to reach the first stop. Perhaps this was the time to do it. He could wait outside the washroom door—it was a legitimate place for someone to be waiting—and when the door opened, if there were still no one else around, then he could save everyone the time and trouble of further searching. It would be easy to wait in the washroom until they came to the first stop. Then he would leave the train. With luck he'd be well clear before they discovered the body.

It was true, of course, that Lermontov wanted to take the target alive. Against this, however, was the risk of interference from the Americans. There'd been one on the train, and, for all Pogrebin knew, there might be others. The same risk might exist in Locarno. In trying for everything, he might win nothing. He considered his idea again. The more he thought about it, the more he liked it.

He moved toward the washroom, feeling in his coat for the switchblade he kept snug in an inner pocket there. Withdrawing the knife, he pressed a button in the handle. The blade sprang out. He checked to make sure it was locked in place, and put his hand, still clasping the knife, back into his pocket. Then he waited.

The man was taking his time. Pogrebin heard the toilet flush, the sound of water jetting into the hand basin. Then nothing. He tensed himself, pulling the knife out of his pocket and holding it low by his side in a grip, thumb on top, pointing down the handle to the blade, that would direct his thrust up under the ribs toward the heart.

He heard the inner catch click back, saw the sign in the space above the lock slide from *"Occupe"* to *"Libre."* Then he hit the door with his shoulder, driving forward with all his force.

Before he was halfway through, he knew something was wrong. There was no resistance, nothing to strike at. But he was off balance, and though, in the moments that followed, he could observe the succession of events with an awful clarity, he could do nothing at all to arrest it. The door swung violently open, hit the rubber stopper at the base of the wash basin, and slammed shut again. His momentum carried him forward, helpless, until he hit the toilet bowl, tripped, and pitched headlong across it. Then a knee drove into his back and a knife jabbed his kidney.

A voice, speaking Russian said, "Move, and I'll kill you."

He lay still. The knife was still in his left hand, but in a grip that prevented his striking backwards. The blow upwards over his right shoulder was impeded by the cistern. In any case it would be blind and without force.

"Drop the knife." For emphasis there was another jab in his kidney. He felt the point pierce his skin, and he winced.

"Pitch it backwards, toward the door."

He did so.

"Now the gun."

"There is no gun." He doubted the gun would help him; the silencer was not fitted. It would be suicide to use it. But it was his only remaining weapon. He hated to give it up.

The response was a searing pain in his right side. The voice said coldly, "If I have to, I'll kill you. Hand me the gun. Reach for it slowly. Take it by the butt, and hand it back over your left shoulder. No sudden movements. Remember. If you force me, I will kill you."

He felt with his left hand under his jacket for the holster. Drawing the gun out, he handed it back as instructed. At some point, he thought, he will have to let me up. The gun will do him no good, any more than it would me. When he was on his feet, he was confident, he could take care of the knife.

These thoughts were interrupted by a violent blow on the back of his head. His vision blurred; he struggled feebly. Then another blow, heavier this time, hit him, and he blacked out.

Wylie got quickly to his feet. He turned and bolted the door. I should have killed him, he thought. Anyone could have walked in on us while I wasted that time on the gun. He knew, though, that he couldn't have. In haste or anger, perhaps, in the midst of a struggle; but not coldly, the way the Russian would have killed him. And he couldn't do it now, although he knew it was the safest thing.

He should kill him, get off the train, and leave the gun, and the documents the man presumably carried, to mislead the police. But he was new to all this. He couldn't do it. He began to look for alternatives.

In the midst of looking, he noticed an alteration in the rhythm of the wheels beneath him; the train was losing speed. I have to get off at this stop, he thought, or someone will find him and connect me with him. That would create a furor, with police and officials all over the place. He couldn't afford to be involved in that.

Bending down to the figure on the floor, he turned him over. Quickly he went through the pockets, finding a passport, a wallet containing cash, and a driver's license. In an attachment to the empty holster he found a squat metal tube which he recognized as a silencer.

Stepping back, he put the silencer in his coat pocket along with the automatic. He took the cash from the wallet, but left the driver's license. Then he removed the man's trousers, wrapped them into a bundle around the passport, and, opening the small sliding ventilation window, pitched the bundle out. The wallet and the driver's license he left lying next to the prostrate body. When he was found, without trousers, passport, or cash, the man would have a lot of explaining to do. The task wouldn't be made any easier if they also found the wallet with the Russian driver's license. With luck the predicament would tie him up for days.

When the screech of the train's brakes announced the stop, Wylie stepped out into the corridor. There was an injunction, he had noticed, printed on the washroom door in French, German, and English, prohibiting use of the facilities while the train was in a station. It was unlikely, in Switzerland, that anyone would defy it. He hurried back to the compartment to collect his suitcase.

When the train stopped he got out. He thought about waiting at the station for the next train, but decided against it. The next train was not due through for more than two hours. Undoubtedly, the man he had left in the washroom would be discovered fairly soon, probably before the next stop. And any policeman with a minimum of intelligence would be interested in passengers disembarking at the previous stop, especially if the passengers in question were foolish enough to hang around the station. He was relieved to see that more than a handful of other people had gotten off the train with him.

As he moved toward the exit he caught sight of the station sign. SCHWYZ. It was not where he wanted to be. But it was not bad, considering the alternative.

CHAPTER XXIII

■

Locarno lies at the head of Lake Maggiore where the River Maggia, sprung and nurtured in the mountains to the north, tumbles into the lake. In 1925, it was the site of the European disarmament conference, chosen in preference to Lucerne, at the wish of the French Foreign Minister; his mistress, it was rumored, considered the atmosphere conducive to romance.

Wylie, reading these facts in a guidebook while taking an early breakfast at a lakefront cafe, received them with impatience. His one wish was to get out of the place as soon as possible—atmosphere or no. To him, the lake, whose charms the guidebook expounded at some length, was simply an obstacle. It lay before him, steel-blue and glittering in the morning sunshine—an expanse of territory, inconveniently full of water, which intervened between him and Italy. He could even see Italy, about twenty kilometers down the lake. The problem was how to get there.

Geography offered two options. He could go down the lake and cross by boat from the neighborhood of the villages of Brissago or Ponte—a crossing of not more than five or six kilometers, *if* he could find a boat. Or he could hike up north into the mountains and try the frontier there. Unfortunately, the guidebook, relentlessly eloquent about the scent of wisteria in the Piazza Grande and the architectural distinction of the Castello Visconti, was silent on the only subject that really interested him—how were the frontiers protected?

It was a question he would have to resolve fast. It had been a risk, after failing to kill the Russian on the train, to stick with the original plan. By now the Russians would probably know that he had been on the train, and even though they wouldn't know precisely where he had left it, their attention would undoubtedly be drawn to Locarno simply because it was so close to the frontier. By lunchtime the place would presumably be crawling with Russian agents. For all he knew, it already was.

Perhaps he should have doubled back. That would have averted the immediate danger. But it would also have put him back in the position from which he'd started three days before—or rather, not the same, because the three days had given them the time to get organized, and some useful clues to his intentions. He couldn't afford to stay in Switzerland. It was too small; it gave them too many advantages. But unless he left soon, he might not be able to. If he gave them the time to regroup again, he might find the exit sealed to him, as tightly as a tomb.

The elation he had felt the night before, on his arrival by the late train from Schwyz, had mostly evaporated. Then, with the adrenaline stimulated by his encounter with the Russian still flooding his system, he had felt himself a match for them. Had he not, in two confrontations, outthought them? And did he not now have the gun? Its weight in his pocket, especially, had given him confidence. He'd found himself, every so often, reaching in to hold it, as one holds a charm—as if the cool touch of the metal were itself a source of strength.

Those feelings, he now realized, were unfounded. Certainly he had done well so far—for one thing he was still alive—but his survival had been, if he analyzed it coldly, largely a matter of luck. If the owner of the Pension had not been greedy . . . if he had not spotted the Russian on the train . . . if the Russian had not been overconfident . . . but for these ifs he would probably be dead; or worse, on his way back to Russia. As for the gun, it might help if they were obliging enough to announce themselves. But they would know now that he was watching for them, and they'd be more careful. They had blundered once. He mustn't expect them to do it again.

He was also engaged in a battle with fatigue. For two days he'd slept little, living on his nerves, drawing heavily on his reserves of energy. Now, when he needed to act fast, to gather his wits and physical resources for an attempt at the next hurdle, he felt curiously listless, inclined just to sit there and wait for them to show themselves.

With an effort he pulled himself together. It was pointless to sit around speculating. He could only find out about the frontiers by looking. The thing to do was take the Corniche road past Ronco toward the land frontier. Then, when he had a better idea of the obstacles, he could make his decision.

When he got back to his room he unpacked the purchases he had made in Schwyz: a small canvas knapsack, a length of rope, sneakers, wire-cutters, a flashlight, and some heavy woolen socks. Changing out of his suit into Levis and a T-shirt, he put his purchases in the knapsack, together with some spare clothes. On top, wrapped in his leather windbreaker, he placed the gun. Then he repacked his suitcase and placed it on the stool at the foot of his bed. It contained, among other things, his traveling chess set, which he would be sorry to lose. He thought about trying to squeeze it into the knapsack, but dismissed the idea almost at once. It was too heavy. He no longer had room for it.

Downstairs he told the clerk that he planned to go hiking and would be back in the evening. In fact, he thought it unlikely that he would return. He didn't plan to spend another night in Switzerland, and if he had to, it wouldn't be in a hotel. Locarno was much too small to permit him that luxury.

As he left to look for a taxi to drive him to Ronco, he was surprised to find he had no qualms at all about not paying the bill.

Ezio Pittore was nineteen years old. Present circumstances found him driving a taxi, but he had plans for that to change. For years now he had cherished the desire to attend the university in Geneva. He would become a doctor, perhaps, or a businessman. It didn't matter much—so long as he could secure for himself a reasonable share of the affluence he saw so casually displayed by the tourists he drove in his father's Fiat.

His father didn't pay much; but he was allowed to keep what he made in tips. It wasn't bad: two thousand, sometimes twenty-five hundred, francs a summer. At that rate, however, it would take him years to save what he needed. He couldn't wait that long. Life was too short; his horizons too wide. So he had taken his capital and set himself up in business.

He sold mostly to tourists, chiefly Americans—an ounce here, half an ounce there. Not a volume business; but the margins were attractive. A pound of Colombian, in Italy, cost him three thousand or thirty-five hundred, depending on the state of the market. Retailed, and mixed with a judicious amount of cheap Mexican, it brought him in close to eight thousand. It was risky, of course, but not very. He was careful about whom he approached; and most tourists—the Americans at least—when they were not receptive, were at least tolerant.

He glanced in the rearview mirror. The man's appearance was encouraging—Levis, a T-shirt, the neck of a wine bottle, opened and re-stoppered, sticking up under the flap of the knapsack beside him. He did not seem the type to be—what was the American expression?—uptight. Besides, his Italian was excellent, and this eliminated what had proved, in the past, a major source of misunderstandings.

He felt in his pocket for the cigarette case. Opening it, he placed it on the seat beside him.

"O.K. if I smoke?"

The passenger nodded.

On one side of the case there were caporals; on the other side, two slender paper cylinders, uneven in thickness, the ends twisted loosely to prevent the contents spilling. In fact these, too, contained tobacco. He was not stupid enough to carry the stuff around. One could be wrong about people, after all.

He took one of the cylinders and held it up for his passenger's inspection.

"You're sure it's O.K.?"

"O.K. with me. Go right ahead."

"You want some?"

Wylie shook his head. "Not today."

"Do you get high?"

"Sometimes. When I feel like it."

"You need some? I know where to get it. Good stuff. Not cheap, but good."

Wylie was about to refuse when an idea struck him. "Maybe. How much?"

"Five hundred an ounce."

Wylie whistled.

"Remember. It's good stuff. Colombian."

"Yes, but in the States we get it for half that price."

"Sure you do." Ezio shrugged. "But in the United States it's easy. Here there are problems. Importation, transportation . . ." His hand, describing circles in the air, hinted at difficulties too numerous to mention.

"Where do you get it?"

Ezio stiffened. "Why do you want to know?"

"Italy? Do you get it from Italy? Do you bring it across the border?"

Shit. . . . Ezio jammed on the brakes, wrenching the wheel over to bring the car to a halt at one of the scenic lookout points placed at intervals along the road. A narcotics agent—an American working undercover for the Swiss. He'd heard about them. He took the unlit cylinder from his mouth and untwisted one end. Then he tapped the contents of the cylinder into his open palm.

"Look," he said. "Smell it. It's tobacco. I don't have any Colombian. I don't have it, and I don't know where to get it. O.K.? I was just joking when I offered to sell you some. I don't even smoke it."

Wylie took a bundle of currency from his pocket and selected a fifty-franc note. Putting the bundle back into his pocket, he rested his hand on his knee, the money held loosely between his forefinger and thumb.

"Listen," he said, "I don't care about that. I don't care what you sell or who you sell it to. I need some help. Some information, I think you can give it to me."

Lermontov was having a hard time. The night had been bad, and the morning was no better. It seemed the telephone had never stopped ringing, and, each time he answered, it had been the Consulate in Geneva or the Embassy in Bern, expressing, at a new level of seniority, a greater degree of outrage.

"Yes, Comrade Ambassador." He had now reached the top.

"I understand I am to receive a formal note protesting certain activities of Soviet nationals in Switzerland. I wonder if you can guess what these activities are?"

"Yes, Comrade Ambassador."

"Then perhaps you can offer a suggestion as to how I should respond to these complaints?"

"In your place, I think I would deny responsibility altogether." Really, on top of everything else, did he have to teach this fool his job?

"In my place?" The Ambassador's tone suggested Lermontov had just set a new record for presumption. "In my place you would deny responsibility? And precisely how am I supposed to do that when a member of my staff is discovered unconscious in a public lavatory with an automatic pistol, obviously his and totally illegal, lying by his side? And what am I supposed to say to the fact that a member of the American Embassy was discovered several hours later at the foot of a railway embankment between Geneva and Schwyz with his skull smashed in and his neck broken in two places? And how do you propose I should comment on the fact that another Soviet citizen, whose driver's license identifies him as a member of the Soviet Armed Forces, was found on the Geneva–Schwyz express, minus his trousers and his passport? Do you wish me, on top of everything else, to make a public idiot of myself?"

Why not? thought Lermontov wearily. It wouldn't be the first time. Aloud he said, "I was merely pointing out, Comrade Ambassador, that at least two of the incidents were clearly the result of action by the CIA. I have no information on the death of the American, but the conclusion that it was caused by one of my subordinates is not supported by any evidence.

"I suggest," he continued, "that since the balance of responsibility for these incidents clearly belongs with the CIA, you should respectfully request the Swiss government to direct its complaints to the proper quarter."

"I shall do that, of course. In the meantime, I intend to send a report to Moscow, conveying in the strongest possible terms my censure of the manner in which you are conducting this operation."

Do that, thought Lermontov. Do that, by all means. It won't make any difference. If we succeed, you'll be ignored. If we don't, there will be censure that will make yours seem like a pat on the head.

"I understand, Comrade Ambassador. But might I suggest that, when filing your report, you make sure to direct a copy to the attention of the Minister for Defense. There are issues of national security at stake here of which you are obviously ignorant. Their importance, if I may say so, transcends that of any minor disturbance in the smooth course of our relations with the Swiss. The Minister will, no doubt, be willing to confirm that."

He hung up. Diplomats! God preserve him from them. The morning was almost wasted and they had made no start on Wylie.

It had taken all night and most of the morning to obtain the release of Pogrebin. At first the police had been inclined to accept the story that he was an innocent tourist, set upon and robbed, on his way to Locarno. The discovery of the American's body however, had complicated matters. Thank God Pogrebin had had the sense to get rid of his knife and holster. Thank God, also, for the Resident's continuing influence with a certain official in the Ministry of the Interior.

Pogrebin's report had been both encouraging and depressing. It was encouraging to Lermontov that he'd been right about Locarno. He was beginning to get a feel for the way Wylie's mind worked. He was still convinced, despite the incidents on the train, that Wylie would not change his plans. Locarno still offered the best chances for crossing the frontier, and, after yesterday, Lermontov was sure, Wylie would be feeling the pinch. Lermontov was willing to gamble on this, anyway. In support of that gamble he'd pulled agents out of Geneva and summoned them down to Locarno.

The trouble was, if Wylie had stayed on the original train, he had almost a full day's start on them. Lermontov was inclined to think he hadn't—he wouldn't have done so himself—but he couldn't be sure. It was also clear that Wylie had been expecting them. He'd been somehow able to take Pogrebin by surprise—Pogrebin's report of that encounter had been understandably vague—so it was possible that he'd identified Lermontov himself and the agents at the station. Wylie had also shown himself to be resourceful and determined. He was now armed. He would not lie down and die for them. He would not be easy to catch, especially if he made it to Italy.

CHAPTER XXIV

Pittore lived in the village of Ponte about two kilometers from the frontier. The best way to cross, he told Wylie, was up in the mountains behind the village. The lake was more risky. It could be done by boat at night—if a boat could be found. But patrol boats with searchlights were fairly frequent, and water provided no cover. For this reason they were unlikely to find anyone in Ponte willing to risk his boat in the attempt. In any case the mountains were easier. There was a guardpost up there, at the highest point between the Corniche road and the road running from Locarno to Borgnone, and the guards did sometimes patrol at night on the Italian side. However, the intervals between patrols, though irregular, were fairly long, and the frontier itself consisted merely of a chain-link fence, about three meters high, with barbed wire running across the top. It was no problem to climb, and the barbed wire could simply be cut.

The crossing would have to be made at night. In daytime there were too many hikers around, attracted by the view from the guardpost. Moreover, most of the frontier was visible, through binoculars, from the guardpost or the customs posts at Borgnone and on the Corniche road. He would be happy, he said, to direct Wylie to the best place to attempt a crossing. However, it would probably be better if he himself went along as a guide. If Wylie decided to use him—this was said with lowered eyes and a certain amount of hesitation—the charge would be five hundred francs: three hundred for the loss of fares on the taxi; two hundred for his own services.

They were sitting in the kitchen of Pittore's house. The stone walls were unplastered and hung everywhere with pots and pans, scrubbed spotless, but dented and worn from constant use. On one wall was a rough wooden sideboard, its shelves stacked with earthenware dishes. In the corner, a small arched alcove, leading up into the chimney, contained a wood-burning stove of cast iron.

Wylie looked around him. He had already paid two hundred francs to hire the taxi for the morning. Another five hundred, at a guess, would purchase the entire contents of the kitchen and leave enough over for a down payment on a new passport. It was a lot to pay, and his cash was not inexhaustible. Nevertheless he decided to accept. Company would be reassuring, and he would feel safer if he could keep an eye on Pittore until he was safely across into Italy. Besides, it was one thing to look at the mountains in daylight and at a distance—the route seemed obvious. But in the dark, and up close, it would be quite different. He had never been good at following directions.

They set out at three, taking a path which led past the back of the cottage, through a meadow, to a stream that tumbled out of the mountains to the north. When they reached the stream, they left the path and followed the course of the stream toward the heights. It was not the easiest way, Pittore explained, but it was the safest. It was too late in the day for normal hikers to be setting out into the mountains, and the ravine they were following would take them close to the frontier but shield them from the binoculars of the guards.

As the crow flies, the walk was little more than five kilometers; but, on foot, the wanderings of the creek bed nearly doubled the distance. In the course of it they would also have to climb twelve hundred meters. It got dark around seven, Pittore said, and it was important to be out of the ravine by then. In the open they could pick their way by moonlight; in the ravine they would have to use the flashlight, or risk breaking their necks. He did not have to explain why it would be better to avoid using the flashlight.

At first the way was easy. Wylie was inclined to look back and admire the view. The stream cascaded through large gray boulders mottled with the delicate olive and green patterns of moss and lichen. The meadow below was sprinkled with wild flowers, tiny points of white, yellow, and blue against a background of green, tinged with gold. Beyond stretched the lake, still and shining, laid like a sheet of gun metal between the mountains. Soon, however, the route grew steeper; the boulders became obstacles to be skirted or clambered over, and he was forced to keep his eyes on the ground to avoid tripping over tree roots or loose rocks. His breath came shorter, the straps of his pack chafed at his shoulders, and his thigh muscles began to ache and burn.

They climbed in silence, stopping at intervals, but only long enough to catch their breath. Wylie was glad of the time he had put in swimming; but it had made him fit, he discovered, only by the standards of his sedentary profession. By the end he was exhausted, his lungs sucking great gulps of the thin air, his legs, trembling with fatigue, able to stumble only a hundred yards or so between rests.

It was dusk when they reached the top. They were about half a kilometer from the frontier, but hidden from it by a small ridge. A slight breeze had sprung up, and they took shelter behind a half-circle of boulders. There they took off their packs.

"Time to eat," Pittore said, "and to rest. The moon is almost full tonight. It starts to come up around nine-thirty. Then, before it gets too bright, we'll go to the fence." He opened his pack and took out a loaf of coarse bread and a hunk of cheese. He divided the cheese and tore a fair-sized piece from the loaf. The rest he handed to Wylie.

"You should put on some clothes," he said.

Wylie shivered. He was still wearing only a T-shirt and Levis. While he had been climbing, they had kept him warm enough; but the sun was behind the mountains now, and the T-shirt, damp and sticky from his exertions, was cold against his skin. Laying aside his food, he reached for his pack and started to fumble about inside it for a sweater.

The sweater was near the bottom. Too tired to take everything out, he simply felt for it and pulled. As he did, a thread caught on the zipper of his leather jacket, rolled up on the top of the pack. The jacket unfolded. The automatic slid out, hit the ground with a clunk, and slithered across the pebbles, coming to rest at Pittore's feet.

For a moment neither moved. Then Pittore stooped and picked up the gun. Balancing it on the palm of his hand, he looked at Wylie and then back at the gun, his eyes focusing on the squat tube of metal attached to the barrel. He frowned.

Wylie waited.

"Trouble." It was a statement.

Wylie nodded.

"Police?"

"No. I told you. Politics."

Pittore thought some more. Then he said, "Listen. Five hundred francs is for showing you the frontier. Not for getting shot."

"I know." Wylie's voice was level. "I'm not expecting trouble. But if it comes, I'm not expecting you to help. If we see or hear people, you can leave. They're not looking for you. They won't bother with you."

Pittore said nothing.

"Leave now if you like," Wylie said. "I can get across on my own. Only, I may need that. Please give it to me." He held out his hand.

"You said politics." Pittore didn't move. "Whose politics? Our politics?"

"No. The Russians'. They want something I have."

"Then why not go into Italy the usual way? Like a tourist?"

"I can't do that. That's just where they're looking."

"How do I know you're telling the truth?"

Wylie thought.

"You don't," he said at last. "You can look at the gun, if you like. It's Russian. I took it from one of them. But it doesn't prove anything."

There were perhaps three paces separating them. Pittore still held the automatic in the open palm of his hand. I could jump him, Wylie thought. I'd be on him before he could fire. But he waited. He couldn't predict the outcome of a struggle and, anyway, what would he do with Pittore afterwards? He couldn't kill him.

Abruptly Pittore relaxed. Taking the automatic by the barrel he handed it, butt first, to Wylie.

"I believe you," he said. "I'll stay for now, but if anyone comes, then I'm leaving. Russians"—he shook his head—"those bastards are everywhere."

They ate in silence. Wylie was too tired to be hungry, but he ate anyway. It would be a long time before his next meal and he needed the energy. When Pittore proffered a flask of spirits, he took only a sip. The warmth felt good, but a clear head was more important.

After the meal, Pittore got up and said he was going to scout around. It was almost dark. Wylie's legs were jelly and his feet hurt. He nodded and grunted, not having the energy for anything more. When Pittore left, he laid his pack on its side, and resting his head on it, stretched out on the ground. Within a few minutes, in spite of the cold and the flints sticking into his side, he was asleep.

He awoke with a start. Someone was crouching over him. A reflex made him reach for the gun; but, as he did so, a hand restrained him, and a whisper came out of the darkness.

"It's me. Ezio. Shh."

"Is it time?" He struggled to a sitting position. His joints had stiffened, and a spasm of cramp speared him between the shoulders.

"Shh." Pittore laid a finger to his lips. "It's them. They're down there, I think."

"Where?"

With Pittore leading, feeling his way up the incline, searching out a firm foothold with his front foot before transferring his weight to it, pointing to the loose rocks and obstacles in their way, they crept to the lip of the ridge. The moon hung low in the sky, covering the landscape with a ghostly wash in which the boulders, their outlines smoother than pebbles in the half-light, provided points of relief in silver and black.

Pittore pointed down the slope to a patch of shadow sixty meters below them and perhaps four hundred meters away.

"There," he whispered. "There's someone down there. I'm sure I saw a light."

"Maybe a frontier guard?"

"I don't think so. Too far from the frontier. Wrong side, anyway."

"Shit." He turned to Pittore. "Ezio. Listen. It's time for you to go. This is my problem now."

"I don't know." Pittore hesitated. "What are you going to do?"

"I'll handle it somehow. I have the gun. Listen. Don't get involved in this; it's not worth it."

"O.K. But let me do this. I'll work round away from the fence and get behind him. It's shadow there. So if I make a noise, maybe I can distract him. He'll never see me. I know this mountain blindfold."

"It's too risky." But Pittore had already left, flitting down the slope like a ghost. Within moments, he was lost in darkness.

Wylie waited. He should give Pittore time to get clear. He also wanted to give whoever it was down there another chance to reveal himself. He needed to know the man's position before deciding whether to move to the fence.

He felt in his pocket for the automatic. Gingerly he pulled back the breech and eased it forward, feeding a shell into the chamber. The action cocked the weapon; but a spring plate in the back of the grip would prevent it from firing unless the butt were grasped firmly. It was an effective safety catch, except that the firm grip needed to release it would tend to destroy accuracy. Too firm a grip, he recalled, made one pull to the left.

It was then he remembered his pack. Twenty yards down the slope behind him. His spare clothes were in it. So was the rope. And someone might find it. He wished, if possible, to avoid leaving traces. He'd have to go back and get it.

He was halfway down when he slipped. For an instant, he swayed at the point of balance, flailing his arms backwards in an effort to recover. Then he fell. His right foot, shooting out in front, dislodged a shower of pebbles which rattled down into the gully. In the stillness they sounded like an avalanche.

He froze, listening for movement from below. For a moment there

was nothing. Then he thought he detected something—a barely perceptible series of muffled clicks, the kind of noise that might have been
made by delicate, well-oiled machinery, by someone working the action
of a gun. But the sound, if he'd heard it at all, had not come from
below. It had come from above.

Wylie was still in shadow. If someone was above him, he could sit
still and wait for the other to make a move. But the man below would
also have heard his fall and, presumably, would work his way up. On
the far side of the ridge the moon was rising. Presently it would illumi-
nate the slope and expose Wylie. At the very least they could stay
where they were and wait for dawn. Then he'd be defenseless against
them—assuming there were two—especially if they had rifles. He was
sure they would.

The best chance, he figured, was to cross over the ridge and work his
way up the far side, around and behind the noise he'd heard above. This
would mean exposing himself in the moonlight where he might be spotted by the man below. As far as he could gauge, though, that man
should still be a good way off. Perhaps as much as two hundred and
fifty yards. There was plenty of cover; and, if he offered a shot, it would
take a superlative marksman, in that light, to hit him.

With infinite caution, using hands and feet, making sure that three
limbs were anchored before moving the fourth, he crawled back to the
top.

Further up the ridge, close to the crest, Tovarov waited. Someone
was down there. The question was who. It was a question that needed
an answer. "No shooting," Lermontov had told them, "without positive
identification. There may be campers up there, or frontier guards, or
smugglers. No more unnecessary corpses. . . . We have problems
enough already."

Tovarov had a flashlight attached to his rifle. He could use it to identify the target—if it was the target down there. But the problem was he
could use it only once. If he used it without firing, it would betray his
own position; and the target, he remembered, was now armed. So he
would have to work down close. But his partner was still too far below.
The target could still slip out between them. He needed to be flushed
into the open.

He groped around in the darkness behind him until his hand closed
around a rock about the size of a walnut. Drawing his arm back, he
straightened up and hurled it in the general direction from which the
noise had come, but slightly to the left. It struck thirty or forty meters
below him, above and behind Wylie, dislodging a shower of gravel

which hailed into the gully and produced a gratifying amount of noise. Then he watched the moonlit side of the ridge, waiting for someone to come out.

He was rewarded, a few seconds later, with the sight of a man coming over the top of the ridge and moving swiftly to take cover behind a boulder, about fifty meters below. He was facing down the mountain, with his back to Tovarov. Evidently he believed Tovarov was in the gully and was more concerned about the threat from below.

Tovarov settled the butt into his shoulder, slipping off the safety catch and aiming between and slightly below the man's shoulders. The man was the height and build of the target. He was bound to show his face presently. Tovarov watched intently, his finger resting lightly upon the trigger guard.

The man moved again, stepping crabwise between the boulders, crouching low and using his left arm to steady himself. From his right hand there protruded a black tubular object, which could only be a gun. Only the target, thought Tovarov, would be up here armed, playing hide-and-seek in the moonlight. It couldn't be anyone else.

This time, however, the man had settled on the far side of a boulder. Only part of his head was showing, and it was in shadow. At that range, Tovarov was confident he could hit him. But he held his fire. Positive identification, Lermontov had insisted, so positive it would be. The next time the man broke cover he'd take him in the open like a rabbit.

Confident now, Tovarov shifted to a more comfortable firing position, squatting behind the rock that had been his cover and resting his elbows on it to steady himself. He lined up on a spot about two meters to the right of where he expected the man to emerge and moved his finger onto the trigger, all his attention focused upon that spot.

The rock caught him low in the small of the back. It was a hand-sized boulder, thrown with all the force Pittore could put behind it. Taken off balance, Tovarov staggered, his rifle discharging as he fell. The recoil hurled him backwards. He crashed down heavily, his head smashing against a rock, and lay still. The rifle, torn from his grasp by the fall, slithered a few meters further and came to rest.

Pittore waited until the dirt and pebbles dislodged by the fall had completed their rackety descent to the gully. Then, hearing nothing further, he emerged cautiously from his hiding place. Pulling out his flashlight, he ran it rapidly over the ground below him, illuminating the prostrate figure of Tovarov and the rifle several yards beyond. Keeping the light on Tovarov and arming himself with another rock, he approached. Satisfied that Tovarov was unconscious, he used the man's belt to pinion his arms behind his back. If he woke up it wouldn't hold him long, but the man would certainly make plenty of noise trying to get it off. Having done that, Pittore collected the rifle and went off up the ridge to look for Wylie.

Wylie had completed his circle to the north. He'd heard a muffled thud, followed immediately by the thunk characteristic of a shot fired through a silencer, then the noise of a heavy fall. Taking advantage of the moment, he'd sprinted sixty or seventy feet up the slope, finding cover a few yards from the crest of the ridge. His assumption was that whoever had fired had been unbalanced by the recoil of the rifle and had fallen down the slope. Hearing nothing further, he had then moved to the ridge to reconnoiter. He crouched behind an outcrop, holding the automatic at the ready.

There was movement below. Someone was working up the ridge toward the crest. He trained the automatic on the spot from which he thought the man would emerge, his left hand cupped beneath the butt to support and steady his right.

"Arden?" A hiss from below.

"Ezio." He lowered the pistol. "Where the hell are you?"

"Down here."

"Christ, I almost shot you. What's going on?"

"I got one. Come and look."

Wylie clambered down.

"I thought you were leaving."

"So did I. Then I heard you slip, and this guy moving up above. I figured they had you, between them, so I came back to see what I could do."

"What *did* you do?"

"Hit him with a rock."

"Hit him with a rock? Jesus! He had a gun. He could have killed you."

"Not me. He never knew I was there. He'd have killed you, though. He was just about to when I nailed him."

"Christ." Wylie reached out and squeezed Pittore's shoulder. "I don't know what to say."

"Don't say anything. . . . There's still the other one."

Pittore knelt down beside the still unconscious figure of Tovarov and lit a match. The man was breathing, but in shallow gasps. Around his neck was a slim cord which disappeared beneath the lapels of his jacket. Pulling it out, Pittore discovered a small metal whistle which he handed to Wylie.

"For signaling?"

"I guess so."

Wylie examined it. It couldn't be anything else. Drawing a deep breath, he put it to his lips. The sound which emerged was thin and shrill, not loud, but piercing, almost painful to the ear. They waited. From the far side of the ridge, quite a long way off, there came an answering whistle.

"He's still down there. Listen, Ezio. Let me handle this now. Someone's going to discover these guys sometime and start asking questions. You'd best get out of here."

"Take this." Pittore handed him the rifle. "It's better than the pistol."

"Thanks." Wylie touched his arm. "I'll owe you forever. But this time really leave. O.K.? You're much too involved already." He put his hand into his pocket and drew out something which he handed to Pittore.

"No. It's not necessary," Pittore protested. "The five hundred was enough."

"Not for getting shot at. You said so yourself. Take it, Ezio. I may not live to spend it anyway."

Pittore put it in his pocket. *"Ciao, amico,"* he said, "and take care." He turned and crept back into the gully.

Wylie put the whistle to his lips and blew another blast.

It took the second Russian five more minutes to get up the slope. He must have believed Tovarov had been successful, for he climbed quickly and in the open, careless of the noise he was making. Wylie waited, crouched behind the boulder that had given Tovarov cover. When he was thirty yards away, the man paused to recover his breath. He called out. "Sergei." And Wylie, taking no chances this time, shot him between the eyes.

The moon was rising, illuminating the landscape more than Wylie would have wished. He still had the fence to cross, but he couldn't afford to wait until the moon went down. The Russian, Sergei, could not be relied upon to stay unconscious forever. He could kill him, of course, but, although waiting might give him better cover, he'd need time before dawn to get clear on the other side of the frontier. He could kill if he had to—he knew that now. But in this case it seemed pointless.

Instead he emptied the magazine of Sergei's rifle and put the shells in his pocket, noting as he did that they were hollow points, designed to mushroom on impact. Then he wiped the weapon carefully with his handkerchief and covered it with the fingerprints of the unconscious Russian before leaving it on the ground next to him. Having done that, he searched him for other weapons. Finding none, he went down to look at the other one.

The man he had shot lay on his back in the short grass. There was no question he was dead. The force of the bullet had thrown him over backwards and blown half his head away. Wylie was not surprised; hollow points would do that. Nor, beyond the desire to heave his guts up— a natural physical response to the oozing, pulpy nightmare he had made of the man's face, did he feel much. The hollow points had been intended for *him*. It was *him* they had been hunting, up here in the mountains; him they would have left here, to rot until some hiker happened upon the corpse, had the luck not gone against them. Regrets were pointless. So was guilt. Both were just emotional excess baggage he could not afford to carry if he wanted to survive. He could not risk the hesitation which, if the situation ever recurred, they might cost him.

He took the second rifle and its ammunition with him. It would be foolish to leave it around for Sergei to find when he woke up. Otherwise, he left the man as he was. The Swiss police would now have a reasonably obvious scenario to follow—someone had shot the Russian for reasons unexplained, but easy to guess at. There were several suspects more obvious than Wylie—the CIA, for example—and there would be no reason to look beyond them unless he left a gaping hole through the fence.

He reached the fence in five minutes. He was a kilometer below the guardpost—certainly invisible from it at that distance. The barrier was as Pittore had described it: about ten feet high, with a V-shaped trough formed by strands of barbed wire running along the top. He waited for several minutes behind a boulder, fifty yards back, but could detect no signs of patrolling on either side.

Using the rope, which he looped over one of the uprights, he was able to scramble over without having to cut the wire. He tore his hand in the process; but it was worth it to avoid disturbing the simple and obvious conclusions he wished the police to draw.

He walked almost two kilometers into Italy before he hid the rifle and ammunition he'd taken from the dead Russian. With any luck it would be months before it was found. In any event, the finder, coming on something so valuable, would probably not notify the police.

He waited until midmorning before he entered Traffiume. There were plenty of tourists around, and, as Pittore had predicted, his presence was not noticed.

Fifteen hours later, he was in Rome.

PART III

PART III

CHAPTER XXV

It was some time after she left the subway before Anne Crossland realized she was being followed. Once or twice since she'd turned off Flushing Avenue she'd seemed to catch the scrape of a footfall in the distance behind, but she'd paid no attention. It was seven-thirty and still light—too early for muggers; somebody's path had simply coincided with her own. The explanation reassured her for a while, but when the footsteps remained faithful through all the windings of her route, drawing obstinately closer despite the gradual quickening of her pace, she began to get seriously alarmed.

She didn't turn around—no point in inviting trouble—she just lengthened her stride. The man—she was sure it *was* a man—was still twenty yards behind; ahead, not much farther away, was the corner of her street, and beyond it, only a few more steps, her home. If she started running as soon as she was round the corner and out of sight, she could be there before he had time to head her off.

She was at the corner and about to bolt when he called out.

"Mrs. Crossland . . ."

The voice was bland, educated, with overtones of Boston. The shock of hearing her name was followed, instantly, by recognition. It was Hunter.

"I hope I didn't startle you."

He loped toward her, smoothing back a wisp of hair that had fallen onto his forehead. He was smiling, she observed, but without much conviction.

"The resurrected Mr. Hunter." She stared at him coldly. "Yes. You did startle me, as a matter of fact."

"I was waiting for you at the subway," he explained. "I'm afraid my attention must have wandered. . . . You were way past before I spotted you."

It occurred to her to ask him how he had known what time she'd be home, but she didn't bother. All she would get would be some facile lie.

"So why are you following me?" she asked. "Trying to find out what I get up to?"

"Oh, no." He looked surprised. "If we wanted to know that, we'd be less obvious about it. I was just trying to catch up with you. . . . I *am* sorry, though; I should have called out sooner. You must have thought I was a mugger."

He smiled, inviting her to share the absurdity of that suggestion.

"Yes." She didn't respond to the smile. The present alternative to mugging, she thought, was not too welcome, either.

"I see you're angry with us."

"Yes."

"I can't blame you; you've every right to be. That's why I got in touch with you. . . . I felt, on reflection, you were owed an explanation."

Owed an explanation? Did he think she was stupid?

"I don't buy that." She shook her head. "I don't believe you ever feel you owe anyone anything. I think you want something."

He was silent for a second; figuring, she guessed, trying to decide if the time were right for candor.

"Yes . . ." He appeared to conclude that it was. "I do want something, as a matter of fact. But the explanation is part of it. . . . Why not listen, at least, before you turn me down?"

She said nothing.

"What can you lose?" he persisted. "There's no obligation. I can't force you to help me. . . . Just listen and decide. It's all I ask."

No obligation? He sounded like a salesman. What line was he peddling today, she wondered: patriotism? enlightened self-interest? or just the usual shopworn charm? . . . Her impulse was to turn him down flat, to walk off and leave him standing there clutching his merchandise, but she resisted it. She really wanted to know—didn't she? She wanted, at least, to resolve her doubts about Wylie. Why let anger deprive her of the knowledge?

"I'm listening," she said. "So go ahead. Explain."

"Here?" He looked around him. "It's a little public, isn't it?"

She shrugged. "Come into the house, then. . . . If you think it's worth your while. I should warn you, however, that it almost certainly won't be."

"It's the business, really," Roskill said. "It makes us very suspicious. It's forced on us, mostly, by the people we deal with. We develop reflexes, in self-defense, and we forget they're not always appropriate."

She let this pass without comment. It was an apology of sorts, she supposed, from a man not used to apologizing. Since entering the house, she'd noticed, he'd become less sure of himself, as if in her territory he'd lost the initiative and didn't know how to deal with her. He looked almost lost, standing there beside the sofa, his eyes wandering uneasily around the room. . . . What was he doing here? she wondered. Why had he trekked all the way from Washington to see her? Couldn't he simply have picked up the phone? . . . Defensive reflexes, she supposed; he probably worried about the line being bugged. At that, she warmed to him a little. How lonely, she thought, to go through life and not to trust a soul.

"Sit down," she said. "If we're going to talk, we might as well be comfortable."

"Thank you. . . . I was wondering," he hesitated, "if I might use your phone. . . . I should call my office to let them know my movements."

At this hour? Her hostility returned. Was he one of those tiresome men who imagined that his world ceased to function if he were not around to direct it?

"Certainly." She started heading for the door.

"It's not private. . . . There's no need for you to leave."

"I was going to get myself a drink. . . . May I offer you one?"

"Thank you. A Scotch would be welcome, if you have it. On the rocks, maybe? With just a splash of soda."

Roskill. From the kitchen she heard him give the name together with her number. She could only pick up snatches of the ensuing conversation, and she didn't strain to hear the rest. She made a point of not straining, in fact. Eavesdropping was the sort of thing he might be expected to do; it was important to her, just then, to feel herself above it.

The call was over when she returned with the drinks.

"So your name is Roskill?" she asked. "Or is that another alias?"

"No." He shook his head. "It really is Roskill."

"Then why didn't you tell me so before? . . . And why all that stupid business with the phones?"

He said nothing.

"You didn't trust me, obviously. . . . And now you've thought better of it. Or been forced to for some reason. I'm still waiting to hear your explanation."

He remained silent; trying to decide, evidently, where to begin.

"I assume," he said at last, "that you haven't heard from Wylie since you made the contact in Moscow?"

She shook her head.

"Well, I have. . . . Not directly, I think. But at least he sent me a message. . . . He has what you asked him to get for us, he claims. But he doesn't want to give it up."

"Doesn't want to give it up?—whyever not?"

"He wants to sell it to us . . . for a great deal of money."

So *that* was it. After the first shock she didn't know whether to be angry or laugh. The bastard! she thought, to leave her there dangling, ignorant and panic-stricken, just for money. . . . Well, that resolved *one* doubt—she now knew exactly what their romance had meant to him. . . . But on the other hand, there was a certain poetic justice to his action. Roskill, after all, had used him, had risked them both quite shamelessly—like poker chips. Why shouldn't he be made to pay some compensation? . . . She had a sudden vision of Roskill and his henchmen receiving the demand: their shock, their righteous anger, their ludicrous dismay.

"You find that funny?"

She realized that she was smiling.

"I'm afraid I do. . . . I almost wish I'd thought of it myself."

He frowned and pursed his lips. He looked prim, she thought, shocked at her levity—like a minister who spots a member of the faithful giggling during the Creed.

"In any case," she went on, "I don't see the problem. . . . He has it, and you want it. If it's worth it, you pay. And if it's not, you do the other thing."

No response. He was staring at her, but the disapproval had vanished; his eyes were simply appraising.

"And I don't at all see where I fit in. . . . Nor why you found it necessary to give me the cold shoulder."

He looked embarrassed, said nothing.

"You thought *I* was in it? . . ."

Now she was angry again. You fool, she thought; you stupid little man.

"Not exactly," he muttered. "That's what I meant by defensive reflexes. . . . You're a journalist, for one thing. We have a horror of *them*."

"I see." Her tone was scathing. "He gets his cut directly. And I get mine from a series of nasty articles—'Special to the *New York Times*'—is that it?"

"Something like that," he admitted. "Not that I really believed it, having met you. But such things *have* been known to happen."

"Well, you can put your mind to rest. . . . I'm not going to write this up. My own part in it was too silly, for one thing. And for another, I can't. I don't have the backup."

"No," he said. "You don't. And that business with the alias and the telephones was our way of making sure you didn't get it. . . . It wasn't very nice of us, and I'm sure you didn't deserve it. But as you've discovered, this isn't a nice profession."

"It stinks," she agreed. "But that's neither here nor there. . . . I still don't understand why you won't pay."

"We don't know if he really has it. And even if he does, he's asking way too much. . . . In any case," he shrugged, "it's not my decision."

"Then what will you do?"

But the question was barely asked before she, herself, supplied the answer. "You'll find him, of course, and when you do, you'll . . . persuade him to lower the price. In fact, now that I know you, it wouldn't surprise me at all if you were able to *persuade* him to give it up for nothing."

"Ah. Now you're being too hard on us." He was reproachful. "We'd like to negotiate is all. We'd like to satisfy ourselves he really has it, and we'd like to talk about price."

"And you think I can help?"

"It crossed my mind."

"Well, I can't. I have no idea where he is. . . . I met him precisely once. I passed on your message, and afterwards we had dinner. . . ." She was conscious of an omission from the account that made her feel, inexplicably, a little guilty. "Then I had to leave Moscow for the provinces. When I returned he was gone."

"So you cut short your own trip?"

"I got scared, don't you see?" She stared at him defiantly. "When he just left without a word, I thought something was wrong. So I bolted, too—while the going was good."

"Probably wise." He smiled. "I don't in the least doubt what you say. And I'm very grateful for all you've done—not least for agreeing to talk to me after I treated you so shabbily. . . . I have only one more small favor to ask. If he does get in touch with you, for any reason, will you let me know? And would you let him know we'd like to negotiate?"

"I don't know why he'd contact me." She felt another little prick of guilt. "But if he does, I can pass on your message about wanting to negotiate. . . . I don't know about the other, though. . . . I think I'd rather you found him without my help. He obviously doesn't trust you. To be frank, I'm not sure I do, either."

"Understood." He gave a bleak little smile. "And of course that's your decision. But before you make it final, there's something else I think you should know."

"Yes?"

"Something *did* go wrong. In Moscow, I mean. I don't know what it was exactly. All I know is that Moscow is somehow onto our friend Wylie. They seem to know that he hasn't made a deal with us yet, and they're out in force, combing Europe for him. Unless we find him quickly, I don't give much for his chances. In fact . . ." he paused, "I'd say you could measure his life expectancy in days."

"She's not in it?"

"I don't *think* so." Roskill shook his head. "At least, if she *is*, she's a better actress than she has any right to be. . . . She seemed to think it was funny, for one thing. And when I got hold of her first, she was too genuinely angry. . . . But then I rather like her, so I suppose we must discount my intuition."

"Well, you never did plan to rely on it." Holland grinned.

"No." Roskill reached for the thermos that always stood on his desk and poured himself a cup of coffee. "You mustn't rely on intuition. Not ever. When you can, you make sure. It's tiresome and expensive, but there's really no alternative."

"You had no problems?"

"Not really. . . . For a while I was afraid she wouldn't let me into the house. She didn't want to—she wanted to tell me to go to hell—but curiosity got the better of her; curiosity and good manners"—Roskill smiled—"a very vulnerable combination. . . . Is everything set up?"

"Yes. The DCI himself okayed the tap with Justice. . . . We've a listening post down the street, and it's manned round the clock. . . . You really think he'll call her?"

"I don't know." Roskill shrugged. "Probably not. But we just can't afford to ignore the possibility. . . . There *was* something, however. They'd evidently made a date to meet again when she returned to Moscow—at least she tried to contact him and discovered he'd bolted. . . . It's intuition again, but I got the impression that something was going on between them."

"More than likely," Holland nodded. "It's a shipboard-romance–type situation. She's attractive and so is he; they're in a strange city and sharing a secret. Add a little stress, and you have all the ingredients. Nothing like that combination to get the libido working overtime."

Roskill stared at him.

"Tony," he asked, "how old are you?"

"Twenty-six. Why?"

"Twenty-six. . . . Jesus," Roskill sighed. "Sometimes I wonder about your generation. Three years out of school and already a hardened cynic."

"I'd call it a hardened realist." Holland shrugged. "But what's in a name? . . . Either way, it's not very surprising. After all"—he flashed Roskill a grin—"I've been sitting at the feet of a master."

CHAPTER XXVI

The American Embassy in Rome is located on the Via Veneto at the point where the avenue, having made a leisurely S-bend, straightens out and heads toward the Viale delle Mura and the massive ocher brick-work of the Aurelian Wall. At this end of the avenue the tree-lined side-walks are straddled by a number of cafés from beneath whose um-brellas and striped awnings the leisured and the curious, observers of *la dolce vita,* may watch the comings and goings of that odd world.

In one of these cafés, hardly more than a stone's throw from the Em-bassy, Wylie, toying with a Campari soda, sat watching a woman.

The closeness of the Embassy did not bother him. It was six o'clock; most members of the Embassy had probably gone home. He was confident that his appearance, transformed by a few careful purchases from the clothing stores on the Via Frattina and truly impenetrable sun-glasses, would enable him to survive all but the closest scrutiny. Against that he relied for protection upon the principle of careless assumption—that common habit of mind which assures someone who has lost his hat that the last place to look for it is on his head.

It was not, however, any intention of thumbing his nose at his pur-suers which had brought him to the avenue from his *pensione* on the far side of the Tiber. He felt confident, but not to the point where he was tempted to oppose the principle of careless assumption with a strategy of pointless risk. He was there with a purpose. Experience had taught him that the Via Veneto was the most likely place to achieve it.

The focus of his interest had been deposited fifteen minutes earlier, on the sidewalk close to his table, by a white Cadillac whose elaborate chromework and baroque radiator grille proclaimed it a custom model, built for someone whose tastes were eccentric and showy. In New York he would have identified it, unhesitatingly, as a pimpmobile. In Rome the name was probably different; but the function, he concluded after observing the woman's behavior since her arrival, was unquestionably the same.

She did not particularly look the part. Her linen skirt, hemmed just above the knee and nipped in at the waist, emphasized, but did not exaggerate, the contours of her hips. The cotton shirt was unbuttoned a little below her throat, permitting glimpses of prominent, delicately molded collarbones—but nothing more. Her shoes and purse, in matching dark brown leather, were expensive, obviously, but not flashy. And her manner, as she wandered past his table, had been only faintly provocative, betraying little more than a complacent awareness that she was attractive and had been noticed.

It was only when she strolled toward him for the second time, threading her way between the tables on an erratic, apparently random, course which managed nevertheless to take her past the line of sight of every unattached man in the place, that Wylie became certain of her purpose.

When she sat down, it was facing him, at a table adjacent to his. As she did, she raised her sunglasses from the bridge of her nose, rested them on the top of her forehead, and smiled directly at Wylie.

"Hot," she said.

He accepted the gambit. It was very hot, he agreed. Perhaps the *signorina* would permit him to order her an iced drink.

It seemed the *signorina* would. And, it was soon established, without too much beating about the bush on either side, that the *signorina* would also be happy to have company for the evening.

Her name was Clara. She lived in the Trastevere, not far from the Vatican and the Castel Sant'Angelo, in a one-bedroom apartment whose furnishings, to Wylie's eye, exactly suited her calling.

The room was large and dimly lit. The walls were covered in wood paneling, painted a pastel green and trimmed with gold. The ceiling was high and vaulted, decorated with a mural of a pastoral scene in which nymphs and cupids, clad in fig leaves and little wisps of ribbon, engaged in rural pastimes. In the center of the room on a low dais, partially hidden behind a Chinese lacquer screen, was an enormous bed.

He had scarcely time to take in all this sumptuous suggestiveness before she flung herself on him, pressing her body against him and reaching up to take his head between her hands and draw it toward hers.

"*Caro*," she whispered. Her hips, thrust forward, worked in slow circular motion against his, and her tongue flickered in and out of his mouth.

He disengaged himself and leaned backwards, holding her shoulders. "Not now," he said. "Later. Now I want to talk."

Her ardor ceased abruptly. She looked at him coldly, her expression a mixture of suspicion and contempt.

"Talk? Talk about what?"

"Sit down and I'll tell you."

"Look." She sat on the bed, pressing her knees together and smoothing the skirt across them. "We agreed on a price. That was the regular price. Deviations are extra."

The thought amused him. He was tempted to ask for the tariff. But it was going to be expensive enough as it was; he hoped it would be worth it.

"The man," he began, "the one in the big white car, is he"—he searched for an acceptable euphemism—"your protector?"

"What's that to you?"

"I have a problem." He hesitated. "It concerns the authorities. I need some help."

"The authorities? You mean the police?"

"Not exactly, but near enough."

"Then he can't help you. He doesn't do that sort of thing."

"What sort of thing?"

"Whatever it is you want. He doesn't need trouble with the police."

"Listen," Wylie said gently. "We agreed on a price. Right?"

She nodded.

"Well, I'll double it. All I want you to do is call him. Tell him there's someone here who wants to discuss a business proposition. He has nothing to lose. If he doesn't like it, he can just refuse."

"He won't like it." She was reluctant. "He'll just get angry."

"Not when he realizes there's money in it. Call him. Put it to him, and let him decide."

Eventually she consented. She disappeared behind the screen. He could hear a protracted telephone conversation, conducted, on her side, in vehement whispers. At length she reappeared.

"O.K. He'll meet you here. But he can't make it until after ten. You want to come back later?" She lowered her eyes. "Or will you wait?"

She was standing in front of him. He reached out and unbuttoned her shirt. When it was open to the waist, he eased it off her shoulders.

"I think," he smiled, "I would rather wait."

* * *

Cesare Umberto di Lasso claimed descent from an aristocratic Roman family. His claim was unsupported by any patent of nobility; but his girls, of whom there were many, accepted it without hesitation. "Il Conte" was what they called him and they contributed, to his easy and magnificent existence, not only a portion of the fruits of their labors, but also certain other tributes of a nonmonetary nature. In return, he offered them his protection, negotiating the leases for their apartments, settling territorial disputes, arranging legal assistance when necessary, and in general relieving them of the administrative burden of their profession, allowing them to concentrate on what they were best at.

Il Conte was not in a good mood. He used his own set of keys to let himself into the apartment, entered without warning, and, ignoring Wylie and Clara, strode over to the telephone beside the bed. Picking it up, he dialed.

"Cesare di Lasso. Until further notice I can be reached at four-six-four five-nine-two. After that direct callers to the usual number."

Still ignoring Wylie, he turned to the girl.

"It was whispered to me," he said softly, "by an old and valued acquaintance, that a certain young person, young, but nevertheless old enough to know better, attended a certain political meeting yesterday. Is that correct?"

There was no reply. Crouching on the bed, the sheet drawn up around her shoulders, she stared at him with large, frightened eyes.

"Is that correct?" The voice was silky, but it held overtones of menace that made her cringe and turn her head away.

"Is that correct?"

She nodded. He stepped forward. There was no change in the calm expression on his face; but his hand shot out, the open palm catching the side of her head with a force that knocked her sideways onto the pillow. She lay there passive, her knees drawn up to her chest, her face turned away, her eyes screwed up tight in anticipation.

Wylie made no move to intervene. If he was shocked by the sudden eruption of violence from the elegant figure who stood before him, he did not let it show. He was there for business. It would not do to begin by antagonizing a man who might help him.

The idea had been sparked by his dealings with Pittore. It had struck him then that the safest entry into the criminal world was at the point of contact between petty crime and the ordinary citizen. There was a marketplace, he'd realized, where certain services, technically illegal but hardly criminal, are demanded by the public and supplied by small-time crooks. Dealing, in most countries, was one such service. Prostitution was another. Where there were prostitutes, he'd reasoned, there were also pimps. Make contact with a pimp, and you entered a world of broader possibilities.

Il Conte did not strike the girl again. Instead he turned to Wylie and said, as if by way of introduction, "This silly bitch, God help me, is trying to help organize an association. A kind of whore's union, for Christ's sake." His voice, abandoning its monotone, rose an octave in anger and incredulity. "They wish to dispense with my services and do everything for themselves. Next thing we know they'll have shop stewards, strikes, minimum hourly rates, that kind of shit.

"What are you, anyway," he turned back to the girl, "a Communist? Shit, I hate those people. They've brought our country to its knees. They're deliberately tearing it apart—and when they've finished, they'll hand it over, gift-wrapped and tied up with bright red ribbon, to the Russians.

"Are you a Communist?"

Clara, still lying on the bed, sniffling quietly into the pillow, shook her head.

"Lying bitch. You listen to me. You go to one more meeting—just one—and I'll have you messed up so badly that when they're finished, you won't even be able to give it away. Now get out of here. I have business to take care of."

She started to gather up her clothes. Wylie, now half-dressed, found his wallet and began to take out money. Il Conte waved it away.

"Put it away, my friend. She doesn't deserve it. Perhaps if we find we can do business together, I'll allow you to leave it for her. For now, keep it—as proof of my good faith."

They waited until Clara left. Il Conte, lounging on the bed, occupied himself by polishing, with a corner of the sheet, the immaculate surface of his loafers. Wylie finished dressing. When they heard the door close, Il Conte addressed him.

"She mentioned some kind of problem. What makes you think I can help?"

"I don't know that you can, but I don't know where to go. I need to get advice from someone who won't go to the police about it."

"I think," Il Conte smiled, "I can guarantee at least that. What kind of advice?"

"I need a new passport. I want to know where I can get one."

"Ah." Il Conte smiled again. "You're lucky. It happens I have a friend who has a friend . . . but, you know, that kind of thing is expensive. The passport itself will cost . . . I don't know . . . maybe a thousand dollars. Then there are commissions. For my friend, and, of course, for me. Let's say two thousand altogether. Do you have that kind of money?"

"I suppose so." In fact, he thought it was outrageous. But he was dealing in a seller's market. He had no choice. His success in getting into Italy had postponed but not removed the need for a new passport. His present one was not stamped. He had no Italian visa. So, even if the Italian authorities had not been briefed to look for him, he would be unable to leave Italy except by frontier-hopping. His last experience had left him with a permanent aversion to that. Beyond which, there lay the necessity for a permanent change of identity. When he began his new life it could not be as Arden Wylie. The Russians had seen to that.

"Two thousand? O.K. But it's my limit. If it can be done for that, good. If not, I'll have to think again."

"It can be done." Il Conte spoke with assurance. "But I'll need photographs, of course. Do you have them?"

Wylie gave him the two he had obtained earlier in the day, and a list of personal particulars.

"Good. This will take perhaps two days." He handed Wylie a small card. "This is my answering service. Call tomorrow evening and leave a number where I can reach you. The terms, of course, are cash. U.S. dollars. Payable in full upon delivery."

He got up. "And now back to work. They drive me crazy, these girls, with their stupidities."

He smiled suddenly, pointing to the bed. "But we have to make do with what they've got, eh? If you want, you can leave her something, the little Clara. She's not so bad—as long as she remembers not to think."

CHAPTER XXVII

"Five hundred?" The old man shook his head. "Impossible. What you ask involves great difficulties. I couldn't do it for less than a thousand."

Il Conte smiled. He enjoyed bargaining. It gave him a chance to display the qualities on which he prided himself: a sense of style, a flair for the dramatic, an extensive knowledge of human weakness. It was much like a very good game, requiring strength of character and force of intellect. But, unlike most games, it was not without point. For all the pleasure, there were real advantages to be gained. Il Conte never lost sight of this.

"Difficulties." He sounded amused. "Claudio. Remember who you're talking to. I am your good friend, Cesare di Lasso, and I know that in that thing over there"—he pointed to a heavy combination safe that stood in a corner of the room—"you have a stack of passport blanks at least one meter high."

"Cesare." The old man ignored this gambit. "Why did you come here? I'll tell you why. You came because my work is the best. Impeccable. And it's the best, because my passports are not forgeries"—he paused for effect—"they are real.

"You talk to me about blanks," he continued, "as if it were simply a matter of the right paper, the right binding, the right ink, and knowing the format. But that's not the problem. If that were the problem, then any moron could make his own passport. The problem is serial numbers. They record them on issue, you see, and feed the information into a computer. If any of the blanks go missing, the numbers are deleted and that information, too, is recorded. So for a reliable U.S. passport, one which will survive any inspection, you need a blank with a valid, active serial number—one that will not alarm the computers. And you don't make those things. You buy them.

"Blanks," he shrugged. "Yes, I have blanks. I have, in fact, three U.S. blanks. I couldn't afford any more. If you want a cheap passport, take a French one, or an Italian one. For five hundred I can give you either. But U.S. . . . Do you know how much it costs to buy just one U.S. blank?"

Il Conte did not bother to ask. Any answer he got would certainly be overstated by several orders of magnitude.

"Are you telling me," he demanded, "that the U.S. passport officials are so much less corruptible than the others?"

"Not at all. Just more expensive." The old man smiled. "It has to do with their standard of living, or their security. I'm not sure which.

"Besides," he continued, "you need extras. An Italian visa. That's easy. I have a stamp for that. Immigration Control at Fiumicino. I have that stamp, too. But I'll need to make one for Kennedy, because my old one is out of date. That will take time. And time, as you know, is money."

Il Conte did not contest that obvious point. Instead, he said, "You're too much of a perfectionist, Claudio. I don't need a perfect passport. Just something good enough to convince our client. So take the five hundred. Give him something that looks O.K. One with a deleted serial number . . . I don't know . . . something like that. With luck it won't be spotted. And if it is"—he shrugged—"he can hardly take us to court."

The old man looked at him coldly. "I don't have anything like that. I don't deal in shit. I have three perfect U.S. blanks. Each one cost me more than four hundred dollars. My price to you is one thousand for the passport, the visa, and all the proper stamps. Take it or leave it."

Il Conte did some rapid mental arithmetic. He tended to question whether what the old man had told him bore any but a very distant relationship to the truth, but even assuming it did, the price he'd paid for the blanks had certainly not been more than two hundred. Allow another hundred for the stamp, and you had a cost of three hundred, maximum. Allow a hundred, perhaps a hundred and fifty percent for profit, and that gave you six, or seven fifty. Somewhere in the middle was the number to aim for.

"He can't pay a thousand," he said. "He hasn't got it. In any case, there's another problem. He wants it tomorrow. If you can't do that, there's no point talking."

"Pictures?"

Il Conte produced his notecase, a slim envelope of black crocodile, reinforced at the corners with thin strips of gold. Extracting the photographs, he handed them, with a flourish, to the old man.

"*Ecco,*" he said, "I came prepared."

The old man studied them, drawing them close to his face and peering intently through the thick lenses of his spectacles.

"Particulars?" he said, at length.

So it was not going to be a contest after all. Il Conte was faintly disappointed. He wouldn't have a chance to exercise his skill.

"He wants to be Charles Porter," he said. "Born June 14, 1939. Washington, D.C. Height, five foot eleven. Hair, brown. Eyes, brown. Unmarried. Profession, business executive."

"He can't be Charles Porter. I don't have a blank for that name. The rest of it I can manage. He'll have to be Robert Thompson. I have a blank issued for a Robert Thompson, the particulars match, more or less. In any case they never look at the descriptions. They look at the photographs."

"Six fifty," Il Conte offered. "It's the best I can offer. As it is, it leaves practically nothing for me."

The old man ignored this. Leaning forward, he scribbled something on a scrap of paper he had located, after some searching, among the muddle of ink bottles, stamps, pads, and engraving tools on the desk beside him. His shirt collar, di Lasso noted, was frayed and grimy. There were flecks of dandruff on the shoulders of his coat. Seedy old bastard, di Lasso thought, what does he want with money? He never spends it. His own case, he reflected, eying the Vitucci suit with some complacency, was entirely different.

"Six fifty," he repeated.

The old man put down his pencil.

"Cesare," he said mildly, "you surprise me. So much good breeding. Such distinguished Roman ancestry. And yet—the instincts of a Venetian moneylender. . . . Seven fifty."

"Seven."

"Seven, then." The old man sighed, his words heavy with reproach. "For the sake of an old friendship, and in memory of a once profitable business relationship."

Il Conte rose from his chair and held out his hand. "Seven," he said. "But you misjudge me, Claudio. Every penny over five comes out of my own pocket."

Of course it does, thought the old man as his ears followed Il Conte's footsteps down the stairs. But how much remains in your pocket afterwards? That's what interests me.

It did not, however, appear to interest him very much. He was singing quietly to himself as he gathered up the photographs and took them over to the safe. The tune was from *Figaro,* and it exactly suited his mood.

"Se vuol ballare, signor Contino. . . ."

He fiddled with the dial and tugged at the heavy door. From within he extracted a photograph and held it up beside the one Il Conte had given him. The hair was different, but there was still no doubt about it. The photographs were unquestionably of the same man.

He returned to the desk and reached for the telephone.

"Signor Anderson, per favore. . . . Ah, Mr. Anderson. I have some information which may be of interest. . . . No. I don't wish to give my name. Listen . . ."

He was smiling broadly when he put down the receiver. That moron, di Lasso, with his phony nobility, his silk suits and handmade shoes—for all that he was was just a pimp, with a pimp's mentality. No doubt he was, even now, congratulating himself on a bargain. The thought pleased him, and he took up once more the refrain from *Figaro.*

> You want to go dancing, my little Count?
> Let me be the one to call the tune.
> Yes. I'll be the one to call the tune.

His voice was soft at first, but, catching the lilt of the melody, it picked up as the verse proceeded. He ended, forte, in triumph.

Anderson arrived at the café at five of two. A blue suit, the caller had said, a red tie, and a white carnation in the buttonhole. There was more than a suspicion of the ludicrous about this meeting, and it made him uncomfortable. But they'd contacted a number of dealers and the man insisted on negotiating with him, personally. If he insisted on anonymity, they'd just have to go along.

What he really disliked was paying. Mercenaries were unreliable, at best. And in this case it was difficult to see how he was going to verify what he was supposed to be buying before he parted with rather a large sum of the Agency's cash. It was no consolation to him, a New Englander of Scottish descent, to recall that the Agency had, on occasion, spent much larger sums and received nothing at all in return.

He scanned the tables. No carnations. He ordered an iced tea and sat down at a corner table. He disliked waiting and was glad he had brought a magazine with him.

"Signor Anderson?"

He looked up to confront a large white flower. The suit might once have been blue. Now, threadbare and shiny from repeated dry cleaning, it hovered uncertainly between deep gray and black. The tie was maroon, red at a pinch, and covered with food stains. But the carnation was undeniable, so obviously a badge of identity he wondered why the man had not simply carried a placard.

"Yes?"

"My name is Giuseppe." Without waiting for an invitation, the old man pulled up a chair and sat down beside Anderson. "Is that iced tea you have there? A good idea in this heat. Perhaps I will join you."

They waited in silence until the waiter had brought the tea. Then the old man took an envelope from his pocket and handed it to Anderson. He leaned forward, conspiratorially close, and Anderson had to repress an impulse to back away. It was one of the things about Italy he had never managed to get used to—the habit of conducting every conversation at whispering distance.

"Is this the man?"

Anderson studied the photo. Then he consulted the one in his pocket. No question.

"Yes," he said. "This is the man. But I'll need more than this to convince me you can tell me where he is. I'm not authorized to pay out large sums just for this."

"Of course not," said the old man. "But look. This one I gave you, it's a passport photo, isn't it? Full face. Approximately four centimeters by three. Unflattering, of course. They always are."

He smiled. Anderson nodded impatiently.

"Go on."

"Well, this picture was brought to me yesterday by an old acquaintance of mine. This man, he told me, needs a passport to go with the picture. He also needs an Italian visa, stamps for Fiumicino and Kennedy. And here"—he fished in his pocket again and brought out a small green booklet with the familiar eagle crest in gold on the cover—"this is what I was able to get for him. Look at it."

Anderson did so. It seemed like a perfectly genuine U.S. passport made out in the name of Robert Thompson. The photograph was identical to the one the old man had just given him. He made a point of memorizing the serial number. It wasn't much, but it might help, and at least it was free.

"Does that convince you?"

Anderson nodded. "It convinces me that this man tried to get a new passport and that he applied to you. But I still don't know whether you can tell me where to find him."

"To be honest, I don't know where he is. But I do know this. In two hours someone will call for this passport—incidentally, that is why I need it back." The old man removed it deftly from Anderson's grasp and replaced it in his pocket. "When he does, you have only to follow him—he will be very easy to follow, believe me—and he will certainly lead you to the man you wish to find."

"Who will call for it, and where?"

"Ah." The old man leaned forward, his eyes gleaming with amusement. "That is what I think it would be correct to call the two-thousand-dollar question. Do you have the money?"

Anderson hesitated. He was about to speak when the old man continued.

"We have arrived, as always, at the question of trust. You wonder if I am reliable. Perhaps I will take the money and lie to you. How do you know if you should trust me? To this there are two answers. The first, obviously, is that you have very little choice. Without the two thousand, I shall not tell you a thing. The second is this. If you are not willing to pay, someone else is. More than one group of people, it seems, is interested in Robert Thompson."

"And this other group, have you spoken to them?"

"Not"—there was a pause—"as yet. To be frank, I expected that you would pay more."

Anderson felt in his pocket. Removing a bulky white envelope he handed it to the old man.

"When you count it," he said, "try not to make it too obvious. That carnation now . . ." He wrinkled his nose in distaste.

The old man held the envelope under the table. Opening it, he pulled up a corner of one of the banknotes. The denomination was one hundred dollars. He pulled up another at random. The wad looked about twenty thick. He put it in his pocket.

"In the matter of trust," he said, "I suppose we must both expect to make a contribution. Very well. I shall leave the passport with that waiter over there. At four, someone will come to collect it. He will be of medium height with brown wavy hair. Impeccably dressed. A silk suit, probably, and Gucci loafers. He will be driving a white Cadillac, custom-built, with an entirely unnecessary amount of chrome on the bodywork. Follow him and you should have no problem."

"Wait a minute." Anderson's voice rose. "That's not worth anything. How can you be sure he won't take it home or give it to someone else to deliver?"

"Very simple. He will deliver it in person, because he will be paid on delivery. He will wish to collect, himself, because, like me, he is apt to be careful in matters of money. He will deliver it immediately, because it is due today and because he will be in a hurry to get the money. Unlike me, he is greedy."

Anderson got up. They might end up short two thousand dollars, but those were the breaks. At least they were closer than they'd been so far. And if all else failed, he had the serial number memorized, and the name.

"Good-bye." He did not offer to shake hands, but when he got to the cash register he found he had picked up both checks. I should have left them for him, he thought; the old bastard can certainly afford it.

The old man waited until Anderson had left. Then he put the passport in an envelope, sealed it, scribbled a name on it, and beckoned to the waiter.

"Antonio," he said. "This will be collected around four o'clock by Conte Cesare di Lasso. Please give it to him, and him only. Here," he handed the waiter a five-thousand-lire note. "And would you be kind enough to fetch me my suitcase."

In the street he looked around carefully. When he was satisfied that Anderson had gone, he hailed a taxi.

"Fiumicino," he told the driver.

His flight for Lisbon left at four-thirty. By that time he would be able to verify that di Lasso had made, as agreed, the deposit to his bank. Altogether, from this one transaction, he had made four thousand seven hundred dollars. He could afford a small vacation. Besides, some parties to the transaction believed they had dealt with him on an exclusive basis. When they found out they were wrong, they were likely to resent it. For the sake of his health, it might be wiser to be out of the country for the next week or two.

CHAPTER XXVIII

The rendezvous was Clara's apartment. Di Lasso had specified three o'clock, but Wylie arrived forty minutes early. A necessary precaution, he thought, for though mercenary instincts might ensure that di Lasso would show up with the passport, they did not guarantee he would show up alone. It seemed wise to prepare for surprises.

Clara didn't seem happy to see him. She greeted him coldly, retreated promptly to the bathroom, and emerged a few minutes later dressed to go out. Her manner implied that, on her side at least, their previous encounter had been strictly business; this casual requisitioning of her apartment was an invasion of privacy—not to mention a breach of good manners. She left without saying good-bye.

As soon as she did, he reconnoitered. The windows faced onto the street, and by opening a sash and leaning out a little, he could command a good view of both approaches to the building. On the far side of the room was a door leading to the kitchen, whose one window, he discovered, opened onto an outside staircase at the back of the building —evidently the fire escape. The apartment was on the third floor, so if danger approached from the front, he would have plenty of time to depart by the rear.

Stationing himself at the front window, he lit a cigarette and settled down to wait. . . . It was fraying his nerves, all this watching and waiting; it was too passive a strategy for a temperament better suited to attack. He was getting impatient and therefore careless. The rendezvous, for instance, was just plain dumb—much too like a box. But he'd accepted it, at di Lasso's suggestion, and it was too late to change his mind. So if problems arose, he would have to improvise—just as he always did, just as he had at the frontier and on the train. The trouble was: improvisation required a lot of luck. And his supply of luck, he thought, must be nearly exhausted.

But that was not the main point. Luck or no luck, the plain fact was that improvisation would take him nowhere. It might buy time, perhaps, stave off catastrophe for another move or so, but it couldn't reverse his present hopeless drift. For, as it was now being played, the game could have only one outcome: it might take a week, or two, or only a matter of days, but it would end quite certainly in his defeat. . . . There was no way of winning: that was the point. He could only *avoid losing,* and however often he did it, he could never do more than preserve the status quo. The game would simply continue. It was hide-and-seek with no rules and no time limit—no adults to tell them playtime was over and order them in from the dark.

There *had* to be a way. There had to be *something* he could do to neutralize the CIA and send the Russians scuttling back to Moscow. . . . He could remember the message, for instance. That would certainly help. Once the CIA had it, ways could no doubt be found of informing the Russians, who would then, presumably, discontinue the chase. In any event, if the CIA could be satisfied, they would probably protect him. In certain circumstances—the irony rose up to torment him —there was no place he'd be safer than in the Agency compound at Langley.

The trouble was he couldn't count on remembering. The message had been gone for a week now, and it showed no sign of returning. He was beginning to fear it had gone for good.

So the solution, the way of winning, would have to be something that didn't depend on the message. That was a tall order, for without the message he couldn't imagine the Agency's *ever* being satisfied, and if they kept hunting, the Russians would, too. And in the meantime, if his luck didn't run out, his money would. He was down to six thousand dollars now—at the current rate of spending, a mere twelve or fifteen days. And after that . . .

There was no after that. The future, that normally unbounded succession of vaguely hopeful tomorrows, had dwindled for him to a couple of desperate weeks.

At this low point, just when his thoughts would go no farther, they were interrupted by the arrival, at the far end of the street, of a white Cadillac which came cruising majestically toward him. No doubt there were several white Cadillacs in Rome, but none, he guessed, were quite as spectacular as this. It was unquestionably di Lasso—well ahead of schedule.

His early arrival bothered Wylie. But when the Cadillac pulled into a parking space, just below the window, it yielded up only di Lasso, and he, Wylie noted, was careful to lock up. Evidently he had come alone. Nevertheless, Wylie remained at the window.

He was thankful he did. For when he looked back up the street another vehicle was heading toward him—a Buick, this time, and traveling at speed. It slammed to a halt alongside the Cadillac, and almost before it stopped moving the driver was out and sprinting into the building.

In Lermontov's exasperated view of it, the situation was becoming a farce. No less than six cars, by his reckoning, had followed the white Cadillac into the traffic snarling down the Corso Trieste . . . and only three of them were his. The other three—monstrosities of some American make or other—belonged, obviously, to the CIA. The passport dealer had sold them *all* down the river. So the tailing of di Lasso, planned originally as a careful stalk, had turned instead into a crazy procession: all of them strung out behind the Cadillac like ducklings scrambling after a mother duck.

In a sense it was lucky, he thought, that his own people had started behind. There was still a chance that they had not been spotted. Indeed, the Americans had been so intent upon their quarry that they could easily have neglected the elementary precaution of looking around. In another sense, however, starting behind could turn out to be disastrous, for despite a cleverly contrived traffic accident in the Viale XX Settembre that had left two American vehicles *hors de combat,* it was a Buick that stood double-parked beside the Cadillac in the street up ahead of him—not one of his own VWs. He had started behind, and unless he did something about it rather quickly, he would also finish behind.

Di Lasso and the driver of the Buick had disappeared, presumably into the building the Cadillac was parked outside. . . . But where in the building? And what to do about the man who was waiting in the Buick?

He could wait, of course, hope to jump them as they came out of the building. A single well-placed bullet would put an end to Wylie. But beyond the risk involved in a public assassination, there was another, more powerful objection to the strategy: he couldn't afford to wait; he couldn't afford to give them time to talk to Wylie. For if he did, they might recover the message.

There was really no choice, he reflected; he would have to go in after them.

Once out on the fire escape, with the window shut firmly behind him, Wylie took time to look around. The staircase, a rickety spiral in wrought iron, descended into a courtyard whose only exit was a narrow alley that led out, presumably, into the street. It was a relief to find the courtyard deserted: he would be in the alley, he figured, before di Lasso —or his pursuer—set foot in the apartment, no one would know he'd been there. . . . He regretted the passport, of course, the thousand dollars he was turning his back on. But the passport might turn out to be recoverable. Other losses might not.

He started down the staircase.

He had taken no more than a step or two when his eye was caught by movement—a flash of color—below him. A Volkswagen was backing into the courtyard.

By now caution was instinct with him. Ducking down, he edged back against the wall, keeping the body of the staircase between him and the car, which had stopped almost immediately below. With luck he could hope to stay hidden—at least until the Volkswagen had made its intentions clear.

They became clear at once. Through a gap in the ironwork he saw the doors open and two men emerge. They were wearing raincoats. . . . Raincoats? he asked himself. In this heat? . . . and they kept their hands in their pockets. After a quick glance around, they settled themselves comfortably against the side of the car facing the fire escape.

They were planning to wait. But for whom? . . . That question was easily answered. The courtyard, he saw, served no other purpose than to house the fire escapes. They were waiting for someone to make an unconventional exit.

And that meant, of course, they were waiting for him.

Il Conte was halfway up the second flight of stairs when a door slammed in the hallway and footsteps, running, sounded on the stairway below. Children, he thought benevolently, their whole lifetime ahead of them but always in a hurry. He proceeded, untroubled, up the stairs.

Only when he was outside Clara's apartment and the footsteps were almost upon him did he spare them further thought, and even then his main concern was to avoid being trampled. He stepped to one side, half turning toward the onrusher, and with a graceful, deferential gesture, yielded the right of way.

As he did, he caught sight of the gun.

Kneecapping . . . That first, panicked reaction was followed by another, equally chilling . . . police. Plainclothes police. But the man confronting him seemed neither terrorist nor policeman. He looked foreign, Il Conte thought, probably American—tall, fair, crew-cut, barbarously tailored.

"Don't move."

Definitely American. An American gangster? . . . What the devil would an American gangster be doing in the Trastavere?

"I have no intention of moving." Il Conte reached into his inside pocket and produced his notecase. How fortunate, he thought, that this had happened *before* his transaction with Wylie.

"I have very little money," he apologized, extracting a sheaf of bills and pushing them at the American. "But you are welcome, obviously, to what I have. . . . May I perhaps keep the notecase?"

"Put that away!" The man sounded affronted. "And let's get moving."

Il Conte complied with the first instruction. His alarm had subsided into curiosity by now. This was confusing, he thought: first an order to stop, now an order to do the opposite.

"Where?" he inquired.

"In there." The man jerked the gun in the direction of the apartment. "Open it up."

Il Conte did so and then stepped aside once more. He wondered if the man would go through the door shoulder first, the way they did in the movies, but a movement of the gun prompted him to take the lead. He was always respectful where guns were concerned.

They made a silent tour of the apartment, Il Conte always in the lead. This had something to do with the other American, he thought—but what, exactly?

"Who are you?" he asked. "And who are you looking for?"

"Burrows. CIA," was the reply. "I'm after the man you came to meet."

"The man?" Il Conte feigned surprise. "You're mistaken. I came here to see a woman. And not"—he smiled—"for any purpose that would concern the CIA."

"Turn out your pockets." Burrows eyed him coldly.

"What?"

"Turn out your pockets." For emphasis Burrows leveled the gun at Il Conte's stomach. "Turn them out, one at a time, and dump the stuff on the floor. Move very slowly."

Il Conte turned out his pockets. He doubted the man would shoot him if he didn't, but there was no point in taking chances. He did, however, decide to risk overlooking the right hand jacket pocket. If he made enough of a production out of the others, Burrows might not notice the omission.

"The right hand coat pocket."

Il Conte slapped the pocket.

"See," he said. "It's flat. There's nothing in it."

"Turn it out," Burrows repeated patiently. "And drop the passport on the floor."

Shit, Il Conte thought. That bastard Claudio. No wonder it had been so easy to make a deal.

Motioning him back, but keeping the gun always on him, Burrows kneeled down and retrieved the passport. Flicking it open, he held it out so Il Conte could see the photo.

"Where is he?"

Il Conte was silent.

"This passport is stolen," Burrows said. "It was stolen from our Embassy here two months ago."

Claudio again. All that smooth talk about perfect blanks and active serial numbers. The next time he saw Claudio, Il Conte promised himself, he'd tattoo a serial number on the bastard's foreskin.

"I found it on the street," he shrugged.

"You bought it," Burrows said flatly. "So you can take your choice. . . . You can tell me where and when you are meeting this man, or you can tell the police how you came by this passport. . . . Forgery," he added. "Conspiracy to contravene the immigration laws. Receiving stolen property. Three years, at a guess. Longer, if you already have a record."

It was not a decision that cost Il Conte much thought. He'd made three hundred on the passport already, and the other thousand was gone, either way.

He consulted his watch.

"He'll be here in about twenty minutes," he said.

"Smart," Burrows nodded approvingly. "So we'll wait. If he shows up we'll forget about the passport."

Il Conte smiled.

"He'll show up. . . . In the meantime, perhaps, you could put away the gun? It makes me nervous to have it pointing at my stomach. . . ."

But Burrows wasn't listening, he noticed, wasn't even looking at him any longer. The CIA man was sniffing at the air like a pointer. Then he was staring toward one of the windows.

Il Conte followed his gaze.

An ashtray had been left on the window ledge, and from it, rising in a thread that twisted as it rose and came apart finally in a thousand airy filaments, there issued smoke.

"Someone's been here." Burrows turned to him, accusing.

"Probably Clara." Il Conte shrugged. "She went out, perhaps, and left it burning."

Burrows crossed over to the window and stood examining the ash-tray.

"No," he said. "The other stubs are covered with lipstick. But not this one. . . . A man smoked this. And he didn't leave by the front. We'd have met him on the stairs. . . . Where's the back entrance?"

"The kitchen window . . . he must have used the fire escape."

"Stay here," Burrows ordered. "And don't try anything. Don't forget I still have the passport."

It was then the doorbell sounded.

CHAPTER XXIX

Lermontov considered. The two other apartments had contained only mystified housewives; it had to be this one. But though, approaching the door, he'd seemed to hear the murmur of voices inside, now there was only silence.

What to do? He could retreat downstairs and return with reinforcements, but that was open to the same objection as waiting in the street: it would give them too much time. And too many minutes had already been wasted getting rid of the man in the Buick and ringing doorbells. . . . What, then? Shoot off the lock and burst in, hoping, while they were still off balance, to get in the shot that would silence Wylie? There was an element of the suicidal in that. He'd hoped to come out of this with a whole skin—not that his skin would stay whole very long if he didn't also come out with Wylie. But perhaps Wylie wasn't there. Perhaps he had left by the back. Perhaps they had all left by the back. Perhaps . . .

The hell with perhaps. All this perhapsing was just wasting time. The thing had to be done. And since he was the man on the spot, he would have to do it. His job and his country demanded it. Pride demanded it.

Withdrawing the Makarov from his pocket, he took a step back. He would wait half a minute to make them think he had gone. Then, as soon as he'd fired, he would rush the door, diving to the right as soon as he was through it. Though ringing the doorbell had certainly alerted them, surprise—one or two seconds of it—would still be with him. He would get his shot off, he resolved, before they got off theirs.

He waited, focusing himself, clearing his mind of the doubts that might cause him to hesitate. He wanted to be relaxed yet totally committed, to achieve that state of mental blankness where thought is supplanted by will.

So when the door burst open and Burrows erupted from it, it was Lermontov who was taken off guard. He had no time to think, far less to move. The butt of Burrows' automatic crashed down on his head; his knees gave. He folded up like a collapsible chair.

Burrows retrieved the Makarov and stood over the inert body. The chest was rising and falling evenly. The man wasn't dead, which was good; but he wouldn't be moving for a while, which was even better.

"Drag him inside." Burrows turned to Il Conte who now appeared in the doorway.

"Who is he?"

"Russian, I guess," Burrows shrugged. "I didn't have time to stop and ask. . . . Drag him inside and let's find out."

Il Conte obliged. His respect for Burrows, high to begin with, had increased very considerably in the past half-minute. The man was a lunatic, perhaps, but a dangerous and very competent lunatic. He would need careful handling, this Mr. Burrows.

"Tell me," he asked, conversationally, "how did you know it wasn't the milkman? . . . I realize you looked through the peephole, but still, you *could* have been making a mistake."

"He didn't have any milk." Burrows permitted himself a moment of smugness. "And when he stepped back I saw the gun. . . . Know any milkmen who carry guns?"

"You could have let him come in."

"I could." Burrows nodded curtly. "But I didn't choose to. . . . Initiative," he added, "I like to keep the initiative."

This was a sentiment with which Il Conte could agree wholeheartedly. He'd have liked the initiative himself, for Wylie was gone, obviously, and Burrows still had the gun . . . and the passport. So Il Conte's future rested, to an extent that disturbed him, on the goodwill of Mr. Burrows. He was looking for ways to give it a surer foundation.

"Tie him up," Burrows said.

"With pleasure." Il Conte spread his hands in a gesture of helplessness. "But I appear to have come out without any rope."

Burrows thought.

"Nylons," he said at last. "Your girlfriend . . . she must keep nylons around here somewhere."

Really, Il Conte marveled, the man was infinitely resourceful. . . .

He crossed over to the dresser that stood between the two front windows and started to rummage through the drawers.

The first drawer contained cosmetics: an unbelievable litter of tubes, jars, and bottles. The second was filled with a jumble of underwear—most of it dirty, he suspected. No nylons were visible on top, but perhaps there were some underneath. Reluctantly, he began to pick through the muddle. . . . What a slut the girl was, really.

When his hand first encountered it he was simply curious. Something solid, something heavy, something that when moved went clunk softly against the side of the drawer. A bottle, probably, displaced from the drawer above. But when, exploring further, his fingers touched wood and metal, closed around a shape that perfectly fitted his hand, he revised this opinion and retracted, mentally, all the ill he had ever spoken or thought about Clara. She was a princess, an angel, a pearl among women.

He glanced around.

Burrows was squatting beside the Russian, ferreting through the man's pockets. The automatic lay at his feet. He looked up and caught Il Conte's glance.

"What's taking so long?" He frowned, irritably, and returned his attention to the pockets.

Il Conte wheeled, leveled the pistol.

"Look what I found," he said.

"Don't be a fool." Burrows didn't move. "Don't mess with me. You'll only regret it."

"Stand up."

Burrows stood.

"Kick the gun over here."

Burrows did.

"Think about it," Burrows warned. "Remember who you're dealing with. The CIA . . . not your usual troupe of clowns."

"Screw the CIA."

This was bravado. He might have the advantage for now, but could he keep it? Burrows was clearly an expert in violence; *he* was not. Neither was he sure he would be able to pull the trigger if Burrows did decide to resist. He was not even sure the pistol was loaded. And in the meantime the Russian would probably wake up . . . all of which facts, he suspected, would shortly occur to Burrows—if they hadn't already.

"Turn around and face the wall. Stand with your legs apart and put your hands on your head."

Burrows shook his head in disbelief. Which movie did you get *that* from? his look said. . . . He hesitated perceptibly before obeying.

But Il Conte knew exactly what he was doing: he disliked fighting, and he disliked guns, disliked any activity, in fact, that might spoil his suit or muss up his hair, but there was one technique the rivalries of his profession had forced him to master. He stepped smartly forward and, before Burrows could take any more time to think, kicked him hard in the genitals.

Burrows ceased, temporarily, to be a problem. He half stunned himself, anyway, hitting his head against the wall when he doubled up. A couple of taps from Il Conte's pistol—the first rather tentative, the second more businesslike—were enough to complete the process.

Il Conte recovered the passport and at once felt better about his predicament. "No corpus delicti; no crime"—he remembered reading that somewhere—so one of his problems was solved. But there were others. . . . No doubt these two thugs had left henchmen downstairs. How the devil was he to get clear of this mess?

A glance out at the street confirmed his fears. There was a Buick double-parked beside the Cadillac, and a VW immediately behind it. If they had discovered the fire escape, he was trapped. Without much optimism, he went to investigate.

He took care raising the sash window. If there were watchers down there, he mustn't alert them; curiosity might bring them up. So he couldn't afford any squeaks. He eased the sash up centimeter by centimeter, and only when it was fully open did he venture, very gingerly, to take a look.

He was interested in the courtyard. But his gaze never got that far. For immediately below, crouched down on the staircase and huddled back against the wall, was the last man on earth he expected to see.

Wylie.

Wylie, chalk-faced and startled, his look of relief turning instantly to warning; an index finger on his lips, and the other, in urgent stabbing motions, pointing downwards.

Lermontov awoke to a world gone crazy. His head felt three or four times its normal size; the pulse in his ear beat like a kettle drum; there was blood in his hair and all over his forehead, and a large craterlike indentation—unbelievably tender—in his scalp. But all that, after a moment or two of recollection, made sense. What didn't was that he found himself lying in an empty bathtub and that on the floor next to it, trussed up with nylon stockings and gagged with what looked like a pair of women's panties, was a man he had no memory of having seen before.

He himself was not bound—another mystery—so he levered himself out of the bathtub and staggered over to the door. It was locked. He gave the handle a couple of impotent rattles and retreated, baffled, to sit on the edge of the bathtub. There was no sound from the other side of the door.

The man at his feet was not Wylie; he was therefore presumably, an American—a CIA agent on the same mission, roughly, as Lermontov himself. The situation struck Lermontov as faintly ludicrous: two intelligence officers, a Russian and an American, beaten half-senseless and imprisoned in a bathroom. It could stand as a microcosm of the Cold War.

But jokes aside, he had to get out of this bathroom. No doubt his men would rescue him before long, but he preferred to avoid that indignity. The only alternative to the door, however, was a small skylight. It was out of reach. And besides, he decided, there wasn't much point in escaping to the roof. . . . It would have to be the door. It looked flimsy enough. A couple of charges should be enough to tear it off its hinges. He didn't relish the prospect, however. His head was threatening to burst already; it didn't seem wise to give it further provocation. Nevertheless, he prepared for the assault.

Once again he was spared the necessity. A key scraped in the lock, the handle turned, the door swung gently open to reveal di Lasso, gun in hand and looking apprehensive. He signed to Lermontov to come out.

Mystified, Lermontov did so. He was eager for explanations, but communication was going to be a problem. His Italian was almost nonexistent. So, he assumed, was di Lasso's Russian. He groped around for some phrases of English, but finding none adequate, settled, instead, for a name.

"Wylie?" he asked.

Di Lasso didn't seem to understand.

Poor pronunciation, Lermontov decided. He tried again.

He was greeted this time by the dawn of comprehension.

"Aaaah . . . Ouailee . . ." The rest of the speech was made in body language, but the meaning was unambiguous: di Lasso didn't know . . . he didn't care.

Then Lermontov was treated to the biggest surprise in a day already overfull of surprises. Keeping Lermontov covered, di Lasso retreated to the front door, opened it, stepped back, and with a peremptory gesture, gave the Russian his dismissal, accompanying the move with a simple word of English.

"Go!" he said.

* * *

The explanations given to Lermontov's startled associates when he got downstairs were noticeably laconic. He'd been jumped by the American, he said, and rescued by the Italian. Wylie had been nowhere to be seen. Obviously he'd been alerted somehow and had made his getaway in time. They had missed their chance at him and would have to think again. Probably he would not try again to make contact with di Lasso, and if he did, it would not be here or soon. In the meantime, Lermontov said, more Americans might show up, and his head hurt. There was not much point in sticking around.

CHAPTER XXX

"You were right," Il Conte said. "They've gone."

"I figured they would." Wylie nodded. "The one we released will have assumed I got wind of them and bolted. He'll have told the others. . . . Why would they bother to stick around now?"

"So that takes care of the Russians. . . . However"—Il Conte frowned—"the Buick is still there. We may have another American to deal with."

Wylie shook his head.

"If there *was* one, the Russians must have dealt with him. They wouldn't have risked leaving him around to get in their way."

That made sense, Il Conte thought. In any case there was no future in staying at the apartment. He had the passport back, and though the deal with Wylie was blown, obviously, he'd still made three hundred dollars in profit. Not much, certainly, but considering the alternatives offered in the past few minutes, not bad either. It was time to make an exit. For whatever else about this tangled situation might be obscure, one fact stood out. . . . This man Wylie had too many enemies. Continued association with him was potentially lethal.

"In that case," he murmured, "it's time for me to be going."

Wylie stared at him.

"What about the passport?"

This was a question Il Conte had been hoping to skip. Wylie might feel that the ethics of the situation demanded the return of his thousand dollars—a view to which Il Conte could not, in all sincerity, subscribe.

Beyond which, it was possible that Wylie might harbor some lingering resentment at the arrival of so many of his enemies, hot on Il Conte's heels.

"The passport?" Il Conte shrugged; his hand strayed casually to his coat pocket. "You still want it? . . . I doubt it will do you any good. The man I dealt with betrayed us, obviously, so both of us are faced with a loss. Naturally I regret this. And I regret also that I shan't be able to help you any further. But I prefer to retire from the passport business. The margins are unattractive, and the risks are far too great."

Keeping his eyes on Wylie, he started to edge, crabwise, toward the door.

"So I shall say good-bye," he went on, "I wish it could be 'until we meet again,' but to be honest, I hope we don't. . . . You're too dangerous to be around."

The Makarov, he noticed, was on the table. Within easy reach of Wylie. But Wylie didn't move.

"You think you can walk out—just like that?"

"Yes." Il Conte's fingers closed around the pistol in his pocket.

"It's not that easy."

"No?" Il Conte stopped. "Why not?"

"Think about it. . . . I'm dangerous to be around, you say, and you're right. I have a lot of enemies. . . . The CIA and the KGB, to be precise. The two most powerful intelligence services in the world. . . . And so far as they know, you've been helping me. At the very least, they have to see you as a link—their only link—to me. You think they'll leave you alone?" Wylie shook his head. "You're dreaming. From now on they'll be looking for you as hard as they're looking for me."

Il Conte thought.

"But I'm not helping you any longer," he objected. "So if they find me, I'll just explain everything as it happened. After that they'll leave me alone . . . they're in business, after all. In business one doesn't waste time on the irrelevant."

"Oh, of course," Wylie mocked. "You'll explain everything. . . . And they'll believe you, of course. After all, why wouldn't they? You're so obviously reliable."

Il Conte was silent.

"Go ahead," Wylie prodded. "Leave. . . . And when they pick you up—as they surely will—you can tell them you don't know where I am. And—who knows?—maybe in the end you'll even convince them.

"Of course," he added, "the meantime is likely to be rough."

Il Conte wavered. . . . Wylie had an ax to grind, of course, but there was a lot in what he was saying. If he had some suggestion to make, it would do no harm to hear it.

"You have an alternative?"

"I think so," Wylie nodded. "I think I can get you clear of this. And I think I can make it financially attractive."

"How attractive?"

"Five thousand dollars."

"Then I'm willing to listen." The reply was very prompt.

"Not here." Wylie shook his head. "We need to get out of here. . . . Do you know anywhere we can be safe for a while?"

"Certainly."

"Then let's go."

"What about the man in the bathroom?"

"Leave him for Clara."

Il Conte grinned. He had a sudden vision of Clara discovering the unfortunate Burrows—her indignation when she learned of the unorthodox uses to which her underwear had been put. He liked this man Wylie, he thought; the man had a sense of style. He also, apparently, had a lot of money.

"So there you are," Wylie said. "I'll need an apartment for three or four days—say four, to be on the safe side—and the other stuff I listed. . . . Can you get it?"

"Certainly." Il Conte nodded.

The items Wylie needed, he thought, were not readily purchased at the average hardware store, but they were always available to those with the right connections. As to the apartment . . . he had the keys to half a dozen suitable apartments right there in his pocket. This was one of the advantages of his profession; one always had somewhere to go.

"And as I said," Wylie continued, "when it's done, you're home free. Nothing more to worry about. And five thousand dollars in hand."

This last comment, in Il Conte's view, brought matters to the crux.

"About payment . . ." he began. "Since you won't be around to see the end, it seems best that we settle in advance."

"No way," Wylie grinned. "I'm out of pocket from the last time."

"You think *I* did that?" Il Conte looked hurt.

"Probably not." Wylie shrugged. "But it has certainly occurred to you that you could take the money and save yourself trouble by selling me out."

Il Conte thought of remonstrating, but decided against it. The look on Wylie's face convinced him he'd be wasting his time. And besides, Wylie was right; the thought had occurred to him. It had occurred, in fact, at the very first mention of the money.

"So how *do* I get paid?"

"Money order," Wylie said promptly. "I'll buy you one from American Express. You'll get it in advance. Only it won't be made out to you. . . . I'll buy it in her name. So you'll have to take her with you to get it cashed. And she won't go with you unless you carry through on your end of the deal. . . . That way we're both protected."

"Protected! . . ." Il Conte was scandalized. "We're both in the hands of a woman. I don't call that protection. She'll probably sell us both."

Wylie shook his head.

"Not her," he said. "You might, and so might I. But not her."

"Well"—unwillingly, Il Conte capitulated—"but it's a huge risk. . . . Are you certain she'll even show up?"

"Yes."

Wylie spoke confidently. But in fact he was far from certain. It all depended on whether he had read her right, on whether he had read *them* right. If he hadn't, he was as good as dead. . . . But if he had, then he could turn the game around.

In a way, he thought, it was the classic chess problem in reverse. He didn't know exactly when the idea had come to him. He simply knew that at some point during the hair-raising minutes he'd spent on the fire escape outside Clara's apartment, while his conscious mind was coping with the problem of staying alive for any longer than he could hold his breath, his subconscious had somehow assembled and fitted into place the elements of a solution to the larger problem. . . . Sui-mate. The king sacrifice. He'd staked five thousand on getting a pawn in place. Now he just needed a queen.

It all depended on Anne.

PART IV

CHAPTER XXXI

The noise of the telephone, drilling obstinately through the layers of sleep, nagged Anne Crossland awake. Dazed, she groped around for the receiver, upsetting, in her fumblings, the clock beside her bed. . . . One-thirty. Who the hell could be calling at that hour?

Italy, the operator informed her. If she were Anne Crossland, there was a call for her, person to person, from Rome, Italy.

Flustered, she started to protest: she was sure there was some mistake; she'd been confused with someone else; she knew nobody in Rome. But the operator was no longer on the line. A new voice answered her. It belonged to Wylie.

"Anne? . . . Listen . . ."

No word of apology, she noted. Just the complacent assumption that what she was doing—sleeping or whatever—could be dropped to accommodate his schedule. Or did he imagine, perhaps, that she lay awake nights, waiting for him to call?

"Do you have any idea what *time* it is here?"

"Yes. I'm sorry. But it's not easy for me to get to a phone. I had to be sure of reaching you."

"What do you want?"

It had better be important, her tone implied. The unfriendliness was quite deliberate. He wasn't, at that moment, one of her favorite people. In fact he was high on the list of her least favorite people, vying with Roskill for the number one spot.

"I need help."

That sounded familiar. They *all* needed help, it appeared, and they weren't at all backward about asking. When they didn't need help, of course, they left her entirely alone.

"Help?" she inquired coldly. "You've got a nerve, haven't you? After dumping me so thoroughly in Moscow? Not a word of explanation. Not even a couple of lines to say good-bye."

"I had to leave"—he sounded impatient—"I wanted to get in touch, but it wouldn't have been safe. . . . Look. I know I have no right to ask, but I'm asking anyway. There isn't anyone else."

Had to leave . . . What a lie that was. She was tempted to hang up, but curiosity held her. She'd heard Roskill's version; she wanted to hear Wylie's.

"What do you want?"

"I want you to meet me in Rome. I can't explain why. Not over the phone. I'll tell you when you get here."

The outrageousness, the sheer cheek of it, took her breath away. When she recovered, her impulse was simply to laugh.

"When I get there? . . . You must be out of your mind. Do you honestly expect me to drop everything—just like that—and chase half-way across the world simply to listen to some crazy proposal from you? You're either mad—or intolerably conceited."

As soon as she'd spoken she realized she'd said rather more than she'd meant to, that the mere fact of protesting undercut the protest. The oblique reference to their night together, at any rate, told her—if it didn't tell him—that he was still very much on her mind.

"Not mad or conceited, just desperate." In fact he sounded quite calm. "I've booked you on a ten A.M. flight tomorrow with Pan Am. The ticket's prepaid. All you have to do is be there. You can fly in, listen, and if you decide not to help, fly out again. I'm asking for a couple of days, that's all—three at the most."

It might help if you asked for a little bit more, she thought; if it weren't quite so baldly a matter of being of service.

"No."

Silence.

"No," she repeated. "Because, quite apart from anything else, I've been in contact with Mr. Hunter. So I know why you had to leave—as you so tactfully put it—and I know all about your little game. And I don't want any part of it—or you. . . . So please forget what happened between us in Moscow. It was just a casual encounter: fun while it lasted, but nothing serious. And it's over. . . . I'm not going to meet you—in Rome or anywhere else. I'm going back to sleep."

But though her exit line had been delivered, for some reason she didn't hang up. Part of her seemed to want to prolong the conversation, wanted, perhaps, to hear him deny—at least for vanity's sake—her description of what had happened between them in Moscow. Or maybe it was simply guilt, the small twinge she always felt when forced to a point-blank refusal. Whatever it was, it was enough to keep her on the line and impel her, when his silence persisted, to continue.

"So I won't come to Rome. But I will give you some advice. . . . If I were you, I'd jump in a cab and hurry on over to the American Embassy. Because, according to Mr. Hunter, some people from Moscow are trying to get hold of you. . . . I imagine you know who I mean?"

This did get a response.

"Yes," he said. "I've already run across them."

Already run across them . . . In spite of the casual phrasing, there was something in his tone of voice—a sort of calm hopelessness—that told her he wasn't lying. Her anger died. She was afraid for him, suddenly, and the rush of fear was stilled hardly at all by the ensuing realization that, since he was calling, he'd survived the encounter. . . . For if he was still out there, so presumably were they.

"Already run across them? . . . Then are you . . . all right?"

"I am so far. I managed to fend them off."

"Then for God's sake!" she burst out. "You *have* to go to Hunter."

"I can't."

"Why not?"

"I can't explain now. Let's just say that if I did, it would be as bad as the alternative."

"But your life is in danger. Don't you understand? Those people are trying to kill you."

"Yes," he said. "I understand perfectly. They made their intentions very clear. . . . But I don't think *you* need worry. They're not after you. They won't harm you, because if it ever comes down to that, I won't let it happen."

You won't let it happen. . . . Sure, she thought sardonically, but if it ever came down to that, just how, exactly, would you stop them? . . . But again there had been something in the quality of his voice that cut through the skepticism and reached her. She knew what he meant, at any rate, and though the knowledge did little to reassure her, she gave him credit for good intentions: no harm would come to her, he was saying, because if it came right down to it, he would give himself up. . . . She more or less believed him; she believed, at least, that he believed himself. But that, unfortunately, was not nearly enough.

"Look," she said. "I can't. I just can't. I don't want to get involved. . . . The truth is I'm scared. I was scared in Moscow, and I'm still scared. . . . Go to Hunter. Please. Hunter won't kill you, but the others will. . . . I don't want you to be killed."

"I can't go to Hunter," he said patiently. "If you can't help me, you can't. I can understand your reasons, and I accept them. As I said, I have no right to ask. . . . The ticket's bought, however, so if you change your mind, it'll be there for you at Kennedy, at the Pan Am counter. I've booked you into the Grand. I'll call you there tomorrow."

"No," she said. "I'm sorry. But no."

She did hang up then. But for a long time she couldn't sleep. The trouble he was in—if Roskill could be believed—was of his own making, but the knowledge did little to relieve her sense of guilt. And when she did drift off, finally, her dreams were peopled with men from Moscow.

So when she awoke, earlier than usual, to greet the tarnished glory of sunrise over Manhattan, she was depressed and grouchy—in no good mood to deal with whoever was leaning on her doorbell. . . . And in no mood at all to deal with Roskill.

It seemed to her that she had never been so angry. Had she possessed a gun, she thought, she'd have pointed it between his eyes and pulled the trigger, savoring particularly the moment, just before she fired, when his complacency turned into shock and panic. But of course she had no gun, no weapon of any kind; nothing but words to meet him with. And words, she knew, had lost their power to reach him. She was helpless— he could do what he liked and nothing could touch him—and it was the helplessness that chiefly fueled her anger. It was like trying to deal with the phone company, she thought, or with the IRS: you weren't confronting a real person, simply the embodiment of function; instead of human reactions you met with statements of policy.

"You can just sit there"—she stared at him with hatred—"and calmly tell me that for the past week you've been listening in on my phone calls?"

"It's all above board." Roskill met the stare without blinking. "We okayed it first with Justice. There *is* an issue of national security involved. And of course, only the tape of Wylie's call was kept; the others have been destroyed. We don't pry more than we have to. And we don't —believe me—enjoy doing that."

"Don't enjoy it? . . . You never do, do you? But somehow you always manage to overcome your reluctance. How awful for you to have to do so much you don't enjoy."

"I can live with it." The shrug was audible.

"And, of course, you couldn't risk trusting me to tell you. . . . I said I would, but that wasn't good enough, was it? You had to lie your way into my house, accept my hospitality, and when my back was turned plant your loathsome bugs."

"Trust." He stared. "We're not very good at it. I told you that before."

She said nothing. But the look on her face spoke for her. Of all the bugs in her acquaintance, it implied, he was the most loathsome.

"But none of this is to the point," he continued. "The point is: will you go?"

"You heard the phone call. Or at least you read the transcript. The answer I gave *him* was unambiguous, I thought."

"Then I'd like you to reconsider."

"You'd *like* . . . Who cares what you'd like. The answer is no."

"I'm not asking for me, you know." His voice was low-key, reasonable. "I'm really asking for him. . . . Look. You said it yourself: they're going to kill him. They've tried twice already, to my knowledge, and each time they damn near succeeded. Next time, or the one after, they'll get lucky. . . . Do you want him to be killed?"

"Should I care?"

"I don't believe that," he said. "And neither do you."

She didn't reply.

"Then is it that you're scared?"

"Of course," she looked at him defiantly, "of course I'm scared."

"Well, I don't think you need be. I think he was right about that. . . . After all, they let you out of Russia, didn't they? And they'd hardly have done that if they'd thought you were involved. . . . They *know* you weren't—don't you see?—because when Wylie made the contact you were a thousand miles away in Georgia. And before you came back he'd left. . . . And besides," he added, "we'll be there, too. We'll have people around you all the time. We won't let you out of our sight for a minute."

"How reassuring . . . a cortège of goons dogging my every footstep. Guards on my door at night. Someone in the next bed, no doubt, watching over my dreams."

"So you see"—he was impervious to sarcasm—"there's nothing to worry about."

She changed tack. "No reason to worry about me, perhaps. But what about him?"

"But that's just the point, isn't it? . . . He'll contact you; you'll lead us to him. Then there won't be any need to worry about him. He'll be safe."

"Funny *he* doesn't seem to see it that way. . . . He knows the Russians are after him. He knows they'll kill him if they catch him. Yet he still won't come to you. In fact—you can check this in the transcript—he doesn't think he'll be any better off."

"Oh, Jesus." He sounded disgusted. "You don't really swallow that crap? You don't seriously believe he's in any danger from us?"

"I don't know what to believe." She looked at him steadily. "Right now I don't think I believe him or you."

And certainly not *you,* she thought, because there isn't much you wouldn't do to get what you want. And nothing you wouldn't say. And you'd do it, or say it, without a moment of regret. . . . And that's what galls me most, she thought; I'd give almost anything to cause you a little regret.

"The radical press . . ." he sighed. "All that garbage about torture and assassination and experiments on unsuspecting citizens with psychedelic drugs. It's ninety-five percent pure fiction, and the rest of it so twisted you could never untangle the truth. But what can we do? . . . If we deny it, we just give it currency. So we can only shut up and hope that the adults of this world, the people with the guts and the smarts to do their own thinking, will know it for what it is.

"I'd hoped you might be one of those," he continued. "Because if you aren't, I think Arden Wylie is going to die. . . . And please don't kid yourself that when he does it'll be a simple bullet in the head. It won't. . . . They're going to need to find out, don't you see? They're going to want to know what he knows and whom he's told. And they won't just take his word for it; they'll sweat it out of him drop by drop. They'll put him through hell until they're certain they've got it all. And even then they won't kill him. There'll be the usual show trial, the usual abject public confession, the whole thing dragged out until the last shred of dignity is stripped away from him, the last whimper of remorse extracted. So the bullet in the head—when it comes—is going to seem like a mercy."

He paused then to let his words sink in, his gaze pressing on her until at last she was forced to meet it.

"It's your choice," he said. "I can't force you to do anything. I just want to be sure that when you choose, you understand, fully, what you're choosing."

For a long time she said nothing. But the struggle showed in her eyes. When she lowered them, finally, it was in capitulation.

"You bastard," she whispered. "You total bastard."

CHAPTER XXXII

∎

Pogrebin was bored. Lermontov was punishing him, for "errors of judgment" in Switzerland, with airport duty—a menial form of surveillance that consisted chiefly in padding around the terminal at Fiumicino, trying to look inconspicuous. It was a chore, in Pogrebin's opinion, ill-suited to his talents and all the more tiresome for being, also, pointless. The business with the passport had certainly alerted Wylie; the man would have to be a moron—and he obviously wasn't—to risk the airport after *that*. But Lermontov had insisted. Wylie, he said, had an undeniable talent for doing the unexpected; it would be just like him to try sauntering out, right under their noses, by just the exit they now assumed was barred.

So Pogrebin had been at Fiumicino since ten. And he would stay there until Lermontov remembered to relieve him. But all things considered, he wasn't inclined to blame Lermontov; for though the tribulations he had suffered on being discovered, trouserless, in a lavatory on the Geneva–Schwyz express were punishment enough, in his opinion, for any errors of judgment he might have committed, airport duty was still a lot better than a number of alternatives he could imagine. Lermontov was a reasonable man and, within the limitations of his profession, a humane one. Pogrebin had, therefore, resolved to deserve the consideration shown him and stay awake.

It was hard. After three hours of lounging behind a newspaper, scanning the crowds that hurried through the lobby for a face he knew perfectly well was not going to appear, a certain hopelessness descended.

The faces blurred, merged into one another, formed into an image which, like the composite portraits of wanted criminals put out by the police, bore not much resemblance to anybody. It was difficult, not to say exhausting, to cast his eyes, impartially, for hours on end over a constant flux of humanity; he could only keep going by cheating somewhat, by picking out an individual and giving fantasy a little play.

He concentrated, though his task dictated otherwise, on women—attractive women. An individual, detaching herself from the throng, would capture his attention. He would follow her with his gaze, speculating, from the walk, from the curve of the lips or the tilt of the chin, about how good she'd be in bed. Sometimes, under provocation, his imagination would get more specific and he would recreate in his mind's eye the satin texture of an inner thigh or the precise undulation of a hip. All of which, he occasionally realized, might help him get through the day but didn't do much to make the process less frustrating.

All the same, it paid off. At one-forty exactly—his glances at the clock were very frequent—his interest was aroused by a woman in her late twenties or early thirties whose style of dress he took to be American and whose qualifications for his attention were in other respects perfect. She was accompanied, he noticed with a twinge of inexplicable regret, by a middle-aged man in business gray whose company she didn't entirely seem to welcome. She walked a little ahead of him, head rather in the air, at a brisk pace that suggested that he might keep up, if he could, but she wouldn't much mind if he didn't. But though her attractions were undeniable and her situation intriguing, it wasn't these, after the first glance, that held him. . . . He had seen her, or her picture, before. In fact he had seen her recently.

In another moment he recalled exactly where. It had been on Lermontov's desk in Moscow. In a file requisitioned from Intourist. She was Anne Crossland. Wylie's girlfriend from Moscow.

Lermontov, he now recalled, had been inclined to dismiss her. She and Wylie had had a one-night stand apparently, but before Wylie's contact with Ivkov. When the contact had occurred she'd been in Georgia, only returning to Moscow several days after Wylie's departure. Despite her inquiries about Wylie and her own premature departure when she learned that he had gone, Lermontov believed she was not involved —at least not more than romantically—with Wylie. In any case, by the time Ivkov's treachery had been discovered, she was in New York, beyond their normal reach; they'd concentrated on locating Wylie. Now, however, she was in Rome.

She was in Rome. Wylie was in Rome. One didn't have to be much of a mathematician, Pogrebin decided, to make *that* add up.

Unfortunately, he didn't have much time to decide what to do. She swept on past him to the exit and the waiting rank of taxis, her companion almost trotting to keep up. Pogrebin knew he should follow—his instructions to remain at his post until relieved were obviously superseded by developments like this—but following in one car in Rome traffic was a low-percentage proposition; he would lose them in a snarl-up somewhere and earn nothing for his pains but further censure. It was the curse of his two-edged luck, he thought, to be granted, on one hand, such a splendid opportunity and denied, on the other, the means to take advantage of it.

This time, however, he was mistaken. Having chosen, at the risk of revealing himself, the only course that to him made any sense—parking himself directly behind them in the line for taxis—he was rewarded by hearing her give, in crystal tones, instructions to the driver.

"The Grand?"

Pogrebin nodded. "Corso Vittorio Emmanuele Second."

"Describe *him*," Lermontov said.

"About fifty. Lanky. Height, about five feet eleven. Wispy reddish hair. Gray suit, white shirt, dark tie—the usual uniform . . . Odd face, though. Not boyish, quite, or even young-looking. But somehow . . . immature. Middle-aged but immature, if you know what I mean."

"American face," Lermontov nodded. "They don't like to get old, so they never grow up. . . . They were definitely together?"

"No question. Same taxi; same hotel. . . . Not the same room though. He's in one-fifty; she's in one-fifty-two. I don't think it's a question of *that*. She didn't seem very pleased to be with him."

"Not room . . . suite," Lermontov corrected, without thinking. "They don't have *rooms* at places like that. Only at our kind of hotel."

He cast a sour glance at his surroundings. His operational headquarters were at a good remove, in luxury, from the Grand. There were no fresh flowers or marble bathtubs on the top floor, rear, of the Soviet Embassy; in the attics they'd given him there were not even windows.

"You've checked on him, of course?" he asked sharply.

"He's registered as Hunter. Profession, business executive—what else? I sent a cable to Archives, but he's not in the Rogues' Gallery—not under that name, anyway. . . . Archives did say, however, that the description tallied with what they know of a Robert Roskill. He was Chief of Station in Rome at one time, apparently. Now he's a desk man at Langley. Very senior. In fact . . . Archives has him listed as the head of a section of Operations. The Soviet and East European Section, to be precise."

Lermontov studied him for a moment.

"So you think that Mr. Roskill, head of the Soviet Section of CIA Operations, is in Rome with Wylie's girlfriend, on some business connected with Wylie?"

"Yes," Pogrebin said firmly.

"So do I," Lermontov grunted.

He lit a cigarette and for a while he sat puffing at it, his eyes hooded and far away.

"There doesn't seem to be any muscle around," Pogrebin ventured. "We could pick them up, if you wanted."

Lermontov frowned.

"You like it, that picking them up business. You like it, don't you?" Pogrebin said nothing.

"So go ahead," Lermontov growled. "Pick them up. . . . And then what will you do?"

Pogrebin looked blank.

"Well?"

Pogrebin thought.

"I see," he said.

"Good," Lermontov said. "What do you see?"

"We *don't* pick them up. . . . At least, not yet. Because she doesn't know where he is. If she did they wouldn't be sitting around in a hotel, would they? She must be waiting for Wylie to make contact. And that means we wait, too."

"Good," Lermontov nodded. "Now get out of here and start rounding up people. . . . I want everybody. The people at the hotel should stay, of course, but I want everybody else."

Pogrebin turned to leave.

"Grigori Petrovich . . ." Lermontov's voice stopped him. "You ignored your instructions again, didn't you? . . . You were supposed to remain at the airport, not mess around here, sending cables to Moscow."

Reluctantly Pogrebin nodded.

"You did well." Lermontov's smile flowered suddenly. "Thank God someone around here has the balls to do it occasionally."

"I haven't seen any sign of your goons," Anne said.

Roskill looked up from his paper and peered at her over the tops of his reading glasses.

"Good," he replied. "I'd worry if you had."

He went back to his reading.

"Are there any?"

"Oh, yes . . ." He looked up again and smiled. "The wait getting to you?"

She nodded.

She'd once seen a movie, she recalled, in which Hell was imagined as the experience of being stuck forever in a shabby hotel room, surrounded by people one thoroughly detested. At the time, this conception had struck her as contrived and unconvincing; now she was willing to grant it some force. Not that her suite in the Grand could be described as "shabby" nor Roskill as "people," but the principle was the same. Her only quarrel with the movie now was over the omission of a detail. To make the experience complete, she believed, one also had to be waiting for a phone call.

Added to the intrinsic tedium, there was, in her case, also guilt. Roskill's presence was a disturbing reminder that Wylie considered him as bad as the alternative. Nor had it helped that he'd gone off, shortly after their arrival, to do, as he put it, "a spot of phoning," returning later with the air of a cat that has just caught a bird. She could keep telling herself that she was here to deliver Wylie from the hands of the Russians, but that didn't stop her wondering, with an anxiety that lurched occasionally into outright panic, exactly what she was delivering him *into*. . . . "We want to talk to him" was all that Roskill would say on that score. But given the lengths they'd been willing to go to to arrange the conversation, she doubted, if the conversation proved unsatisfactory, that they'd be willing to leave it at that.

"You do understand that I'll be going with you?" Her question contained more than a hint of challenge.

"You will? . . . Why?"

To be there, she felt like saying, to make damn sure that all you do is talk. . . . But instead of saying it, she just looked at him.

He studied her thoughtfully.

"I think I should tell you," he said at last, "that there's a good possibility we were spotted at the airport. There was a man behind us in the line for taxis, apparently, but when we went off, he didn't get into a taxi. Instead he raced off in search of a phone. . . . What I'm saying is this could be rather hazardous."

Sure, she thought; and what you're saying could also be pure fabrication, to rid yourself of a potentially troublesome witness.

"I'm still going," she said flatly. "If it's safe enough for you, I'm sure it's safe enough for me. . . . And just to make sure you don't ditch me at the last moment: you don't get the address until I'm in the car."

As soon as she said it, she felt foolish; no doubt they could cope very smoothly with any small problems she might be able to cause.

Roskill, however, just nodded wearily.

"Very well. . . . If that's what you want."

Then the phone rang.

"It's for you," Roskill said.

CHAPTER XXXIII

You could say this for Roskill, Anne thought, he was certainly organized. One quick phone call, and within minutes his forces were mustered. The handholding detail consisted of two young men, barely out of college, she guessed, wearing junior executive outfits and an intent, on-duty expression on their faces. It was the sort of look she associated with Marines on parade: concentration, but in the abstract; a kind of high-beam stare directed at nothing in particular.

Roskill introduced them as Kendrick and Malone. They turned their stares on her briefly, nodded, murmured "ma'am," and lost interest. They had eyes, it seemed, for Roskill only.

"Everything set?" Roskill asked.

Kendrick nodded. "The car's downstairs."

He led the way to the elevator, she and Roskill a few paces behind. Malone brought up the rear.

They kept this formation until they reached the elevator, reforming once again to march in phalanx across the lobby. Near the entrance they paused. A third young man, wearing Polaroid sunglasses, was lounging in an armchair, reading a copy of *Time*. He glanced up as they halted, peered out over his shoulder into the street, turned back and nodded, almost imperceptibly, to Kendrick. They passed on into the street.

Roskill nudged Anne.

"Goons," he whispered, deadpan.

She wondered whether all this were staged for her benefit. Or did they, perhaps, have some other object in view? In any case there was an air of artifice about it. It was all happening, and she was part of it, but the odd sense persisted that she'd wake up presently and find it wasn't real.

This feeling that the whole scene more properly belonged in a theater increased when she saw the car they'd provided. It was a black Cadillac, at least half a block long, with CD plates, prominently displayed. Jesus, she thought, why hadn't they sent the Navy?

She headed without thinking for the back seat nearest the curb. But Kendrick forestalled her, taking her by the arm and shepherding her, instead, to the far side. The seat behind the driver, evidently, was reserved for Roskill. It seemed there was nothing impromptu about this production; even the blocking had been carefully thought out.

Malone, she noticed, had made his way up the street to another Cadillac, also black. There was a driver in this one. Malone climbed in beside him.

There was a brief, expectant silence.

Roskill turned to her, eyed her quizzically. .

"The address," he said. "I hope you haven't forgotten."

She had a sudden impulse to refuse him, to get out of the car and simply walk away. But what would that solve? They'd maneuvered her into an impossible position: damned if she did, and doubly damned if she didn't. Besides, the words, at this stage, were not much more than symbolic; she'd already betrayed Wylie when she stepped on the plane with Roskill. Nevertheless, when she spoke them, she felt like Judas.

"Thirteen, Via Ambruscati. Apartment four. . . . He said it was off something called the Piazzale Portuense."

Kendrick reached forward and took a microphone from the dashboard.

"Piazza della Repubblica," he intoned. "Then on down Nazionale toward the Venezia. Take a right around the Monument and head up the Corso. . . . And take it slow and easy, capeesh? The traffic is a bitch."

The lead Cadillac slid out into the traffic. Kendrick followed.

"Aren't we a trifle conspicuous?" Anne asked Roskill.

He gave her an odd, equivocal look: polite attention, but covering an interior smirk, as though he were savoring some private joke. Then he shrugged.

"It sometimes pays to advertise."

She couldn't make much sense of that. Did he mean perhaps that the goons and the Cadillacs were a show of force, intended to discourage interference?

"Well, shouldn't there at least be somebody behind?"

"Oh"—the same odd look—"there is."

Well, at least *he* seemed confident enough. She, however, was not. Her sense of being involved in a farce had vanished, to be replaced by a growing unease. The Cadillacs no longer struck her as ridiculous; they reminded her now of the Mafia, or a funeral.

Their progress down Nazionale was punctuated by snatches of CB dialogue between Kendrick, Malone, and other voices which belonged, she presumed, to members of their entourage.

"Got a VW behind you there. About ten cars back. Little green bug. . . . Cut into line at Esedra. . . ." A new voice, this one. Not Malone.

"Then ease on up and check him out."

"Ten four."

Silence.

"Two occupants. Both men, mid-thirties. Passenger talking a lot on the CB. . . . What do you think?"

"Try picking him up on the regular channels."

Silence.

"He's not on any of the regular channels. . . . Should I hassle him a bit?"

"Negative." This, sharply, from Kendrick. "Just keep him in view. . . . I like them where I can see them."

It was the tone, as much as the substance, that chilled her. A little too calm, a shade too deliberately laconic and laid-back, it didn't quite succeed in disguising the tension underneath.

Suddenly, she was afraid.

Sensing this, perhaps, Roskill launched into a commentary on the landmarks.

"The Victor Emmanuel Monument." He pointed at the huge pile of bronze and white marble now sliding by on their left. "A nineteenth-century attempt to recapture imperial glory. . . . The white marble comes from Brescia; it doesn't mellow like the local stone. Reminds me somewhat of a toothpaste commercial. . . . Rather tasteless, don't you think?"

She wasn't listening. Her thoughts were in the line of vehicles behind. "Is the traffic always this bad?"

"Oh, always. . . . Now this street we're about to enter is the Corso. Also named after Victor Emmanuel. If you look out to your right in a minute or two, you'll catch a glimpse of the Pantheon up a side street."

It didn't help. His effort to take her mind off the people behind them succeeded only in doing the opposite. The Cadillacs would be useless in

this traffic, she thought, totally unmaneuverable. Two large black bee-
tles swallowed up by a great writhing serpent of vehicles that moved, on
average, at not much more than a fast walk. They would never get away
at this rate. Why the hell didn't he stop yapping and *do* something?

Now a new voice was heard on the CB, cutting peremptorily to silence the others.

"Corso Victor Emmanuel . . . Navona just by on the left . . . I've
got a red light . . . moving again."

Roskill abandoned his monologue. He sat forward, scanning the
traffic ahead.

"Moving better now," the voice continued. "In about half a minute
I'll have the Pantheon on my left."

On the *left?* But Roskill had told her to look on the *right*.

"There!" Kendrick was pointing to the nearest lane of oncoming
traffic. "The white Fiat with the dent in the side."

As he spoke the Fiat slowed to a crawl. A chorus of honking broke
out behind it. Kendrick, too, slowed down. A gap of ten or fifteen yards
opened up in front and he surged forward, hitting the brakes just in
time to avoid rear-ending the vehicle ahead. Then she understood, understood everything: why the Fiat was coming *up* the Corso, why Roskill had needed to sit behind the driver.

But by then Roskill was out and running, sprinting up the middle of
the street toward the Fiat. Almost before she could move, the rear door
of the Fiat swung open and he was in it and accelerating away.

"Classic," Kendrick commented. "A classic reverse. Cutting back
against the flow. And nothing those bastards can do but sit and watch.
By the time they get out of this"—he gestured to the traffic—"he'll be
over the hills and far away."

She hardly heard him. Without thinking, she slid over to Roskill's
side of the seat and grasped the door handle.

Locked.

"Now, ma'am," he remonstrated, "you wouldn't want to do that . . .
I mean where would you go?"

He was right, of course. The Fiat was already swallowed up by the
traffic.

"Let . . . me . . . out!"

"Sorry." Kendrick kept his eyes on the street ahead. "Orders," he
added, unnecessarily.

There was no comeback to that, nothing she could do.

"Where are you taking me?"

"Where do you want to go?" He shrugged. "A tour of the sights? Drive around for an hour or so? . . . That should about do it."

About do it? . . . Of course it would. Wylie kidnapped in the meantime, dragged off to Langley, and stuck in some box while they sweated it out of him. . . . Protection, she thought hopelessly; had she really hoped to be able to protect him? How *could* she have been so stupid, so utterly naive?

"Bastard!" she burst out. "You're all just bastards."

"Now hold on, ma'am," he reproached her. "Just think a minute. You don't really want to be there. . . . We think we shook them. We sure hope we did. But if we didn't, there could be violence."

Not bad, Lermontov thought. Not bad at all. But not quite good enough, either.

That was the trouble with Americans, he reflected, they were ingenious, but blinkered by cultural assumptions: incurably automobile-minded, and convinced the rest of the world shared their obsession. But here the conviction had led them into error. For while *their* imagination might be yoked to four wheels and six cylinders, his was not. The switch on the Corso had left his VWs trapped in a line of traffic that would carry them blocks in the wrong direction, but it hadn't left him without resources. The scooters should have no problem coping.

His battle plan, like theirs, had been shaped to accommodate the Roman traffic. It would be stupid, he'd figured, to rely on cars—however many—to stay with their quarry through *that* chaos. So instead of gambling everything on direct pursuit, he'd organized reserves by sectors, one vehicle patrolling each, and coordinated them by radio. So long as the scooters stayed in touch with the target, a backup vehicle could be dispatched to deal with it as soon as it settled.

He'd placed a lot of trust in the scooters. In these conditions they were perfect for the job: able to nip in and out of the traffic like terriers herding cattle, and inconspicuous because the streets were already infested with them. But above all, he'd relied on cultural assumptions—the Americans, he'd been sure, would be looking for cars.

It was gratifying to learn that his trust had not been misplaced. The Fiat had just been reported crossing into the Trastevere. It did not seem to have spotted the scooters. At all events it had made no move to shake them.

The Via Ambruscati turned out to be a short cul-de-sac off one of the long streets that intersect the Trastevere. The house numbers ran from bottom to top, even on one side, odd on the other. Number Thirteen, Roskill saw, was the third down on the right.

He directed the Fiat's driver to park around the corner. Since Wylie might be keeping a lookout, the arrival of any vehicle other than a taxi could alarm him. Sending the second car round to the back to investigate and guard possible exits there, he left the driver in the Fiat to cover and took Burrows with him. Keeping close in to the houses on the righthand side, they started down the street.

Thirteen was a three-story apartment house. From the row of bell-pushes outside they learned it contained six apartments, two on each floor. The front door was locked, but merely with a Yale. It yielded easily to the L-shaped strip of plastic Burrows produced from his pocket.

Apartments one and two were on either side of a narrow hall that led away from the front door. At the far end was a staircase.

The entranceways to apartments three and four were side by side on the second-floor landing. Four was on the right. This door, too, was locked with a Yale. That was good. They could muscle their way in if they had to, but bystanders were always a nuisance; it was best to keep things clean.

Burrows produced his piece of plastic.

Roskill shook his head. He put a finger to his lips. From inside the apartment they could pick up snatches of music. It sounded to Roskill like a Mozart piano concerto, but whatever it was, it provided nice cover for Burrows' operation on the lock.

He nodded to Burrows.

Burrows slid the plastic in between the door and the doorjamb, easing it down to hook around the catch. Then, exerting a steady pressure, he pulled on the plastic and pushed on the door.

The door swung open. They were in a small hallway with three doors leading off it. One of them was open—it revealed an empty kitchen; the other two were shut. The music, definitely Mozart, was playing in the room on the right. Roskill motioned to Burrows to try the other one. Burrows did. It was locked.

The fact struck Roskill as slightly odd. But he didn't have time to worry about it. Fiddling around with the lock would only alert the music-lover.

He pushed open the other door and marched in.

CHAPTER XXXIV

Wylie was sunk in an armchair, so deep in it he seemed to be resting on his shoulder blades. His feet were on the table in front of him. He had evidently been reading, for a magazine lay open across his knees. A cigarette, of which little remained but a long crooked finger of ash, protruded from the corner of his mouth; the eye nearest it was screwed almost shut against the smoke. There was an ashtray perched on his stomach, but it didn't seem to have served its purpose very well; the area of T-shirt around it was speckled with ash.

He barely reacted to their entrance. The eyes flicked up to question them, but he made no other movement. Nor, until they were both in the room, did he speak.

"Who are *you?*"

"My name is Roskill," Roskill answered. "I'm with the CIA."

Wylie did nothing for a moment, then he nodded. He seemed neither surprised nor even particularly interested. He looked drained, Roskill thought, defeated—as if the effort of eluding them for so long had worn him to the point where he no longer cared. His nod had been no more than a gesture of acknowledgment that catastrophe, so long awaited, had at last made its entrance.

"So Anne sold me out." It was a statement.

Roskill nodded.

Wylie gave a wan smile. Then he shrugged.

"You don't seem very surprised," Roskill observed.

"Should I be?" The voice was weary. "Besides, you were bound to show up sometime. It was simply a question of when."

"I'd say it was more a question of who." Roskill found himself somewhat irritated by the indifference. It was bad enough to have been outmaneuvered for the better part of two weeks by this dejected, seedy-looking amateur, without also learning that the whole exercise had been pointless from the start, that the man had never expected to pull it off and didn't much care anyway.

"We could have been the KGB," he continued. "You could have been dead when we walked through the door. . . . As it is, you're coming out of it alive. I'd say you're extraordinarily lucky."

Wylie's answer to that was a faint, skeptical smile.

"But that's water over the dam," Roskill went on. "The main thing is we've found you. In time to save you from your suicidal impulses. There's a car downstairs to take you to the Embassy. You'll be safe there . . . and tomorrow we'll fly you to Langley."

"No," Wylie said.

"No?" Roskill echoed. "What the hell do you mean?"

"I mean no. Negative . . . I mean I'm properly grateful for your concern, et cetera, but I don't *want* to go to the Embassy. And I certainly don't want to go to Langley."

"You don't seem to understand." Roskill's irritation returned. "There are people out there who want to kill you. Without us to protect you, they certainly will. . . . And besides," he added, "you owe us something and you've jerked us around long enough. The fun is over now, and we want it."

Wylie said nothing.

"But you don't need to worry," Roskill pursued. "So long as we get it, the rest doesn't matter. You'll find we're not vindictive."

"I don't have it."

Silence.

"You don't have it." Roskill permitted himself a touch of sarcasm. On top of everything else, did the man think he was stupid? "Look. The game is over. There's really no point in piddling around."

"I don't have it," Wylie repeated firmly.

"But you did offer to sell it to us, didn't you?" Roskill smiled coldly. "And that would have been stupid of you—wouldn't it?—if you really hadn't had it. And somehow I can't bring myself to think of you as stupid. Not after you've given us so much evidence to the contrary."

"I did have it. But I don't anymore. I've forgotten it."

"I see. . . . I must say I find that quite extraordinary. It never occurred to you to write it down?"

"It did," Wylie nodded. "But unfortunately too late. By the time I got around to it, it was already gone. . . . Stupid of me, wasn't it?"

"Yes," Roskill said. "Very."

Wylie still hadn't moved, he noticed; he was still lounging there, calmly uttering these inanities as if he didn't expect to be believed and didn't much care one way or the other. It was almost as if he were deliberately setting out to be provoking. And that was a mistake, Roskill thought; if he kept it up he would regret it.

"So you see," Wylie said, "the offer of protection is misplaced generosity. You might as well go home. . . . I realize, of course, that I've caused a lot of trouble. I don't suppose it would help at all if I said I was sorry?"

Sorry? Roskill couldn't believe his ears. The man had to have a screw loose somewhere; he had to be some kind of clown.

"You still don't understand." He glanced around at Burrows. They moved out on either side of Wylie. "I'm not asking; I'm telling. I don't believe a word of what you say. I think you remember perfectly . . . or at least," he amended, "I'm sure you *will*."

"Telling?" Wylie cocked an eyebrow. "In other words, kidnapping."

"Call it what you like." Roskill shrugged. "But let's be moving along, shall we?"

"No." Wylie's lips compressed around the monosyllable.

"Shit," Roskill sighed. He glanced at Burrows and nodded.

Burrows took a step toward Wylie. As he did, Wylie reared out of the chair like a snake. The ashtray became a discus aimed straight at Burrows' head. Burrows ducked. His fist caught Wylie half out of the chair, and the force of the blow, added to Wylie's momentum, snapped his head back as if it had been on a hinge.

"Jesus," Roskill muttered. "That didn't sound good. I hope you didn't break his silly neck."

Burrows squatted down beside Wylie and felt for a pulse. Taking a grasp on a handful of Wylie's hair, he lifted the head and jiggled it once or twice, experimentally, from side to side.

"He's all right," he grunted.

He took a small metal box from his pocket and extracted a disposable syringe. Holding it away from him, needle upwards, he squirted it once, and without further preparation, plunged the needle into Wylie's arm.

"That should keep him still for a while."

He stood up, gazed curiously at the unconscious figure on the floor, and turned to Roskill.

"Funny," he said. "You'd have thought he'd show more sense."

"Desperation." Roskill shrugged. "The cornered-rat defense. Last-ditch attempt to turn things around."

"I guess." Burrows nodded. "Not that it makes any difference. In fact, I rather enjoyed it . . . the punch." He grinned. "I owed him that."

Pogrebin looked at his watch . . . three and a half minutes since Revin had left. Time to get moving. He stepped out around the corner and started down the street.

He didn't saunter or look casually about—nothing was more suspicious, he knew, than someone acting nonchalant—he simply walked at a relaxed, even pace, like a man heading somewhere but not in any hurry. He was careful not to look at the American in the Fiat.

When he had gone thirty yards or so, Revin appeared from the opposite direction, walking briskly. That was from the textbook: a man moving fast was inherently more threatening than one moving slowly. It was essential that the American pay more attention to Revin. *When the principal is in the contact zone, the threat must seem to come from the backup.*

Timing was the key. A man has only one pair of eyes; the cigarette trick was based on that human limitation. In that sense, it was like a conjuring trick. But in fact it was more like a trapeze act—if the catcher is not in position, his partner hits the net. If Pogrebin went into his routine before Revin was ready, he'd be in the same predicament. Only in this case there was no net.

About twenty meters from the Fiat, Pogrebin permitted himself a glance at the American, a quick, incurious look; nothing more than a point, briefly held, on the arc his eyes traveled up the street toward Revin. The American was clearly edgy—his gaze had flicked quickly from Pogrebin to the rearview mirror and back again—but he was not yet definitely suspicious. He would be shortly, Pogrebin knew. That was why the timing was so vital.

At ten meters from the Fiat Pogrebin went into the routine. The first part was easy: slackening his pace, he groped for the pack in his pocket, extracted a cigarette and placed it between his lips. The move brought him about five meters short of the open driver's window next to the American. He was now in the contact zone.

Now for the hard part.

You must not look. The message had been dinned into him, over and over, by the instructors. *Once you enter the contact zone, you look at the target only when you strike. Only when the backup makes his run.*

So now he was in the hands of Revin. Only Revin could ensure that when he looked, finally, at the target, he wouldn't be looking at eternity.

He stopped. His hands patted his coat pockets in a delicate pantomime of searching for his lighter. No luck. . . . He strayed a step or two closer, hands descending to his trouser pockets. No luck there, either. . . . Another step. His right hand came up to slip inside his coat. The inside breast pocket, the logical next place to look. The move the whole routine was designed to camouflage. . . . His fingers closed around the butt of the Makarov. His ears strained for the sudden pounding of Revin's footsteps. The urge to look was almost overwhelming. . . . *You must not look.* . . . Go on! he silently entreated Revin. Move, for God's sake. Move!

Then Revin was running, dashing in behind the Fiat in a sudden thrust toward the front offside door.

Pogrebin never saw this, of course. He was too focused on drawing and aiming the Makarov. But he knew it was what must have happened, because when he did look, at last, the American had turned to face the threat from his rear. When he turned back, a second later, the Makarov was very steady, only twelve inches from his head.

Textbook. Precision timing. The trick pulled off to perfection in every detail. These thoughts passed through Pogrebin's mind as he savored the bemused, foolish look on the American's features. . . . Only later did it occur to him that perhaps it had been too perfect.

In the back of the gray van, like a leopard in a thicket, Mikhail Grusha waited. . . . No survivors, Lermontov had said, and Grusha, watching the near corner of the Via Ambruscati with the poised stillness of perfect concentration, was there to see that order carried out. The rear doors of the van were ajar, the Kalashnikov at the ready. Presently Wylie and the two CIA men would come into view round the corner. Then the doors would burst open and Grusha would strike. The Kalashnikov was automatic, its rate of fire ten rounds per second; at this range—less than ten meters—it would cut the Americans in half. The thing would be over in less than five seconds.

After that it would be simply a matter of racing away, dumping the van in a nearby alley, and transferring to the VW for the dash to Fiumicino. An anonymous phone call, later, to one of the newspapers, claiming the kills for the Brigate Rosse, would put the incident in its proper perspective. The *brigatisti* would probably deny responsibility, but by that time Grusha would be back in Moscow. Not that he worried overmuch about afterwards—that was why Lermontov had insisted on bringing him: if you got him in position, he would get the job done.

When he first heard the siren, Grusha did not pay much attention to it. Some unfortunate motorist, probably, who'd chosen the wrong moment to run a red light. But the moan in the distance got steadily louder and more strident until at last there could be no doubt. It was coming toward the van, coming up the same street.

"Cops?" Grusha still didn't turn his head or take his eyes off the corner.

"Ambulance . . . heading this way . . . straight for us." The driver sounded jumpy.

"If it's not the cops, it's O.K.," Grusha reassured him. "Just keep an eye on it."

"It's slowing down."

As the driver spoke the ambulance flashed into Grusha's view, disappearing instantly down the Via Ambruscati. The siren stopped.

Shit, Grusha thought. Complications. . . . But there was still no insoluble problem. Wylie had resisted, evidently, and they had had to tranquilize him. That was not altogether surprising, in view of what was known about Wylie. But the ambulance would still have to come back out of the cul-de-sac; and it would have to slow down to take the corner. A burst through the windshield would stop it cold. Then he could scramble out and finish the men in the back. It would take longer . . . thirty seconds, maybe as much as a minute . . . but there would still be plenty of time to get clear. This part of the Trastevere was out of the mainstream of traffic. There was nothing to worry about.

"Stay put," he ordered the driver. "I'll hit it when it comes round the corner. I'm going to have to get out, probably, to deal with the ones in the back. Don't move until I'm back in the van. If you take off without me, I'll kill you, too."

The driver ignored this.

"There's a truck coming up behind us," he said.

Grusha glanced at it briefly. In fact it was a movers' van, not directly behind, but lumbering up the street in their direction. . . . Perhaps it was innocent, perhaps not. They would find out in due course, either way.

"You watch *it*," he snapped. "I'll watch the corner. And remember, don't move until I say so."

The truck resolved the question of its innocence almost immediately. As it drew level with the van it slammed on its brakes and backed, with surprising speed, diagonally across behind them, completely blocking Grusha's line of fire. As it came to a standstill the siren sounded.

"Move!" Grusha yelled.

When the van surged forward, however, the truck did, too. Grusha fired a quick burst into the rear tires. They disintegrated into strips of flailing rubber, but the truck kept moving. Before a further burst immobilized it completely, the ambulance had shot out of the cul-de-sac, slithered through the turn, and roared off down the street away from them, siren blaring.

"Radio!" Grusha barked.

The driver grabbed the mike from the dashboard. "All vehicles pursuit . . . red ambulance . . . headed down Portuense to the Porta Portese."

The truck was still blocking them. By the time they cleared it and made the turn, the ambulance had a lead of at least two hundred meters.

Afterwards, scenes from the subsequent chase would sometimes appear in Grusha's nightmares; it violated every principle of his profession, being disorganized, protracted, and very public. That he emerged from it unscathed was due to the natural reluctance of bystanders to tangle with anyone carrying an automatic rifle, and perhaps also to the awesome reputation of the Brigate Rosse. The ambulance was caught when it hit heavy traffic, less than a kilometer from the Via Ambruscati. Grusha stopped it by shooting out the tires. The ambulance's driver came out with his hands up, but there was no time to worry about him. The target was the men in the back. The back of the ambulance, however, was quite empty. And so, by the time someone slipped back to investigate, was the apartment on the Via Ambruscati.

Both empty. When Lermontov heard about it, he simply nodded. But not nearly as empty, he thought, as his own future.

∎

CHAPTER XXXV

Anne, too, felt empty. Back at the hotel Kendrick stayed with her for a while, bestowing on her the doubtful consolation of his company. Orders, he explained again: evidence of Roskill's concern for her well-being. She suffered him in silence. After her outburst in the car, she had come to recognize the futility of recrimination. He was only a functionary, someone whose life consisted of taking orders; why vent on him the anger that properly belonged to Roskill? Having nothing else, she took refuge in dignity.

After a couple of hours, in which Kendrick watched television and she toyed with a book, Kendrick was summoned to the phone. He returned looking pleased. Everything had gone off perfectly, he told her: Wylie was safe; the opposition was routed. Roskill had particularly asked him, he added, to convey thanks for her help.

"Then he's not coming back here?"

"No, ma'am. They'll be heading straight to Washington. No point in their hanging about."

"What about me?"

Not to worry, Kendrick said. It was over now, and the Russians knew it. They weren't the sort to waste time with reprisals. In any case, they'd be too busy licking their wounds. Just to make sure, however, he and his colleagues would check out the area. He'd be back in a while, he promised, to set her mind at rest.

Surprisingly, he did come back. They'd checked everywhere, he reported, all over the hotel, all through the neighboring streets, but they'd found nothing. If she were still worried, he could arrange for her to stay with someone from the Embassy, but there was really no danger; the hotel was perfectly clean.

She thanked him but refused the offer. She'd had her fill of U.S. officialdom, she thought. An evening spent fending off the curiosity of some diplomat and his wife was too high a price to pay for the exorcism of her slight lingering nervousness. Kendrick was probably right. No doubt the hotel was, and would remain, perfectly "clean."

She wondered, however, how long it would be before she stopped feeling dirty.

Flowers arrived in the morning. Two dozen pink and yellow roses, delivered to her room along with breakfast. A Roskill peace offering, she thought, and characteristically ill-chosen. But the note attached was not from Roskill.

You'll be expecting explanations, but I'm not in a position to give them. Downstairs is someone who is. He answers to the name of Cesare di Lasso, and claims to descend from the Borgias. Very possibly he does. The reception desk will point him out.

He will identify himself with an American Express money order for $5,000 made out to you. Please go with him to the American Express and cash it. The money is his—for services rendered. He will explain.

Please do this for me. I owe you too much already, but once he has the money, Mr. di Lasso will help me repay.

The note was handwritten and unsigned, but it wasn't hard to guess who had sent it. And beneath the text, in place of a signature, was a postscript—added, she imagined, to confirm the note's authenticity.

You told me a kiss on the eyelids meant good-bye. We haven't done that yet.

Apparently, Kendrick notwithstanding, it *wasn't* completely over.

Il Conte was profoundly relieved. Wylie was undoubtedly crazy, but at least he was a man of honor. For two days Il Conte had been running inexplicable and, in his eyes, hazardous errands; now at last he was going to be paid.

He watched her countersign the money order, receive the thick wad of banknotes. He was shocked to observe that she didn't count them, but it didn't matter; he would take care of that himself.

She returned from the counter, handed the money to him, stood there patiently while he flicked through the bundle.

"Now," she began in English, then broke off. The man's command of it was minimal. How could he provide the promised explanations? Perhaps Wylie had forgotten that not everyone had his fluency in languages. . . . She ran an inventory, necessarily short, of her own Italian.

"*Perche?*" she finally managed.

He looked puzzled.

"Fiumicino," he responded. "Now I take you to Fiumicino. . . . 'Take her,' he tell me, so I take. . . . We go now. Please?"

She struggled for a moment with the language barrier, but soon gave up, baffled. . . . Explanations? she wondered. Should she be getting them or giving them? And what the hell did it matter anyway? . . . Wylie, Roskill: she was sick of them both. She just wanted to go home.

Il Conte, however, performed his last errand faithfully. He ran her back to the hotel and on out to the airport. He helped her check her baggage and insisted on going with her as far as the Immigration barrier.

Not until she turned, at last, to thank him, did he hand her the envelope.

CHAPTER XXXVI

"He's at The Farm," Roskill said. "Cooling his heels. *He* doesn't know where he is, though. He was drugged to the eyebrows all the way from Rome."

"Good," the DCI nodded. "What about her?"

"Gone home, I imagine. Not much else for her to do. She isn't"—he grinned—"very pleased with us, but what options does she have? . . . Arden Wylie is just another missing person, last heard of somewhere in Europe. At least, *she* can't prove anything different."

"So much for her, then. . . . How are you making out with him?"

"Haven't really started. I consulted Harry here"—he jerked his head in the direction of Rosen—"and he recommends we try isolation. So we've stuck him in one of those little coffins in area four. . . . No light, no sound, no stimulation whatever. Nothing to do but lie still and count heartbeats. In theory he should be gibbering. . . . But in practice"—he cast a resentful glance at Rosen—"you'd think he was taking a vacation."

The DCI turned to Rosen; his expression combined curiosity and a certain amused skepticism. Rosen knew the look well; it was the normal layman's reaction to the complex ambiguities of his field. In Agency language he was "the Witchdoctor," a name that conveyed perfectly the prevailing attitude to his pronouncements: softheaded mumbo-jumbo, dressed up in jargon, passing itself off as science.

"Sensory deprivation," he explained. "You induce anxiety, a sense of

total isolation. Then, when you start in with the questions, he's practically begging to cooperate. . . . It saves time in the end."

"How much longer?" the DCI asked.

"When he starts gibbering, you'll know he's ready," Rosen said
shortly. "I can't give you a timetable; it depends on his inner resources."

"In the meantime, however," Roskill murmured, "he's taxing mine."

Rosen said nothing.

"So I think," Roskill continued, "that perhaps we're approaching this
wrong. . . . He's obviously not short on inner resources. If we wait for
him to exhaust them, we could be here till Christmas. I think we need
something more forceful. . . . Why encourage him to be tiresome?"

"Tiresome," Rosen echoed. "Maybe he's not being tiresome. Maybe
he really has forgotten."

"Well, in that case"—Roskill clearly didn't consider it likely—
"perhaps you'd like to advise us?"

"I'm afraid not."

Rosen sounded mutinous. He hadn't meant to, for there was something about these men—the unblinking detachment, perhaps, with which
they could consider the unthinkable—that discouraged mutiny, but the
truth was he wanted out. The truth was they scared him, these two; they
scared the daylights out of him. They had too much power, they'd had
it too long, and because they cloaked it in secrecy they answered to no
one. They sat around in their sterile offices, surrounded by secretaries
and "sanitized" telephones, and they spoke in murmurs of the "national
interest" while they traded human futures like porkbellies. . . . Advise
them? He wished he'd never heard of them, never written a single report
or taken a cent of their money. For though they might talk, in their
careful way, of "protective custody" and "debriefing," the real words
were shorter and uglier. And he, Rosen, by advising them, by sitting too
long and hearing too much, had become an accomplice. He should have
quit more than two weeks ago, after the first of these meetings, but
curiosity—and the seductive flattery of their confidences—had held him.
Now there *was* no out. All he could do, though with little faith in his
chances, was stay and do his best to restrain them.

"You're afraid not?" The DCI eyed him speculatively. "Why not?"

"There is no advice, except . . . wait. I've given that, but it seems
you don't want it. . . . Look," he pleaded. "We know that the causes
of forgetting, particularly in cases of selective amnesia, are usually emotional. People forget, very often, because they subconsciously want to
forget. What Wylie's forgotten, or claims to have forgotten, could well
be associated, in his subconscious, with powerful feelings of fear and

guilt. . . . But knowing that is one thing; knowing what to do about it is something else."

"It seems to me," Roskill offered, "that one could try giving him powerful feelings of wanting to remember."

"One could." Rosen shrugged. "It seems to me you already have, but you may be operating at the wrong level. You're talking about conscious feelings. His block, if he has one, will be deeper. . . . You might just make things worse."

"This is academic," the DCI cut in. "If he's really forgotten, we may have a problem. But first let's find out if he's really forgotten."

"Agreed," Roskill said firmly.

"How?" This time the note of mutiny was deliberate.

Silence. Both men turned to scrutinize Rosen.

"We needn't concern ourselves with the details." The DCI's tone was a warning.

"How?" Rosen ignored him, kept his eyes steady on Roskill.

"Scare the shit out of him." Roskill shrugged.

"And if that doesn't work . . . ?"

"*Beat* the shit out of him." Another shrug.

"I see." Rosen's voice was expressionless. "You beat the shit out of him, until either he tells you or you decide he's not faking. . . . And how do you decide?"

"I'm told it's usually fairly obvious."

"Is it? . . . Well, either way you still have a problem."

"We do?"

"We're wasting time," the DCI cut in again. "It's been decided. I don't see much point in going on with this."

"There's every point!" Rosen's voice was shrill. "You're breaking the law, for one thing. I mean, beating the shit out of him is illegal, isn't it? Not to mention kidnapping. . . . So what's to stop his blowing the whistle? What's to stop his going to the press? What's to stop . . ."

He broke off, the words swallowed suddenly by some deep void. The room had become utterly still. The others were staring at him, he noticed, their incredulity mingled with distaste. It was as if he, a guest in their club, had rewarded their kindness with some gross solecism.

"Thank you, Harry." Surprisingly, it was Roskill's bland voice that broke the silence. "You're right. That *could* present us with a problem. However," he went on smoothly, "I'm sure we can come up with a solution."

Solution? . . . Somewhere in the depths of Rosen's subconscious the word joined with another in obscene association.

Shit, he thought miserably: when they're through, they're going to kill him.

When Roskill entered, Wylie was lying on his bunk. He was blinking a little—his eyes had not adjusted to the light—and he was paler than when Roskill had last seen him, the subterranean pallor enhanced by dark stubble on his chin. But otherwise he didn't seem much different: he was on his back, hands clasped behind his head, looking more like a man bent on taking life easy than one tormented by loneliness and fear. . . . Softening him up? Roskill thought sardonically; if they'd listened to Rosen the process would go on forever.

"Enjoying yourself?" He sat down on the edge of the bunk by Wylie's feet.

"I've stayed at worse." Wylie shrugged. "Food's O.K. Service is passable. Plenty of peace and quiet."

"And plenty of time to think."

"Yes," Wylie nodded. "I've thought up a new line in the King's Indian."

"Well, time's up," Roskill said curtly. "So what I'm telling you is this: forget about rights—the Fourth Amendment and all that garbage. As far as I'm concerned, you don't have any rights. There are two hundred and twenty million Americans out there, and their rights are more important. They need that information. You're not leaving here till I get it."

This was received without comment.

"Have you heard from Anne?" Wylie asked.

For a moment Roskill looked puzzled, but only for a moment.

"Unh-unh." He shook his head. "That kite won't fly. . . . Don't look for any help from her. She's on our side. She didn't go to Rome for you, you know. She went for us—to help us nail you. . . . You screwed her"—he smiled—"and so she screwed you. And now, I imagine, she's lost interest."

"You could be wrong."

"Possible." Roskill shrugged. "But after all, what can she do? She can't prove anything, even if she wants to. She wasn't around when we nabbed you, and she hasn't seen you since. All she can do is speculate, and that won't help you much. . . . The bottom line is this: you're on your own. Don't look for help from out there; there isn't any."

"Listen . . ." Wylie said.

"No. You listen," Roskill cut him off. "I'm bored with you. I've wasted too much time and energy already. I've lost a man, and I've spent a lot of money. It's time to cut the crap. . . . Either I get that information now, immediately, or we start taking you apart, piece by piece. And be clear about this: I'm not talking about pentathol, or putting you in a tank, or any of those mind games; I'm talking about pain, pure and simple. And I'm not giving you any more time. When I walk out of here, it starts. And it goes on until you give, or until we're convinced you have nothing *to* give. But I should warn you," he added, "we're not easy to convince."

"And if it turns out I *have* forgotten? . . . That won't bother you?"

"You haven't forgotten," Roskill sneered. "You're not worried enough. If you had forgotten, you'd be in a bind, wouldn't you? Stuck in the hot seat and no way to buy yourself out. But look at you . . . you're not even sweating. . . . Of course," he added, "I could be wrong—maybe you just have no imagination—and if I am, I'll feel just terrible. I may never forgive myself."

He stood and started toward the door.

"Wait!" Wylie said.

CHAPTER XXXVII

When they reached the hotel, Roskill told the cab driver to skirt the main entrance and drop him, instead, at the side door on Fifty-eighth Street; this not from any motive of secrecy but because, being perfectly capable of opening the car door for himself, he saw no reason to tip someone else for doing it—particularly not some hotel flunky in beige livery and a truncated top hat.

It was a while since he'd been to the Plaza. On his visits to New York he stayed with friends or at the Harvard Club, eating out, if necessary, at a steak house and doing his drinking at the kind of bar that made no charge for ambience. The Plaza, therefore, was not one of his normal haunts; it was the sort of place he reserved for the people to whom he owed dinner and hoped to fob off with a drink. Anne Crossland, of course, hardly fell into that category—he owed her nothing, by his reckoning, except possibly a swift backhander—but she had suggested the place, and since it was central and convenient he'd not objected. It was almost over now; he could afford to be magnanimous.

Having paid off the taxi, he made his way along the north wing, through the arcade of boutiques and gift shops, to the front lobby. Ten-thirty, she had said; and Roskill, pausing at the entrance to the Palm Court, discovered he was fifteen minutes late. It didn't bother him much: she would definitely wait for him. She didn't have any choice.

The place hadn't changed much, he noticed, looking around for her. There was still the same not quite convincing suggestion of smartness about it, the same slightly faded chic: the waiters drifting around dispensing drinks as though bestowing favors, the trio grinding out tunes from the forties, the tables filled with the usual midmorning crowd—salesmen snatching a quick one between appointments, middle-aged women taking time out from the rigors of shopping, and a smattering of the conspicuously unemployed. It was an odd place, he thought, to be ending this thing.

He spotted her at a table tucked away behind a pair of potted palms. In front of her, in an ice-bucket, stood a bottle of Cordon Rouge, unopened, and two glasses, tall-stemmed and tulip-shaped. Beside them, he noticed, lay an eight-by-ten manila envelope.

So there it was at last—what all of the excitement, all the wailing and gnashing of teeth had been about. Just two or three sheets of paper, probably, covered with higher mathematics. Exciting enough to Olofson and his friends, perhaps, but hardly imposing enough, physically, to have been the cause of so much trouble. . . . Well, at least, he thought, the price was finally right. He didn't know what astronomical sum the Plaza was now charging for a bottle of champagne, but whatever it was, it wouldn't make much of a dent, surely, in half a million dollars. In fact, he thought, feeling expansive, he might even stretch a point and pay for it himself.

He strolled over.

"Celebrating?" he inquired.

She looked up, smiled, and gave a shrug.

"I thought we might drink to the end of our association. That deserves a celebration, don't you think?"

"The end of it?" he murmured. "Myself, I'd have phrased it less gloomily. Why don't we drink to its successful conclusion?"

"I won't quibble . . . end . . . conclusion . . . whatever. Let's drink to it anyway."

A waiter was summoned, the bottle opened, and the wine poured.

"Well, at any rate . . ." Roskill leaned back and raised his glass in a sort of salute. "I'm glad to see you're not a sore loser."

"Oh, no." She shook her head. "Just so long as Wylie's all right. . . . He *is* all right, isn't he?"

"Very chipper, last time I saw him. Chafing somewhat, of course, at the precautions we've been forced to take for his safety, but otherwise unharmed."

"And now you'll let him go?"

"Why not? Now that this matter is resolved, we won't need to bother him further. Unless, of course . . ." He shrugged and left the sentence unfinished.

"Unless, of course, he talks out of turn. In that case, no doubt, you'd bother him quite considerably."

"Something like that," he agreed amiably.

"You really are rather poisonous." She said it reflectively, without heat, like a herpetologist identifying a specimen.

"Don't let's squabble," he shrugged. "I am if I have to be. I have a job to do, and it's a necessary job, whatever you may think. . . . Besides, Wylie himself is hardly a model of probity. His troubles are all of his own making."

"They are," she agreed. "That *was* stupid of him, wasn't it—trying to steal something you wanted to steal yourselves."

"That's right," he grinned. "Speaking of which . . . may I have it now?"

She nodded.

"There you are." She handed him the envelope. "Enjoy."

It did him credit, she thought, that his expression hardly changed when he saw the photographs. There was a certain narrowing of the eyes, perhaps, a momentary compression of the lips, but on the whole his composure was admirable. He examined them systematically, giving each a judicious appraisal before going on to the next. When he'd finished, he put them carefully back in the envelope.

"So?" he inquired.

"They are good, aren't they?" She could almost have been making a judgment in aesthetics. "The one of you in profile, for example, with Wylie in the background pinioned by your thug. . . . Remarkable definition, I think, when you take into account the depth of field. They'll look marvelous in the newspapers.

"But of course," she went on, "the real zinger is the tape."

She reached into her handbag and produced a cassette.

"You're going to enjoy this." She pushed it across the table to him. "Everything clearly audible . . . even the thump when your goon clobbered Wylie. There should be no problem at all, I imagine, with voice identification. I mean, they have all those machines for it nowadays, don't they? Like the ones they used on those tapes from . . . where was it now? . . . surely you remember? . . . the tapes of Nixon and all those other people."

"Watergate," he muttered.

"That's right," she said brightly. "Watergate."

"The newspapers," Roskill said. "Exclusive to the *New York Times*, is that it?"

"Something like that," she nodded. "'CIA Kidnaps Chess Master—Allegations of Torture.' I've never been good at headlines, but I expect they'll come up with something catchy. . . . With the pictures and the tape, it should run for weeks. Then, of course, there'll be the Senate inquiry. And the trial. . . . There's bound to be a trial, wouldn't you say? I do hope you have a good lawyer."

"How much?" Roskill said.

"Oh . . . I don't know." She pretended to ponder the question. "They'd fetch a mint on the open market. Imagine the *Times* and the *Post* and the Boston *Globe* all bidding away like mad. . . . Shall we say . . . half a million? Each."

"Each?" Roskill's eyebrows shot up.

"Yes. Half a million for me and half a million for Wylie."

"And we get the tapes and the pictures?"

"Not exactly. What you get is a conditional vow of silence. The tapes and the pics go to Wylie's Swiss bank. And that's where they'll stay. . . . Unless, of course, anything odd should ever happen to either of us."

"You mean we pay out a million, and all we get is a promise?" He sounded stunned.

"That's right." She smiled sweetly. "You're going to have to trust us. I know it's not easy for you, but you'll find you can manage it—with practice."

Roskill considered.

"I don't know," he said at last. "A million dollars . . . that's awfully steep."

"Oh, I think you can come up with it all right. . . . Not that it makes any difference to me. You're going to have to let him go in any case. I'd almost rather sell it to the *Times* . . . I've always had a hankering for a Pulitzer prize."

"Just one more thing," Roskill said. "Was it you who set this up?"

"Me?" She sounded surprised. "Oh, no. I just handle the negotiations. It was Wylie's bright idea. . . . You see, he apparently really has forgotten what that Russian told him. But he knew you people would never believe that, and it was obviously no use just going on running, so he decided to get himself caught, but in a way that would get you off his back for good. . . . A king sacrifice, he calls it. I don't quite understand why, but he seems to think it's rather a revolutionary idea."

"And you were the bait?"

"Yes. . . . Unwittingly at first. In fact, I was very annoyed about it when I first found out. But I'm not annoyed anymore," she smiled. "I think things have turned out rather well."

"Rather luckily, I'd say." Roskill's voice was sour.

"Oh, dear . . ." she sighed. "You're not going to be a sore loser, are you?"

"It's the truth. He'd have been up the spout if we hadn't taken his bait. How could he be so sure that we were keeping you under surveillance?"

"I was curious about that myself. . . . But he thought you were bound to be. It was the obvious thing to do, he said; just what he'd do in your position. . . . You know, what strikes me most about all this is how very much alike you two are. Psychologically, you could be twins."

"I'm not flattered by that comparison," he muttered. "Arden Wylie is a thoroughly underhanded little bastard."

"Yes," she agreed. "He is, isn't he?"

CHAPTER XXXVIII

For a moment, it seemed, he didn't know what to do. He stood there dazed, blinking a little in the bright Virginia sunlight, as if freedom, so abruptly thrust upon him, were some new problem—to be approached with circumspection. Behind him the metal gates swung shut, the guard returned to the gatehouse, and the jeep that had brought him from the compound roared off and was lost among the trees. Then he looked across and saw her. Visibly startled, he hesitated, seemed about to call out, but thinking better of it, simply nodded and started to walk toward her.

She didn't get out of the car to greet him, merely watched as he approached—a tall untidy figure, still dressed in the almost-uniform of Levis and T-shirt she remembered his wearing in Moscow, his walk a little awkward now, as if walking were a knack he was trying to recover, and the thin, intelligent face thinner and paler than when she'd last seen it, the eyes brighter and more wary. . . . Existential drifter, she thought; game-player, mercenary. IQ about one eighty. Values—uncertain. Loyalties—other than to himself—unknown. Attractive certainly, but my God, she thought, hardly a promising long-term proposition.

A few feet away from her, he stopped. He still didn't smile or speak; instead his eyes searched hers, seeking clues, she guessed, as to what kind of reception to expect. She gazed back, determined not to help him, not knowing in any case what kind of reception to offer. She didn't, in fact, know why she was there at all, for although there was still—in more than one sense—unfinished business between them, it could have waited. But whatever her reasons, she *had* come; the business *would* be finished. And how it would be finished was largely up to him. Most probably, she thought, he would blow it.

"So it worked," he said at last.

"Roskill didn't tell you?"

He shook his head.

"First I knew was half an hour ago. They gave me a razor, told me to clean myself up because I was leaving. Someone would meet me at the gate, they said. They didn't say who."

"Well, it did work," she said. "It worked perfectly. Even down to the money. . . . I expect you're wondering about that."

He let that ride.

"I wasn't sure you'd do it," he said. "In fact, after the phone call I was afraid you wouldn't. . . . Why did you?"

"Did I have a choice?" she shrugged. "It seems to me that you and Mr. Roskill, between you, made damn sure I didn't."

"Well, anyway"—he smiled—"I'm glad you did. I probably owe you my life. . . . I don't know what to say, except 'thank you.'"

"Oh, any time," she murmured sardonically. "Just call up from wherever and I'll come running. . . . It's been such fun. And also," she added, "*very* rewarding."

And that, she thought, should give you pause.

"So I thought I'd drop by," she went on, "just to make sure Mr. Roskill kept both parts of his bargain. . . . I already have the money, you see. And I think I'm going to keep it."

She paused, waiting for a reaction. Go on, she inwardly urged him, make it easy for me; squawk a little. Show me you are who I think you are, so I can drive off and forget you.

There was a moment when she thought he was going to. Blankness, shock, and a flicker of resentment passed in rapid succession across his face. But the look he turned on her finally was merely wry. After so many surprises, it seemed, he could adjust to another without missing a beat. And again he reminded her of Roskill. . . . That was the trouble, she thought; at heart they were too much alike.

"Keep it?" he smiled. "There's some justice in that. I'd say you've rather earned it."

Part of her wanted to believe him. But it was too easy; he was clearly smart enough to know that pretended indifference was, in this case, the surest route to success.

"I'm surprised," she said dryly. "I thought the money was what it was all about."

"Oh, it was," he admitted. "It was at first. But that didn't last long.

Very quickly it turned into a question of coming out of it whole. Now"
—he shrugged—"I feel like a winner simply for having survived."

"In other words, you don't want it?" She was openly unconvinced.

"Oh, yes." He looked surprised. "Of course I want it. There are a lot
of things I want. . . . But if I can't have them, I'll get along without
them."

"What things?"

He thought for a moment. He was about to tell her, she guessed, but
at the last second decided against it.

"Just things," he said.

"And people . . . ?"

She hardly knew why she bothered to ask. His actions since Moscow,
surely, had given a definite answer to *that*.

"Tell me," she went on, "did it never bother you? Didn't you ever, in
all this time, feel a twinge of regret about leaving me dangling in Moscow . . . or had you already decided, even when you left me that morning, exactly what you were going to do?"

Again he seemed to hesitate.

"Well?" she demanded.

"Talk's cheap," he shrugged. "Whatever I said, you'd think I was
after the money."

"Oh, God," she sighed, "take it. I never did plan to keep it, anyway.
I was going to give it to some charity or other. But now that I consider
things clearly, I can't think of anyone who needs it more than you. . . .
So take it. I hope you enjoy it. At least, it'll get you plenty of things."

He said nothing. His reaction to winning, it seemed, was the same
indifference he'd brought to losing. But this, too, was probably strategy
—just another instance of his intelligence.

"Well, at least smile or something," she prompted. "You won, didn't
you? . . . What more do you want?"

He studied her intently.

"You," he said at last.

But now that he'd said it, she couldn't accept it. . . . And that was
partly her fault—the knowledge came to her like a sudden pain—because
she'd set this scene up on a heads-I-win-tails-you-lose basis; the whole
encounter had been nothing more than a series of tests he couldn't possibly have passed. . . . But it hadn't been *all* her fault, had it? History
counted for something, surely? Distrust was not an affliction you could
simply decide not to have?

At that she remembered the emptiness, and fear, of returning to Moscow and finding him gone. And the anger flared up in her again.

"Oh, Christ," she snapped. "You might at least have spared me that bullshit."

He started to say something, but she didn't want to hear. His words were drowned, in any case, by the noise of her starting the car. She slammed it into gear, let in the clutch with a jerk. . . . He could fucking well hitchhike to Richmond, could Mr. Self-sufficient Smartass Wylie, because she was damned if she'd be suckered into any more of the glorified chess games that seemed to occupy his life.

As she accelerated away, she glanced in the rearview mirror. He was standing, stockstill, gazing after her. Once he half raised an arm in what might have been protest, or, just as easily, a gesture of farewell. Then the arm fell back again, and the gesture ended, characteristically, in a shrug. At last he turned and started to walk toward Richmond.

He was still walking when she returned, five minutes later. She saw, in the distance, a car go by him, then another. But ignoring them, he plodded on, slouching down the highway like a hobo—no immediate destination; no pressing desire to reach one. . . . Game-player, she thought; existential drifter. Wandering into the future armed with nothing more than the willingness to take it as it came. . . . Not much of a long-term proposition, perhaps; but, after all, these days what was?

EPILOGUE

∎

The DCI looked at Roskill and back to the memo. He frowned.

"Resignation? . . . Don't you think that's a little extreme?"

"Not really," Roskill shrugged. "We didn't get it, we lost a man, and we're out a million dollars. That seems to demand the customary sacrifice."

The DCI considered.

"I suppose I should admire the sense of duty that impels you to put your head on the block," he responded. "But I refuse to wield the hatchet. We've lost one man; why make it two?"

Roskill was silent. His offer had been sincere, but it was prompted largely by the desire to jump before he was pushed. The DCI's reaction surprised him, but he wasn't going to insist. He was forty-eight—too young to be condemned to potter in his garden, too old to go out and find other work. And what other work did the world have to offer, he wondered, to washed-up, forty-eight-year-old spies?

"Besides," the DCI went on, "one has to keep a sense of proportion. We didn't get it, perhaps, but there'll be another chance. Even if there isn't, it won't be long, probably, before one of Olofson's colleagues at MIT or Cal Tech leaps out of the bath and starts yelling 'Eureka.' . . . We take our crises too seriously, as if they were all life or death. They almost never are."

Roskill stared at him. He had never seen the DCI so philosophical. The suggestion that the Agency's work was anything less than continuously vital would normally have driven him to the borders of apoplexy.

"I suppose it's mostly a question of habit." The DCI seemed disposed to pursue his speculations. "We're servants of the public. And the public wants a CIA because the other side has a KGB. So we do it because they do it, and they do it . . ." He shrugged. "You see what I mean?"

Roskill did, of course. But it didn't seem a line of thought that ought to be made articulate. It could do them all out of a job.

"I think you should take some time off. Go mess around on your sailboat for a while. When you're rested up come back and soldier on as usual." The DCI smiled, took the memo, tore it in half, and dropped it, like a piece of dirty laundry, into his wastepaper basket. "And let's have no more nonsense about resignation. Where would we be without people like you?"

Roskill couldn't think of any response—he was too stunned. Eventually he managed a muttered "thank you" and turned to take his departure.

He was almost at the door when the DCI spoke again.

"By the way, before you go you might take a look at this." He held out a blue airmail envelope. Roskill went over and took it. It was postmarked St. Lucia, and addressed to "Spooks. Langley, Virginia. USA."

"Came in the mail this morning," the DCI explained. "Questionable sense of humor. And lousy security, of course. But take a look."

Roskill did. Inside was a snapshot attached to the top left-hand corner of a handwritten letter. Also attached to the letter were several pages of typescript. The snapshot was in color: Wylie and Anne Crossland sunbathing on the deck of a large sailing boat. They were looking into the camera, raising glasses of what looked like rum punch, and smiling. They seemed to be making a toast to somebody.

The letter was just a couple of lines.

Dear Roskill,

The picture is to reassure you, in case you were worried, that your money is being well spent. The attachment should be self-explanatory. I wasn't going to send it to you, at first, but then I remembered a certain worried-looking Russian in Gorki Park. He seemed rather anxious you should have it, so here it is.

There was no signature.
Roskill turned to the attachment.
"We are speaking," he read, "of an application of lasers . . ."